OF NOD

OF NOD

A Poetic Novel

by
MARK ALAN MURRAY

An Earth's Seductive Haze Publication
Berkshires, Massachusetts, U.S.A.

OF NOD is a poetic novel. It is a work of fiction, but at times is infused with the author's present recollections of his experiences over a period of years. Certain names, locations, and identifying characteristics have been changed, in addition to the actual occurrences, and certain individuals are composites. Furthermore, dialogue and events may have been recreated from memory and in some instances, have been compressed to convey the substance of what was said or what occurred.

To order additional copies of this title, contact your favorite local bookstore or visit www.lulu.com

Cover design by Mark Alan Murray
Book design by Mark Alan Murray
Cover photo by Alan Murray

Printed in the United States of America

An Earth's Seductive Haze Publication
Berkshires, Massachusetts, U.S.A.

ISBN: 978-1-105-29178-4

30.00

OF NOD

***

The cavernous heart—
Where lions den and lovers roam...
The labyrinth mind—
Where lions pace and lovers entwine...
The ocean soul—
Where lions roar and lovers bathe;
The dreaming Earth—
Where lions tame and lovers wane...
The Heaven gate—
Where lions guard and lovers slay.

My God hath sent his angel, and hath shut the lions' mouths, that they have not hurt me: forasmuch as before him innocency was found in me; and also before thee, O king, have I done no hurt.

Daniel, Chapter 6

The ultimate proof of a tamer's dominance and control over a lion is demonstrated by placing his head in the lion's mouth.

Wikipedia

A truly strong person does not need the approval of others any more than a lion needs the approval of sheep.

Vernon Howard

I am sometimes a fox and sometimes a lion. The whole secret of government lies in knowing when to be the one or the other.

Napoleon Bonaparte

Thou shalt tread upon the lion and adder: the young lion and the dragon shalt thou trample under feet.

Psalm 91:13

Contents

I: LIONS

II: LOVERS

III: LABYRINTHS

IV: EPILOG

LIONS

BLESSING AND CURSE

Upon the bushes that lined our home in Winston-Salem, North Carolina, there were red berries, that mother said not to eat for they were *poisonous,* would make one sick, and so I never let them touch my tongue; but, sometimes, when the urge was great, I would break their skins with my fingers as if they were tiny worlds and gaze upon the glutinous substance within: the seed, portion which could create new birth, secure in the depths.

My blond hair was almost white, and I was unconsciously waiting for my brother to enter the world. The sun, as if it rivaled my blaze, would slowly pull out the yellow during the hot summers when there was no school and all play.

The sandbox, that which my grandfather had built and I had painted a bright red, was where I first learned how to mold the world, how castles could be made and knocked down.

This was the place where I caught wild rabbits and would their hunger quell with scraps from our table.

This is where I would run indoors when lightning struck with its echoing thunder, where I would hide in my parents' arms and wait for tears to stop, rivulets streaming down my face.

As a very young boy, my father would read me The Bible. Samson... his story I asked my father, with his voice of quiet strength, again and again to make his hair, the dark woman he loved, and his rage real in my mind. What a gift both of them gave, Samson and my father, for now my hair has become a cluster of vines that strives to touch the ground, and, when looking through the stray golden strands into the feminine mind, all seem to be a Delilah hatched or waiting to be hatched and, even with the length still intact, my rage grows.

My father and stepmother, Dawn, had been living in Pittsburgh at the time, in a small condo. I believe it was during the first year of their marriage that the fever induced dream occurred. I was visiting. The condo was one room... we slept on the floor together. I believe my brother was there. He and I always visited our father together in those days.

It was dark. My eyes were open and yet it was dark. My father held me in his arms. Over and over again I kept saying "I can fly, I can fly, father...," or at least I believe I was uttering those words amidst tears. Then the darkness would again fade into the other... again, I was the cause... the cause for some great disaster.

I was walking in a park. There was a lush green lawn and a single path which I followed. There were no trees. There was nothing besides the path and lawn. There was no horizon, only a blinding light, like sunlight on the edge of my vision. I knew I had done something of horrible import. I knew I had caused the end to come. So, I bent down and kissed the ground, thinking *"I can only be as good as he will let me."*

And then it was dark again and I somehow knew that I was in my father's arms saying, "I can fly," over and over. And he kept responding, "Take my hand. Take my hand..." and followed, saying "We're making up for lost time. I have not given up in the time in-between. If I had known then what I know now..."

Somewhere along this life's journey I lost a great part of myself. I am now thirty-eight years old and suffer from schizophrenia. But, I do believe this illness is a blessing *and* a curse. Understandings are gained only through some sense of hardship, it seems.

There was a period when everything seemed to be "normal"— through most of my childhood and into my early adulthood I lived a privileged life, with a loving family and enough money for us to eat well and buy most of the material items that we desired.

Something went wrong though, drastically wrong. By the time I was twenty-seven, one horrible night, from a hotel close to Bradley Airport, I picked up the phone in the lobby and called for an ambulance...

There was not enough room on the Psychiatric Ward so I spent the better part of the night strapped down to a gurney, locked in a room by myself. I did not understand exactly... I knew I had told the EMTs I had been hearing voices... and that the voices had been telling me to commit suicide... they were suggestions though, more than voices... inaudible hints... *swallowing that bottle of pills would be a good idea... think about it... think.* But, more than anything, I was just plain scared. I needed help... somewhere in the depth of my soul, I knew I had to get help... for, I was in danger.

~ 13 ~

OF NOD

My mother is a nurse. In the midst of the horror of that
night, when I had driven away from my father's home— then in
West Hartford— without direction, knowing I must escape
that house where the walls were moving... it dawned upon
me... I had to make my way to the hotel where my mother
stayed when she visited just a month before.

It was my mother's voice I heard later that evening, during the
madness of seeing phantoms, of walking in vacant lots. Under
one streetlight I saw a girl with two large copper coins in her
hand... or I thought I saw her, for when I turned my head to
watch the traffic, then looked back, she was gone, had never
been there. When driving to the hotel earlier in the night I
thought I had seen the same girl, standing in the middle of
I84... and I drove through her. She was a spirit that had been
haunting me. She held out the coins as if they were an
offering... and then disappeared. I also felt as if there was some
demon I would have to face if I returned to the hotel... for I
had seen what I did not want to see when settling in earlier that
evening... a disembodied ghost. I was sitting on the bead, but
in the chair across the room there seemed to be something
forming, like smoke and haze— a movement in the still air.
Then, when I was walking in the vacant lot... for I had needed
to leave that hotel where I had found myself alone, dealing with
the crisis of my mind and soul... I heard my mother's voice of
reason— as if she was close or could sense the state of my
mind— say, "Go to the hospital, Marc... you need to go to the
hospital."

I survived. It has been ten years. I have survived. Presently I
am working to rehabilitate people with mental illness. Yes, I am

now on the other side of the fence… I am one people come to when they have lost the most important part of themselves. I help them find their way back to some sense of sanity.

***

When I was about nine or ten years old there was a fantasy which took hold of me. I had just then begun attending Sunday school. I was then beginning to learn about Jesus. Something one of the Sunday school teachers told me got inside and started wreaking havoc with my imagination. She said, "Jesus would return to us one day," that "He would come back as a child," just like me or any of the other children in the classroom, "He would save the world." I took her literally. I believed her. I thought I had done nothing wrong in my life… that I was good… that, in all essence, I might be the next Christ.

One might argue that this event was essentially the beginning of my illness. Or, perhaps the illness began at birth… because I was born into this present day reality. The wars that this nation is part of, the constant bombardment of information about the state of the world— through radio, through television, through newspapers— seems to work one into a mindset of continual anxiety. Humanity, as a whole, is sick. We are killing each other. We are building nuclear weapons, and, in the meantime, we are polluting this planet to such an extent it may become uninhabitable within my lifetime.

THE LOSS OF WHAT IS WRITTEN

The wind and the water grass scraped the outer face of the
canoe which, with buoyancy, carried me to a place of quiet,
where no eyes could watch... face of my mother though—
bright as the sun— hovering in the distance. Hawks flying,
searching for fish to feed upon, waters that mingle, trees
standing, waiting for the wind to course through leafy boughs,
precious moments— somewhere beyond the horizon, symbols
clashing. Naked, canoe resting on shore, I walked into the
water and swam, an essence inside myself for long time not
felt... once more imagined myself as Christ— the turtle who's
shell is sturdy— disembodied, stretching my arms around the
globe and holding Earth as if it was a ball.

Then the descent, loss of what is written, rewriting, becoming
the words...   I struggled back toward the boat tied to
overhanging branches, becoming half dog / half man or some
stick that floats where memory has just begun.

Currently I am staying at my friend's cottage in Tenant's
Harbor, Maine. It is my vacation from work. I have taken this
week off to come here and work on poetry with one of the most
important individuals in my life, Erika.

Every July, for the past four years, I have visited so I might
continue composing with her. She rents a cabin. It is on a
peninsula. The cottage sits directly on a land jut, with the
cove's waves always ebbing, flowing, and breaking directly
outside the bay window in the room where we labor to find the

correct words or phrases that describe my thoughts and experiences.

Erika is a beautiful person. She is sixty-eight years old, beautiful in heart and soul. She has been in theatre her entire life, foregoing college so she could study in Seattle and New York City. Now she directs a theatre company in the Thomaston, Maine area.

The cottage where we stay is simple, quaint, yet exceedingly unique and cozy. There is no shower, but, if I am in the mood to bathe, I begin by wading in the cold water of the ocean, then, wash my hair in a lobster pot, using a smaller cooking pot to pour the warm tap water over the lengths of my hair. There is no better way to bathe. Life is good here. We are happy.

I consider Erika to be one of my mentors. She teaches much more than how to write well. When people ask about this woman I visit, I tell them she is a great reader and thus she has all the knowledge needed to help with editing my work. At her home in Thomaston, she must have ten thousand books. So that people would believe this, I have taken pictures of the rooms of her home to show others how they are filled to the brim with books, each and every room of the four bedroom house... on table tops, stacked on floors, piled on beds, in boxes, on radiators, and arranged on shelving.

Beyond being such an unbelievable reader, she unendingly studies world politics. I joke with my friends, telling them a week spent with her is equivalent to a graduate course in liberal political science; but, this is no joke. Her knowledge on world matters is immense.

I just stepped outside again for another cigarette. It is raining. We are supposed to experience a severe storm this evening, the center of which is moving southward. The storms in the Northeast have been vicious this spring and summer. The weather seems to have taken a turn for the worse in the past few years. Scientists say it might be global warming, that weather patterns are changing. I wonder…

While I was outside, a helicopter flew over this town. That reminds me of this past Memorial Day. In Massachusetts, where I live, I was walking a circular section of dirt and paved roads that exits from one end of Reed Farm and, by twisting and turning, arrives back to the Farm, at the other end of the five-hundred acre lot. It is a beautiful hike any season... and, it was a beautiful hot summer afternoon that day.

About a third of the way into the walk, I was frightened horribly. A low flying jet streaked directly overhead. I thought to myself how strange a jet would be flying so low to the earth. Not three minutes later, another streaked overhead, heading in the same direction. When the third jet, at what seemed a similar altitude, came thundering over, then I was sure the country was at war.

A sick feeling rose up inside of me. I knew there was nothing I could do except go back to the Farm and hope my anxieties were not reality. Far off, then, I saw a sight that brought a smile to my face. Farmer Harold, with his two oxen, in yoke, pulling a cart, was heading up the dirt road in my direction. I walked at an average pace towards them and, when I was close enough, asked the question, "Harold, what the hell is going on? Have you heard those jets?" And he simply replied— in his calm, farming manner, "What, didn't you hear? They're flying low over the whole of Massachusetts... streaking over the parades. Didn't you know? It's Memorial Day."

I wonder what the seagulls will do when it storms. Or, perhaps the storm will blow over and out to sea. The cabin is waiting. I sit here in this library writing. Erika is upstairs showing a film for the benefit of many Thomaston locals.

I know that, in the middle of the night— as always— I will wake from dreams. I will climb out of the bunk, turn on the porch light, and will go outside to smoke. There, in the damp grass I will stand... there in the dark, the only light to my universe being that cast by the porch. If it is anything like last night, I will imagine that a devil is there... but, no, that shadow I see is only the bulbous trunk of some tree... that rustling is merely some raccoon or some opossum close in the brush.

VOICES

I hear voices in the waves. I am in Kemah, Texas, at my mother's home along the coast of Galveston Bay. I hear voices from the trees— the multitudes of birds… a woman's voice… no, many women's voices. What they are saying is intelligible… whispers just audible.

My father drove my truck across this country, south from Connecticut, bringing it all the way here to Kemah, so I might have a vehicle. I am recovering after having been in the hospital. I am seeing a doctor who prescribes medication and whom I talk with about my life. The voices are still there, but they are not bidding me to take my life. Instead, they are pleasing to me in some fashion. They are of the young woman at the Rec center, the life guard in the pool where I swam the other day… they are of the nurse at the hospital where I am volunteering. They are of the stranger I saw walking by the apartment complex down the street… she with blond hair… whom I imagined would have been wonderful to know. And then there are other voices of many a woman who I have never known, who I have never seen. They are in the waves, they are in the birds chirping, and they are in the sound of a car's tires humming over the pavement.

It has been about a month since I was in the hospital. My mother had flown to Hartford immediately and taken me out of the Psych ward, put me on a plane, and here I am… at her home, walking the streets in the development where she resides. I am no longer a danger to myself and had never, never been a danger to anyone else. I had been afraid, but am no more. There is no reason to be fearful. The stress of life has been reduced greatly. I am no longer living at my father's home in West Hartford, looking for work, using substances, and arguing with my stepmother. I am no longer living in that basement room where the walls were telling me the secrets of madness.

My father is here though, in Texas. He drove my truck all this way. It is an old Toyota, black with quite a lot of rust. On the day of his arrival, driving back to his hotel room so he would not have to stay long at my mother's home, he said something about the truck— said I would need a new one soon. And, strange to say, at that moment, the truck seemed to change… visually seemed to become like new in its interior. I cannot understand this… it baffles me, but I say nothing.

I have learned not to speak about these matters, these strange perceptions. Life seems to say to me, "Marc, there are some things that should not be talked about…." When I walk with my mother and her husband, Eugene, about the development, sometimes I yet hear my mother's thoughts, such as, "Was it the right time for him?" I understand this as meaning, "Was this the right time for him to emerge… to become an adult?"

I realize now becoming an adult can be a violent process… that to be an adult has much anxiety and fear, much responsibility as part of the definition. And, I am yet defining myself. I am becoming more human I would guess— no longer choosing to run from my fears, no longer accepting the horrid madness for reality, no longer taking my life for granted, taking medication to cure the sickness of my mind and soul… of emotion.

~ 21 ~

OF NOD

I bow my head to the sunset peeking through the clouds, the universe courses through me for the first time— as a river through a hidden glen.   Cars and children are one in the distance. A crow's call echoes in both worlds. My finger draws a symbol of power in the shore's sand, guided by some god's hand.

A BEWILDERED GOD

In West Hartford, that previous winter, as the illness set-in... a squirrel climbed the steel stair, then twitched and switched directions, hopped from one level onto another, tail a question held behind. My attention divided— a glass of water shared between two men. The half-moon between the winter white snows gathered upon the steeple then emptied back onto the rodent's scurrying efforts to find a place of rest. A man of the church wearing a suit beneath down coat carried a few bound books as if they were a fag of sticks... reached the doors... then found them sealed, barring his entry. Discovering one of the limits of his Earth, he turned— a bewildered god— seemed to trip on a step as he walked down and crossed the icy parking lot to stop beside my Toyota. Slightly trembling, he drew a circle in the chill, bidding me roll down the barrier between. My left hand reached and spun the lever as if cranking an old engine that had forgotten how to run, and, for that brief period— a dot at the end of a sentence— the warmth seeped out and the cold which surrounded him settled upon me. A few words were thrown in each direction and we looked into each other's souls and somehow knew that, on this day, the church would not open easily for either of us. As if he was afraid his footsteps would change the clouds that rested in the sky above, that person who carried his life under his arm— books bound with a leather strap— gently, as if that package was the skull of one of his ancestors fallen from the shelf of the dead, went along with his day— while I sat gazing at the sparrows which jumped from limb to limb in the faltering season. Then, for a turn, behind the frost that was growing upon the window, I sat... listening... to a man, far in the distance, singing impulsively… the sadness of my heart in the nearby streets.

***

This coward, the one who runs from darkness, always believing something better is to be found. My motor has been revving at such a high rate for so long… if I had wings, my feathers would all be frayed; but, now, for my sake, I feel a need for rest. When did I begin to run towards the ensuing moment? Iowa, Michigan, Maine, Texas, Connecticut, back to Maine again... it seems when I lost a love. With the first draft of one of my poems— something that was pure and true floated away on the water, a paper boat. Nightmares are supposed to have an end, which is what I keep telling myself. Common heart, just get over that hill and maybe there freedom will lie; but, like a wasp that's stuck in the space between the screen and the window, a man must at some point say: *"This is my home and so I will make the best of it,"* then call his mother on the phone and let her know in the pauses that follow, in the breath that precedes each word, how wonderful this life is that she has granted him.

***

I am here. I am here at the house in Tenant's Harbor. I have never left and I have always been here. Outside, by the front door… the door leading onto the porch, there is a tree with found beach items scattered about it, including many different colored buoys. On a lobster crate there is a dead lunar moth amidst many patterned rocks and beautiful shells.

I turn now and look up the hill, at the house that sits there with the gray sky as its backdrop. The house is modern, more modern that this humble cottage where we stay. In its front lawn waves an American flag... waving... waving... in the slight breeze of this early morning.

The tide is out. More of the cove's beach is now visible. The waves roll in. In the surf I can still hear a voice, but singular... barely audible... a whisper that is just out of my grasp.

THE SUN HAS RISEN

I did wake in the middle of the night, around two-thirty, from a dream. I was half conscious, dreaming I was there in my bunk, and had a cigarette dangling from my fingers, arm laxly hanging over the edge of the mattress. The smoke wafted into Erika's room. And then she coughed and it woke me with a start... I quickly climbed out of bed, hearing her say in a sleepy voice "Come here, Honey."

My initial thought was she was dreaming, she was disturbed by the sound of me getting out of bed, and she thought I was her husband from long ago. But, no... she must have been calling Chloe... the Jack Russell Terrier whom she loves dearly, whom she has brought to the cabin to keep both of us company, who sleeps in her bed with her.

I have to say that, sometimes it seems this exertion, nights, weekends, while at work and while at play, focusing my thoughts through the hole in the needle, devoting my wings to the way one puts into words that which will tempt the soul or heart of a beast to fly forth into the garden of Heaven or Hell, lacing these threads, doing so, wanting so that I have asked Christian and Pagan shades for assistance. And there were the mysterious thin and great trees on the verge, along the lane the artist must tread, threatening over my shoulders... beneath, the rabbits who lived amidst the rocks; and their whispering fed me, who once allowed to be, burrowed their sinewy forms inside the matter of which I am.

Instead of ravens, I look for angels. Both hover about the dying and living, both carry within claws or cupped palms gifts of water. Drink from black wings and you are the Cyclops with a red eye of greed, whose complex tongue slices like a dagger blade... does not want to be the cause of grief but cannot help what it embitters. Drink from the others, the seraphim, those that seem to hide just beyond belief, that allow no shadows (or, are ravens the shadows of angels?), then you never have to reach with the hand of will in order to touch upon our great mystery. In such a way, God, *I help myself and you help me* just in time— wherever I might be living— so that I might notice what is sacred: the arched leap of the dolphin seen from the beach or the patterned back of the serpent— that slides, an elongated S upon the grass between cemetery's headstones.

The lunar moth's wings are soaked after the rain last night. The left wing of the dead insect is only partially intact. Erika made a gift of the moth to me at the beginning of the week on returning from walking Chloe.

The sun has risen. It is behind a cloud bank. The ocean is the color of steel... its surface is calm... only slight waves come to rest on the rock-strewn shore. A plane is heard far in the distance. A truck shifting gears is also in my awareness... no that must be the sound of a lobster boat out in the cove. Even here, where all seems peaceful, if one listens carefully, he or she can hear the faint reminders...

IN A NEAT PILE

Tomorrow I return. I will eat a little breakfast, make a sandwich, and begin the long drive back to Massachusetts. My heart aches to think of leaving this haven.

I am refreshed... I have centered myself in the work that has been accomplished with Erika. Much poetry was revised. We were at our best this week. Sitting next to her, as she read my poems out loud, many times I would see how they needed to change before she took up the pencil and began marking the pages.

I do look forward to returning home... back to the Farm where I have made a life for myself. The relationships— although complicated— have developed over the spans of four years. I am excited to set my eyes upon those friends, those folk whom have become family to me. There is not one soul at that Farm which I do not love.

The coffeemaker in the kitchenette of this cottage is brewing the dark essence I love so... the light of noon filters through the bay window. The lamp upon this table glows... the poetry books with their notations are in a neat pile sitting by the lamp.

This morning, Erika and I woke relatively early so we could visit the local library where a grand book sale was occurring. Yellow construction tape acted as a boundary so the slew of people wanting to buy was held at bay until the time the sale would begin. When nine o'clock came, everyone on the edge of the tables broke the tape and began sifting through the thousand or so of books.

The people of Maine seem to have a true hunger for books. I was impressed, and thought how wonderful it is that there is such reading happening yet in the world, that people have not forsaken reading for the television.

I have not watched more than an hour of television over the past two years. I do not own a television. There is a TV room at the Farm where I will, from time to time sit and read the Events section of the newspaper, or check my horoscope, but, as soon as someone turns on that screen, I tend to put the paper down quickly and make an exit.

I do not like the news. Any news I do pay attention to is mostly through word of mouth. I find that to learn from others is a most rewarding way to understand the happenings on this globe. If there was one thing about the Earth I would change, I believe it would be to have all the TV sets destroyed, much as all the books were destroyed in that wonderful novel entitled *Fahrenheit 451.*

I keep forgetting I will be leaving tomorrow, and, upon remembering, as time passes, I feel more and more ready for the transition back to the Farm. At Reed Farm, Rosalynn is waiting. She is the oldest member of our community. She has lived ninety-eight years, the greater part of which was spent at Reed Farm. She has seen most of the history of the Farm since its early conception. She knew the founders, and, in a way, I believe she is the heart of the present Farm. She is the great grandmother to the shifting and changing community... to all that live there now, or whatever now has been or will be.

At the Farm, my cats are waiting. A friend, Lane, has been watching them while I've been away, letting them out in the morning, and back in at night. They are beautiful. One is two years old and the other is about seven. Each has an incredibly unique spirit. Some people think cats are all alike, but, no, that is not true. I think, concerning every living animal on the planet— if you spend enough time with their species— you will find each creature has a soul and a way of being that is its own.

Now, though, I am here at this cottage, and I will make the best of the remaining time. I will have a long talk or two with Erika. I will listen to many waves come rolling and crashing to the shore. I will begin reading one or two of the books I found at the sale....

The lunar moth, I have noticed, is now on its back. Its wings have dried. It is sleeping, and will always be sleeping... even after a gust of wind has come and let it fly briefly again through the air... she— the Siren I heard whispering in the waves this morn— is sleeping... Erika sits on the porch, reading....

THE OCEAN

Just outside the cove's mouth are two lobster boats. The men on those boats are hauling their gear. . one lobster pot at a time. Scattered about that entire area are hundreds of buoys, all of varied colors. Further out, a sail boat cuts the surface of ocean, pushed by wind.

I can remember. I know what it is to be working, at this time of year, on a lobster boat. I was a stern-man on a boat for two years, in my early thirties, which fished out of Port Clyde, just down the road from where I now vacation.

Noah was the owner of the boat. He was a man, not so much older that I am today, who was *not* a fair weather fisherman. He and I would fish the waters, up to ten miles off the coast, during the calm days and during many of the rough winter storms.

I can hear the rumbling of the boats' engines even from here.

This has not been a good year for the fishermen of Maine. In fact, during the past few years, they have been catching fewer and fewer lobsters. I was lucky. During the years I was a stern-man, we caught an unbelievable amount of lobsters.

I called Noah this past winter. Having not talked to him in a long time, and not knowing how the fishing industry had been holding up, I was genuinely curious. I could tell though... before I asked the question... subtly I could discern I should not ask. And, he was noticeably not happy to have to answer such inquiry... it seemed as if he was trying to not think about the matter. He simply answered by saying, with his Maine accent, "Well, Marc, you were smart to get out of it when you did."

There is a beauty to the fisherman's love and labor: rising before dawn; drinking a pot of coffee; arriving to the bait house yet in darkness; spilling the huge plastic drums of salted herring and mackerel onto the oily wooden planks; shoveling it into the bins; then, with a turn of the key, the initial roar of the engine... slowly we would steam out of the harbor. I always loved watching the lighthouse, there in the early dawn. After passing the lighthouse, Noah would push the throttle full-forward. The boat's bow would immediately lift out of the water, and, as if we were racing against time, he and I would be carried over the cold vastness to arrive at the line of buoys which we would haul. And we would steam to the next line... and then to the next... all day... sometimes twelve hours a day.

I yet dream... dream of the ocean, of working on fishing boats. I am now an in-lander. I have forsaken the life of a fisherman to become one who would heal others. People question if I miss the adventure of working on the sea. I tell them no, that interactions between people— especially in a community such as ours— tend to have such complexities that there is no lack of stimulation for me. But, as if the waves call me... during the darkest of nights... when the moon and the stars are not visible... then, I yet dream of that work, that labor, that love.

The quiet of afternoon, the peace of early September... my shadow reflected on the pond's water. You, distant from me, oh moon in the blue. You, distant from me, oh woman that I contemplate, that I forced myself to separate from. The day is just beginning. I feel as if I am a caged insect, a lightning bug in a jar; a child peering through the glass. I light the child's face with my pulse. A tinge of regret impedes my ability to enjoy this day. I am no more the lighthouse on the land jutting out from Port Clyde's harbor, that which I watched from the stern of the Rose as we headed out into the great ocean, as dawn was aglow. I am no more the lighthouse in Northport, high that night, wandering about, casting my shadow. I am no more the man of action, of pulse. I am more of the casting, of the rod and lure, of the lonely man.

There were woods by my home as a child. When I lived in North Carolina, in my early years, I found that I always gravitated to the woods. Even when first attending the university, as a young adult, I would spend long days, skipping many of my courses, so I might tramp through the wood, so I might discover new paths, so I might listen to the river that the Nipmuck Trail followed. But, the trees of the woods tend not to call me as intensely as the waves of the sea. The sea is a woman. She, with her strands of flowing seaweed. She, with her motion: raging waters or the quiet ebbing and flowing of the early days' currents. She is beautiful to me and to swim in her brings me back... back through eons of time. I am returning home when I wade in her shallows. I am young again. I am innocent. I am the single-celled body that will one day be the salamander that will one day be the ape that will one day be a man.

OF NOD

As the bumble and honey bees delicately landed on the clover, collecting their pollen, and then silently flew to other clovers, Erika and I talked... there outside the cabin. Distant thunder... dark clouds were forming over the ocean. But, we were both content. "Let it rain... let it rain..." we both seemed to think. We have collected enough pollen this week.

Uninterrupted, we have essentially been on an island— a mental and spiritual island. This has been a gift. The spirits have breathed life into us. The heart of the land has enfolded us. The familiar is what I now seek when thinking about vacations. Knowing a place over time allows one to feel the comfort that is like and unlike home... that is home for a period of time, an interval... it allows me to be myself... to rediscover, to hearken to the call of my soul.

FLUTTER OF A MOTH'S WING

Much happens when we are not there... where the hustle and bustle of lives we've left behind continues. Sometimes, I believe that I may be living many different lives simultaneously... sometimes I contemplate the frightening, the awesome... if only to entertain my active mind. We do seem to be able to direct thoughts to a certain extent. The mental gymnastics one must accomplish in order to maneuver through life is what determines how well a person survives.

I have an active mind. My imagination seems to get me in trouble over and over. So much can come to pass within the collective imagination. I have loved the ghosts of many a woman. I have accomplished much of what others hold as meaningful simply through the experience of waking dreams.

When I look at the beach rocks here, when I hold them in my hands, I can somehow feel their ancient qualities. Each of them is older than the oldest living creature or growth on the planet. They are a testament that Earth will survive regardless of man. Man is but a flutter of a moth's wing.

A severe weather warning was just issued over the radio. It seems hail and tornadoes will hit north of here... around Caribou, Maine. I hope it is north, far north that the storm lands, but there is thunder threatening close at hand.

When there were gusts of wind that blew over the field and upon the open water, that wasn't created by gods, that which was of nature, searching for trees and the feathers of birds to stream across, that which had a mind of its own and might have been a lesser god in and of itself, when that force— once upon a time— first shared the duties of shaping the stone and moving the sand, and seemed to even whistle through the stars and grope through the orifices of mountains in order to entertain itself— what a wonder it must have been! What seeds it must have scattered through millions of years!

***

It is about five days before Christmas. I am out at sea... two hundred miles out, on a seventy-seven foot Gloucester lobster boat. We have been laying into the waves for three days now, but there is no end to this storm. I am in my bunk, trying to sleep because there is nothing else to do.

I am awakened by one of my fellow crew members... he says we are going to have to fish, that regardless of the storm, we are going to fish so the crew can make money and get back to their families for Christmas. I am horrified. The storm is no less raging than it was three days ago. I clumsily put on my rain gear and head out into the frigid, gusty air, onto the deck. The wind is strong, so I must lean into the gusts to keep from being pushed over. When we are in the troughs, the water on each side of us rises taller than a three-story building. When we roll, roll to the top of a great wave, then, looking out across the water, all we can see is huge rolling masses, curling at their tops... the curling foam, the wind that catches at the foam, and lifts it... the smaller waves that crash against the boat's hull, which break overboard sometimes.

I can hardly keep my balance… when my turn comes to break traps overboard, where I will have to stand close to the edge; I go into the cabin and bark at the captain, "We should not be fishing in this. It is too dangerous." And, he replies, "We have no choice… we will run out of fuel before the storm ends. We will lose too much money if we steam-in now."

For a moment, I consider saying that I will not fish, that I will give up and go below deck, but then I say, instead, that if we must fish then I would rather fill bait-bags and band lobsters for the remainder of the storm. He seems to understand, seeing as I am the least experienced on the boat. He lets the crew know. I am tossed around between the bait bin and the lobster banding table for three long days, but I know that I will not fall overboard, there in the center of the deck, close to the cabin.

The sea, raging, as a woman in seizure. I was standing on the deck of the seventy-seven foot boat, leaning to and fro, riding the sway and rock, the vessel's buoyant voyage. "Put your mouth to God's ear," she said, that woman of the deep, she that lives in the turmoil of storm and wave. So I sent the prayer heavenward and listened, hearkening to the forthcoming answer: "Live, live, live," was the reply I heard, a whisper within wind, within storm, and braced myself for the coming of my life that would surely transpire, riding the sway and rock of the vessel's buoyant voyage.

When we return to port, we have a huge catch. But, when the owner of the boat asks if I will be ready to go out again in two days, I smile and say that I need a trip off. He understands, but still gives me a call midway through the next week, wanting to make sure that I will show. I though, on walking away from that boat, had decided that I would never fish the deep sea again.

*****

I sit here petting my cat. I am home now... I have returned to the Farm. It was a long drive. I was tired... too much relaxing over vacation. At one moment I fell asleep while driving... it was just for a split second, but I was well aware of the fact that I had slipped into sleep for that moment. It was frightening... I found the closest rest stop, and bought myself a cup of black coffee... guzzled it down and then was able to drive the last hour and a half back to the Farm.

The cats are happy to see me. The small black one would be completely content if I were to sit petting him forever. It is good to be home. The cabin I live in is just as cozy as ever. The grass has grown since I've been gone... but, there is not the lushness to the woods that was noticeable before I left. I napped all afternoon, and then I awoke to eat dinner with the community. Many people asked about how my vacation was, but in a sleepy manner. I must keep in mind that they have been working all this time... that they have not been listening to the breaking surf for the past week. I must keep in mind that I have changed.

The flow of tears ebbed. I walked upon the shore of a distant land, talking to an ancient woman. She had walked on that shore since the beginning of time. She said "Show your light,

your love, your hope... hold it in your head... find your way."
She touched me and I was calmed. She was spirit... she held
the world within her thoughts, but, for that moment, I was all
she seemed to be focusing on. I had to consciously hold back
the deep sobs, and, later in the night, as the fireflies flickered in
the field where I stood, I could feel that something had opened
within me. The tears had been left on the beach... the fire of
my soul could now burn without being impeded.

BY THE PATH TO THE PAST

Searching, while roaming over this continent of continents, for feathers that still ruffled in the wind; looking for them upon the roadside, upon the still warm figure that I have at this instant noticed, and so I pull the truck over in the hope that it was what it was: a hawk that had just been felled, the yet supple body... it crossed the path of a being which had a mind not of its own... one of those great eighteen wheelers, the sparkling red cabs with their chrome... I have seen many of them rush along in such a heedless way, like mad instruments of destruction, sleepless bodies at the steering wheels, like and unlike me... alone, traveling on the Iowa roads, with the dead corn fields and lonely farm houses... a vision stretched on either side of our journeys. The pickup still running... a piece of cardboard in my hand... trucks and cars passing— without touching, I kneel over the now still body, roll her onto the flat surface and, with both hands make a cradle, carry that carcass back to the warmth of the truck. Home— the place of many windows that lets light in from varied angles. With kitchen knife, I cut the wings, pull out the tail feathers that resist like embedded nails, then remove the beaked head— the eyes have been closed— and hang each of the parts of my totem upon the wall.

***

During the day, the sun goes from one side of my head to the other. The stones that have soaked up my tears were scattered by the mindless nature of the dreamer— seed thrown upon the bare spots of the earth. We had opened the hole in the roof of our heads and let the tempest flow within.... In the light that reached us, we were streamers on the end of a stick— whipping and tattering in the wind, no longer held or able to hold to the bodies discarded. That which was rising, the shore of everything we had ever been, churned, given to a witch's spoon... a flock of birds flying out of the openings, white doves that, once released, eventually returned carrying in their beaks the black parts of our minds. At the end of my arms there hung, like two spider crabs, my hands dripping as if I'd cupped some of the water thick with the salt which was once Lot's wife, that which gives flavor to the black olives, that which is expelled along with semen. Behind us, the street lights' radiance yet shattered upon our heads... we were still shining....

I had for a long time been upon all fours praying to a spirit of power I did not pretend to know, walking alone on the shore of a foreign land, the stage where there are no x's that mark the floor, beckoning when I have forgotten where to position myself, caged by the coast of a continent, isolated from Earth's pride.

Though two friends were standing next to me, it felt as if they had become part of themselves more than I would ever manage, even if these hands were to grab the knife that had been floating in front of me and turn it and slice and dig into my flesh, scoop out my entrails and throw them upon the ground to divine purpose; but, in this passage, I forgot about the promise I had made... and, when we left and the waves had disappeared from our vision, and our altered bodies had taken shelter in the house on a corner of Connecticut's coast, I opened my wallet, procured a piece of Saran wrap which held another square—

like a piece of the puzzle that when put together is the picture of insanity— and, once when everything had been understood, I placed on the tip of my tongue that piece of a tree which had at one time been drowned, boiled and brought to life, embittered as it was, by a tear dropped upon it from God's dismal eye.

***

While there was a bit of light we tried to build a fire. I could no longer feel my hands— the cold had taken them— those knotted roots groping through air… no longer parts of me. Sticks broken off… that action seemed useless… taking each one from those branches when the water they held would never let fire begin. While a hand guarded the flame from the wind, I did my part by shifting from leg to leg and, in a sad way hoped that the miracle would be performed, for all the trees had risen up as if they were a host of gods and, though they freely gave us their lower branches (for I did not perceive an anger at our presence), they could not help but laugh when the mist draped itself around our panic.

Before we had begun to break, when it had dawned upon us that the cabin with its wood stove, our packs and sleeping bags, our food was not where we thought— somewhere in the distance— perched on top of another mountain, the party had split. The young couple deciding to try to find their dark-way, while the person who had led us astray, and I stayed, thinking it would be best to prepare for the night as best as we could. I had a lighter in my pocket and I was wrong in believing in its power to create warmth. Just before Thanksgiving is not the best time to find one's self on a mountain unprepared. Around us there was a maze of paths where the moose had blazed through random growth. The clouds above blotted out the sun and no matter how we tried to make steel roll over flint in a way that would hold flame long enough to dry a section of those twigs and start something more than a little snake-hiss. all that would happen was the cold air seemed to ease its way into the cracks and crevices of our bodies.

We walked away from the pile of sticks, following the same direction we had seen the other two hikers tread into dusk. The endless darkness started to sew her black patch in front of our eyes and I couldn't help but catch my feet on fallen wood. I could hardly keep up with my companion, for his feet seemed to become more able to find their way while mine focused on finding each hole or stick. Then rain began like small drops of horror.

It was time to stop. The arms that reached out to hold me— helped me to stand when I was an infant— were no longer there and I was not sure that I would be able to walk further upon this Earth where we had become lost. In the importance of that moment, I looked through the dark heavens into Heaven itself, and stared at God, my shoulders held back and, in my stance, told that being of consciousness I wanted what was my due and, then, the other face of me bowed down, became smaller than a leaf and prayed for my manhood that had not yet begun.

At once I knew— my feet did not need to take the next step— I took the one, who I had followed in my arms, and he took me in his and we guarded ourselves from the wind and we talked to shed our inner tears; thus we kept our bodies warm until the morning.

As tired as we were, we found a forgotten logging road where the grooves made by past wheels could barely be discerned, but which led us into that other wilderness of paved roads, the many colored signs, the heated abodes. The strong and fragile creatures of us were born then, out of the White Mountains to live— life granted once more.

***

Last night we spoke for the first time in over a year. When my father answered, your voice caused him to hand the receiver over the patterned tablecloth gently— a flower, petals about to fall.

Strange how we can talk as if just last night we swam in Lake Michigan's moon towards the lonely boat. Rigging kept tapping against mast while we tried to sleep, backs pressed against curved walls of the hull. There was not enough room for us to take more than words of friendship from each other while the waves kept colliding against the sides, nudging us toward where we were just beginning to settle into each other's vision.

***

Driving around Oakland, Maine, the darkness doesn't seem so obscure, back roads, the movie theaters haven't been showing what we've been hungry for of late. We enter into each other's bodies, you eighteen, I twenty-six... in some ways it feels wrong, in some it feels just good, you opening your legs to my

~ 44 ~

loneliness and I showing you what it is to be with a budding man.

The moon is full, I remember a pasture... I have not seen the cows grazing there for quite some time. My rain coat as a tarp beneath, me on top, then you on top, the clouds spitting, some hidden animal grunting nearby, then I am grunting, trying to loose my pride into you for a second time, and, when we are done, the hay which at one time was alive— growing into the distance— finally merging with the heavens... all has been reaped and culled into many wheels that sit unmoving in their greatness, while the shadows, those that ever lengthen and relent, play beneath the stars.

***

In my truck, I, like my fellow workers, drink coffee, smoke tobacco, imagine that time is passing, spend time picking the whiskers of glass off my skin, feelers that have been snipped from a cat's nose... watching the pecking order of the flock— who sits in who's cab, what bird eats the most, what bird is dying— until the thin frame of the foreman— he who keeps everyone in line— on his way from freedom back into the vapors of hot resin, lifts his feet so that the serious bent face that he has striven to attain, and has been driven behind, spits twice upon the ground— into the open space, the scavengers scatter before him.

***

There was an attic that I climbed into, crowded with boxes

within which there were books which had never been opened but once— a skimming of the lines— before being packed away to yellow and become brittle over passing years.

There was a barn which I helped clean... the black fungus of long days spent under leaking roof had made the objects that would have been useful unworthy to be saved: lamps with shades, rugs, chairs— harlequins though, piled within a circular screen of chicken wire, which had kerosene poured upon it, which five or so matches brought to an ignominious end.

I have been in the cellar of a Victorian home, where great boulders, unearthed when men dug the foundation— which might have been removed in our modern times with cranes and dynamite— were left to survive, undisturbed, becoming part of the foundation. Like heads of great giants, those craggy faces thrust out from the shadows, peering into my fathomless mind.

I have entered into a cavern, which was burrowed out by water, and needed to be crawled through (at times) for one to reach an end, where moisture lurked and dripped, the stalactites and stalagmites searching, touching to create columns, those which seemed to be supports for the cliffs into which the cave led— where bat dung littered the floors— that place where the scent of dampness was always fresh.

***

Clothes piled on shore rocks, curtains of mist flowing over mountains; she is already breaking the night-calm with her soft skin swimming to a boulder set off-shore that thrusts a pointed back above the waves. Mona must have undressed and dressed herself in nakedness, a state of passion, not caring what would be dry or wet when she returned; so carefully, I place our shoes where they won't get sodden, set my glasses on top of a log, then drape my clothes and hers over the granite warming in morning sun, glittering with shards of quartz. I plunge into her wake, shocked by its warmth— waves mingle…. An outboard cuts the surface further off shore where our feet can't reach bottom, disturbing the quietude, eyes of the owner passing like a storm, leaving only a trail of waves lightly brushing my stomach— like the soft hand of a woman— giving calm water the passion lacked. Now, as a log, I begin to roll over the surface created towards Mona— who has reached her destination and stands upright on the rock's bare shoulders. Glowing by the light from behind, her elbows pressed inward, she looks towards the blue mountains, the horizons unveiled: a piece of sculpture captured, carved so gently skin might be skin— and touching won't tell the difference. Then, close to where she stands, in the dark above lake bed, my feet kicking, scrape tops on rough bottom-stone; blood stains then disperses… *"I will be part of this lake forever,"* I think as I climb and sit next to her dry form, close enough to smell the tarn in her hair.

⇒✲

The shells were bountiful that morning: a walk on the shore, picking rocks and casting them at the waves, hoping that somewhere in surf they would transform into a wish which the seaweed, like maiden's hair, would hide in tendrils throughout the coming cycle. I nodded at an old woman… the silence

~ 47 ~

stretched between us as her face, the moon, passed by and I don't know if the ocean was rising or if it was receding, for I was only a momentary visitor on her coast.

*****

I have been in the back of my truck during showers— the aluminum cap would allow me to hear every part of the rain, each pebble, each pearl that broke. In that place of cluttered camping equipment, with empty jars of peanut butter and candle wax on the wheel wells— a remembrance of the eighteen year old who opened her legs to my loneliness— there, I have sometimes tried to imagine that I was home.

*****

I am in the basement of my aunt and uncle's home. There is a scuffling noise in the garage. We kids go and open the door to find my father being wrestled to the floor by my uncle and mother. There is a shotgun in my father's hands. There is a determined look in his eyes as well as in the eyes of my mother and uncle. Something terrible is happening. I do not understand. I do not understand.

*****

I am in a friend's room in Waterbury, Connecticut. There are two of us there, visiting. I have been traveling through the Midwest, but now am back. I sit looking through a book of etchings depicting the story of Milton's *Paradise Lost*. Satan's army is amassing. My two friends… and a woman… there is a young woman present… partake of a concoction created from morning glory seeds. I do not join them. I am lost in my own nightmare.

**

We walked through the corn field on Horse Barn Hill, a night of laughter, when smoking dope and drinking cheap beer was fun. In moonlight, we all were surrounding her…. It was natural, our nakedness… and I think that *she* enjoyed it, her nipples like two kernels of corn. The moon above was a paper globe lit within. The air was cold against our naked bodies, not used to the sting of fall— we stood in a circle, shivered looking at each other, sometimes letting our gazes shift and witness more. She broke off an ear and pulled at the stringy husk, then passed it around, sharing the white nibblets, bites that were young, sweet.

**

I am in the back of my pickup. There is a cap sheltering me and the eighteen-year-old so that no one can see what we are about to do. We are parked at an overlook. This is somewhere close to Oakland, Maine. I offer her some marijuana. I cannot remember if she partakes. Regardless, though, we copulate… there is cardboard and a sleeping bag under us. She is slight, thin of frame. She is quiet.

**

~ 49 ~

OF NOD

We are in a field. I am naked, walking under the stars. Then, we lie down in the grass... I feel as if I know where she needs me to touch her. I feel as if I am touching the stars that live within her. She is beautiful.

***

I have found a place to sit, upon the broken surface of looming rock, where the edge of this state has crawled forward from the land— the meaning of truth, the cracked fissures, and the patches of quartzite blued by the sky... where a gull moans, maybe its last release of breath. In the waves— lions roaring— loons dive and, for lack of air, rear themselves back into the sun. Scattered orange buoys are tied not only in the ocean-depths, but to some unseen star, securing each device to its dance upon the tidal spread. On looking down beside me, amidst shards of rock severed from their source by past winters' ice, there scurries a little black ant making its way over and under— the depressions and the heights— to that which is manifest, trudging through the debris of eons so that it might carry a piece of sand within the dark hole of its hill. Far above, without sound, the hawk tucks in its wings.

***

Watching the trees through the window... it is raining and cold... it is Christmas. I have been working this Christmas at the Farm; thus, I am unable to visit friends and family. My love is far away— a woman who is part Native American. We are no longer in love. I feel as if I have misused her in some way. We were close for a long time, but now we spend our times together arguing. This cabin though holds warmth. The wood stove is the only heat I have here, and I keep a fire going day and night. To sit by the stove and contemplate… there is nothing better, with the cold wind blowing outside… with the rain and the sadness inside my heart growing.

***

The labor of creating anything of grand design, whether it be a vessel that carries water or that which cuts through ocean pushed by wind, or a body of skin that must create poetry— that which connects each moment with the next and is yet further from the grasp of time— that which is a shelter— that which labors unendingly is what I have found I am becoming.

The two of us working side by side … now, once again, I am the student and a burly man has become the teacher of a would-be college professor who must build boats to survive. I follow behind, wetting out beforehand and afterward so the ten-year-veteran can lay down material where it needs to be laid, so everything is perfect for the foreman who has been reminding us constantly: how much time we are taking, how fast it can be done, should be done, all that we've done wrong, and the little we have done right. When I get a chance to do more, to lay woven or mat, to make some pretty cuts, to learn from my mistakes, sometimes I am able through the process of *not* remembering, to become more of this life— passing dirty jokes back and forth, the repetition of it all— my body sometimes working on its own accord. Thus I am pulled through the dark tunnel of my making, and the factory (and what it produces), the men, boats, materials, tools that we must use, fumes and shards of glass we must breathe— which cause death to arrive early— all have allowed us moments of overlapping significance, and, by watching the laying of glass I have been able to learn that, after the first piece is put down, the next piece and all that come thereafter must be placed in such a manner so all the potential weakest points— the bow, the keel, those radii and flats... where the material ends and where the next begins— will weather many storms.

***

I am at a bonfire. We sit a little away from the others... there are four of us there... four old college friends. We smoke something... a plant's leaves crumbled to a fine black dust. I am taken by the herb. I see the world differently again. The fire, off in the center of the field yet smolders.

***

I am on top of a mountain with numerous people— some from college... some not. We smoke opium. The moon transfixes me, holds me under its gaze. There is a spirit, a magic to this world that I now comprehend. Everyone goes to sleep. I sit cross-legged by the dying embers.

DAMN CIGARETES

The little black cat is eating again. He must have been frightened while I was away. I am sure it confuses him when I leave for vacation. All the sudden he is alone and a stranger is coming into his home to feed him. He sleeps… he sleeps and he seems to be slowly becoming happy again. He does not weigh much, and must have lost a pound or two over the week.

I have lived in this cabin for two years. The two cats and I have a good existence. Sometimes I just lie on the bed and look out through the bay window… when the trees are moving and swaying in a storm… that is when this vision is most pleasant. The depth of night though is not as pleasing. With darkness pressing upon the windows… when I wake with the sleep-stupor still present so I might smoke a cigarette, then it seems there are phantoms that haunt me. I peer out the windows and believe there are faces peering in. Half asleep, I see the world as if it were a nightmare. If I could only sleep through the night, then wake when the sun breaks over this land…. But, I am a devout smoker. When I wake from an intense dream or a dark nightmare, I must have a cigarette in order to fall back into unconsciousness.

Damn these cigarettes. But, thank God for them too. Life— through my twenties— seemed like one sordid episode before I started smoking. I have read that people who suffer from schizophrenia actually benefit from smoking tobacco— that no medication affects the nervous system as globally… or nothing of the sort has been developed as of yet. But I will probably die from this herb…. I will probably have to walk around with an oxygen tank connected to me eventually. I look at my reflection in the dark bay window. I know that this is a fleeting experience.

***

We lie down on a Sunday afternoon, sick of heart, the grandfather now dead in his grave. Each one of us, in some fashion, probably feels as if Emerson Mann is lying by his or her side. The grandmother… I feel most for her… when alive he'd slept by her warmth for some fifty years. What a phantom he must be to Pearl… how she must stop herself from reaching over the comforter to brush her fingers through his hair. And she was such a maiden in her youth… and he was such a gentleman in his demeanor… ever behind the clouds of smoke billowing from his mouth, finally breathing in that last cigarette that sealed his fate with cancer. Now, I loved that man, but yet I smoke cigarettes. Perhaps one day I will lie myself down by the living on the afternoon of my funeral.

***

God's wounded hand strummed the guitar— my heart-strings being played. I looked up at the moon and worshiped her… she was a goddess. The trees were a host of wizards… each one casting his spell on me. The camp fire was where I saw visions. My mind was quiet. There were no longer worries. Adulthood had been forsaken. I was becoming a creature of magic. Only when I was alone could I feel this way. Interacting with people seemed to scare my shadow back to the woods from where it was born. I was strong when alone, but weak when it came to social dealings. I was seduced by the marijuana, by the opium, by the ecstasy, by the acid.

***

I am walking the streets of Iowa City. It is late at night. I am scared. I feel as if I am in some danger. It is close to midnight. I can feel the souls of the men with whom I have been consuming the hallucinogenics press upon my sanity. I do not stop to think that I may be becoming insane. It all makes sense in the reality that I have created. On one avenue, I walk under a modest sized tree. A host of crows is awakened by my footsteps. They were roosting in that tree. They seem to laugh and scream. I have never heard crows at night make such commotion. It seems as if I have walked through a door into another realm and I do not turn to make sure that the door was left unlocked... so that I might be able to return to the place of clarity... until years later.

HAROLD

Dawn is breaking. I slept well last night. The cats wake with me. They eat a little, drink some water, and then go back to sleep.

The floor here is worn. When I first moved into this cabin... one winter day... the floor had a wonderful polish to it. Farmer Harold and I sat there, in the cold, by the wood stove, making the first fire of my two-year stay in this cabin. The experience is very ritualistic, but in a healthy sense. We are both sober. Neither of us partake in the madness of drugs together or when alone. The fire catches with a match put to the newspaper. Slowly, we add to the kindling, closing the door to the stove most of the way to create the draft needed. And the cabin begins to warm.

Harold is a tall man. Although younger than me, he holds himself more like someone who is close to my age. Therefore, we enjoy each other's company. He has lived at the Farm a couple years more than I have. He has been my greatest friend over the years. When we talk, we understand what the other is saying easily. We have walked in the woods together. We have tread down the same path for a time. He will be leaving soon and I am saddened at this thought.

I have become so emotional lately. Tears come to my eyes easily, tears of love. I am beginning to realize I have found myself a home. I no longer need to continue searching. Where I live, the people are amazing. They hold me close... they don't allow me to fall... and, when I stumble, they help me find footing again before it is too late. This is a place of sanity. I don't know how I have found this place, these people. Tears flow.

THE INCIDENT

It was a sawed-off shotgun. That made an impression on me when I was a child. It seems that something very dreadful could have happened... that he had planned it so. I could not understand why he was sitting outside my aunt and uncle's home for what seemed all afternoon, drinking. I could not understand why I was not allowed to go out and say "Hi" to him and, why he would not come inside.

I had been expecting him. On arriving in Wilmington, Delaware after driving all the way from Winston-Salem, North Carolina, I asked my mother why Dad did not come there with us. She told me he had to work and that he would visit within the month. I was surprised at seeing him, parked out front of the house, only a week or so after our arrival.

Well after the police had taken him away... well after he had pulled the trigger... well after my uncle, who had been in Vietnam, stopped the gun from firing by putting the flesh that grew between his thumb and index finger between the hammer and whatever mechanism causes a shotgun to fire... well after I had walked around in a daze in that basement, wondering... crying... with the feeling of a darkness descending... well after my father was released from where he was "getting help"... I had the chance to visit him in North Carolina, at the home I grew up in from the ages of four to seven.

I stayed there a number of days, but, on first arriving, on walking around and re-familiarizing myself with the house, I happened to notice a picture of me on the wall close to what was once his and my mother's bedroom. How can I explain this... since the episode in the basement of that house far away, I had some notion that he had forgotten about me. Perhaps it was because it was such a long time before I had had the chance to visit with him. Seeing that photo— a photo that he himself had taken— I could not keep myself from crying. Deep, painful tears fell from my eyes. He asked me why I thought that picture would not be there. And, when I said "I don't know," he held me, and said, "It is okay to cry, Marc."

UNDER THE WHITE EYE

I have understood the Iowa moon shining in the sky by gazing and watching the pulsing of its full wheel outshine the stars, letting my quiet stance grow its roots and hold to the ground. One night, on an island of snow, in the middle of the cornfield, the rows of broken stalks stretched into darkness like the shattered trunks of trees to which I have bowed my head in the Maine woods; the cars that moved over the road shining their lights into the tunnel of night were streaks upon a pane of glass... distant stars shooting through the shadows. Between the sound of my breath and the wind, there, I could have grown even in the furrowed brow of that winter if I only knew that to go figuratively naked is not the worst way to live. Never minding the cold, I should have broken the sternum of my world, managing with the forceps, my hands, maybe... then I could have opened the wounded land and buried what throbbed deep within my center— the snake coiled around a live rabbit, the marigold, the elements of my childhood that I had yet to revisit, the rebirth, the symbols that were given to me when my father and mother were once one.

The weekend of my brother's marriage, when I was full of memories— of the bouquet cast over the shoulder— when my feet were yet relaxed after the Havah Nagilah and the Electric Slide, when my neck still seemed to wear a bow tie, when the ring that I had carried in my pocket was a fading memory to recall, something I could finger when I wished to disappear, when the hugs and the kisses showered upon me clung— my brother was no longer younger than I, for he had ascended to that altar I have yet to reach— there was the feel of steel within my ribs that was not his— but was of my making— thus, I could not yet breathe that air of satisfaction... that I had been a part of something beautiful in this world— after the airplane had flown me back to a world of building boats, of dreams and friends, after I had driven up the coast of Maine to sleep in my bed, that was when the buzzer had awoken me and I had decided to ignore that call I had made to myself, then, finally crawling out of bed, and setting my mind towards the day, I called and told the foreman I would not arrive 'til noon— too tired from traveling and social convention— it was after such occurrences that I went to the ocean-side and found a piece of driftwood to set within the boundaries of my lawn, walked back and forth and heard the waves that were arriving from distances unknown lap upon the shore which, for the moment, was mine, and... then I bent down, in ritual, over and over again, bowing my head to the morning sun, to the great sea, to the hawk that flew in the gray sky, picking up the shards of green and white sea glass I would eventually put upon my mantle, to call my own.

I can remember standing, a child, ankle deep in the water, holding my father's hand. Sometimes the ocean would rise up to where the legs bend, but mostly she moved around our feet, and, each time the waves retreated— dragging with them fragments of seashells, pebbles, smooth and pockmarked, shattered glass softened over, rounded by sand and salt— I would sink further into Earth. I was holding on to something that wasn't stable— that relationship— for my mother left you and, when we had left the beach, and I no longer saw your visage, instead of the child who walked fearless through the world, I became accustomed to the feeling— without even the strength of your thumb to hold on to— of my feet sinking in sand.

Then, when all of all had succeeded to become still and nothing of nothing was what remained, under the white eye of the moon, I could have yet remembered (even with my heart frozen beneath the corn stalks) enough to make it so I would have become more in the spring than the mound of dirt able barely to cry or groan for God— a work horse plodding forth heedlessly, splitting the earth with each step, dragging behind his faithful plow.

TOWARD WORLDLY MATTERS

There are those objects which have been caused to bare themselves out of the ground. Those whose beginnings once found a place of contentment in the darkness of the earth now thirst, for they may no longer drink the blood of the soil, an endeavor hidden from the vision of those who reach— where wondering about such manners of nature becomes second nature. A flood will accomplish in one day that which some men struggle to achieve in a lifetime and already the waters of the clouds and the rivers have begun eroding their surroundings, leaving boundaries, exhibiting power: trees are pulled out of their earthen bed, all that has been held to for centuries becomes loosened between roots, and what once searched for God's water has now too much to possibly absorb. One by one they came to fall, no longer able to hold onto their stature, groping tendrils losing in one monumental upheaval what had always been provided by stable ground. In my youth, I spent hours gazing into the twisted masses, questing to discern their enigma.

At times I have also walked into the thickness of wood between the cliffs of lime rock where-by the turbulent rivers flowed. Again, I'd find the dying giants, their branches broken and bent beneath them. Portions of the banks dislodged about my awkward stance, some being utterly washed into the far reaches of time. There, I would stumble on the swollen deer carcasses, those that had lost their lives in flight, those whose eyes were white with final madness. And, years later, walking along the same river's bed, after I had left Iowa and then returned, the skulls of the same could be found amidst the leavings, with antlers and without, young and old, pieces of those days that could be taken home or left in the hatchback of the car, to be observed by those who I would woo toward friendship, or to be placed on the mantels of my true friends, and finally to reach the altar with candles lit about each of the fallen gods that I had called and literally wrenched from the gut of Nature, the prayer's object thus becoming tangible in the darkness of my need.

***

It seems as if I have been saying goodbye to my father all my life; the visits so short we barely have time or the necessary impetus to strip the armor which we have pulled from the dead to cage the gentle spirits that live within our forms. I spent years trying to dig past the flesh, through the chest, breaking the boundaries that God had made so I might perceive more than the solid nature of the man that I was becoming. I must admit that I struggled to cope when the stone vase that holds the cut flower, that object which symbolizes the heart, was finally discovered broken. I thought this life was about loving and being loved so much so that I could not understand why I feared until I pried apart those supple curved bones and exposed my hollow inside to the world. The walls that you and I had erected were no longer impassable, people's faces altered as if they were upon a stage, for they would appear to change their masks from moment to moment, becoming someone or other or other than someone... and the voices in my head were quietly becoming louder. Once, in a mad effort towards freedom, I stripped off my clothes and ran naked through the Adirondack woods during a cold rain. I went from flying with God himself rushing in my veins to cupping my eyes with his palms to catch the water which journeyed out of the ducts. And now it is Thanksgiving and everything is not as it used to be except for the fact that we have still not learned how to say goodbye. I am slowly finding the pieces of myself which you and mother and God had given me, and when we hug, this time, you bring your forehead down to touch my skull— which is so close to the skin— as if a bit of your sanity will find its way through that spot which once was soft.

¢

We have entered into a new cycle of the moon, that time when all is not quite balanced, the sickle just begun and the half not yet showing itself, when the rocks that strew the beach are all broken into different shapes; the smallest like gems when wet, colors becoming more apparent when the light of the setting sun falls upon them, the driftwood that has found a place to bed, the seaweed with its strands thrown back and forth even with the slightest of waves. So we have watched, regretting another part of time, the river of light that was created, what appeared to be a stairway that was rising out of the depths of the spirit level, and, as the parts of me have risen and fallen, once more I have been a participant. This is what we have allowed ourselves to become, as if we are the opposite of what has been, that which is stranded upon the shore, but free to fly, the part of all that has died before and yet lives.

¢

I have allowed myself to become dirty; wearing the same rags for
the week that it took to smell like myself, that scent which was
neither honeysuckle nor rose, nor lavender, nor peppermint, but
of the body which craves to rub itself in the clay, to wade within
the waters of the mountain pond, that which had the smell of its
dinner, the grease of the meat still beneath the fingernails, still
in the hair from when I brushed through it with the comb of
four fingers. I have longed to be more like the bear, for he
smells like a bear would smell. I have longed to be more of
what man once was in all of his primal attitudes, and when I had
made myself thus, I then found that space in the woods where I
could see but not be seen, where I could listen but not be heard,
and there I would rub myself in the death of the leaves, in the
decaying lumps of logs, even taking the mushrooms and
squeezing them in my hands... thence I would huddle within the
brush and be the eyes of the hunter who no longer hunts and
watch what might occur where the flow of nature is
unobstructed, where even the light is beyond our imagining...
the way it casts itself, like someone who has become mad,
through the great canopy, there to fall upon the stage that has
existed well before the creation of man. It is there I have seen
the great tragedy taking place— the unmasking of God. There
the deer have fallen and have been prey to the wolf, the hunter
devouring the hunted, there the battle for power has raged most
intense, those packs eating their kill would at times eat
themselves, the flesh of Christ being torn from the bones, the
entrails being pulled and strewn over the fallen debris, the teeth
that are bared to not only consume, but also fend off all the
would-be spirits that grow; the legs that are the sturdiest, the
heart that pounds the quietest, the eyes that shine and the eyes
that cower, the young that are granted the leavings, that which

will allow them to remain young. And the deer, who was she? What made her so docile, so innocent, so worthy to be alive, so almost willing to be destroyed? The heart managing to throb what little blood is left, the legs that kick into the naked air, the eyes seeming to show not only her fear, but that fear which lives within the deepest parts of those who feed upon her, for they seem to know what they have been hell-bound to nourish upon; the prey feeding upon prey. All this I have seen and in my shaded glory I have walked out from the bush and bent down to the ground to bloody my fingers in that which was only half present, wiping them upon my face, in a rite of manhood. I then stood and walked back into the altered world, back into the void that was left.

⁕✿✕

The strength revealed, encompassed all that we once imagined; we sang the first song of the world, brought forth the first flowers and let the dew of our tears settle upon them.... And although initially we knew that which we had added, the perfumes, the bees which gather, the petals that open when touched by light... now, we were grace-given the gift to embolden, perceiving the whole, the roots that grew beneath the ground, the cells that are secured together by force beyond trust and understanding, each part that was sung by the others, each part that was chanted by something older and stronger than us.

✿✿✿

My passivity that has worn holes in me has brought forth these lines. Even though they may seem as but notes, reminders to myself of what I have seen, experienced, and felt, of what I have been, the before and now, still, they hold life within that might pulse if one was sensitive to such things, for each are what help me battle the forces that at times encroach upon my consciousness. These are my children, the creations of my beginnings and endings working together. They are what enable me to strive, by helping my form to perceive further the depths of this struggle, this beauty. And, in each of their completions, I usually pluck the final string of my courage with surprise, for, when the last has been given to me by the Muse, I can almost hear in the distance the sound of a door slamming shut, which echoes over the long passage— the rooms which I have passed through to come here— setting to rest this world and thought 'til poetry might need be called forth again.

LOVERS

OF NOD

HEARTS' LANE

Where I type, cool air of an early, rainy morning comes into the cabin. My gaze fixed on the computer screen, I write without pause. Ania is here. I can hear her sometimes cough in the bedroom where she is curled under covers, where she rests after so much travel.

Yesterday evening, we returned to the cabin from the City, a long drive. Today is Saturday. Later we'll be heading toward Boston to stay at her apartment. I am looking forward to the drive. I did not sleep overly much… but, it was pleasant sleep nonetheless. I rested soundly, by her side, through night.

While in the City, we shared so much with each other, walking through Central Park, rain falling, the crowded 5th Avenue. Now, on remembering, I cannot recall much of the metropolis… for I was by Ania's side. More than anything, she was the land I was exploring— her home country, her future hopes, her sister's family— now living in New England— all her travels. Her life experience was vastly more interesting and comforting when compared to the flash and movement of New York.

The stream beside the cabin runs strong. A gray-blue sky is dawning. I am not alone. It had been three years for me. I left a relationship behind that almost ruined me. After that hurtful experience ended, I began hearing nightmarish voices during odd waking moments— a man's voice, making comments about my daily affairs, in such a loud obnoxious tone those comments could not be ignored. I was falling into the pit of psychosis again. I was losing the stability I had become accustomed to; but, with help from a close friend, I was able to return.

The voices are quiet, they have receded. I wonder why I was so intent on killing all hopes. The quiet mind was not worth the cost. I am on a road, be it in sky or on this planet, it is all the same. I gaze from left to right: fields of madness will always survive on the perimeter. But, here I am surefooted. The path straight, leads toward a future. I am running now, breathing heavily, away from insanity. I have wings secured at my heels (with a bit of wax)— red, taken from that spring cardinal after he collided against a window of a would-be lover's home. When I fly, I must remember to never circle too close.

***

I am in Quincy. It is three in the morning. Ania sleeps soundly in the bed we shared together up until my waking to drink water and begin writing. Outside, the suburb of Boston is quiet, small drops of rain fall.

I do hope we have good weather. We'd like to explore the city... or, perhaps go to the beach. It is autumn... but, I have let her know I have not visited the ocean this year. To see and hear waves, to let sand run through my fingers, to think matters over...

This has been a most exciting vacation— to have a partner, to see Manhattan, to be at the cabin in the Berkshires... and, now, to be in the suburbs of Boston, only a T ride to Cambridge or

Chinatown. We have begun planning to spend other vacations together. Last night, Ania showed me her picture book of Paris… for, she said, in her Polish accent, she wants to "sell the idea to me" to visit Paris in the future… furthermore, saying, "Please take me to Paris…" and, though we are at the beginning, that dream does not seem unattainable.

Rain is falling, which is okay. If we are kept indoors because of rain… well, as it seems, we will have no trouble occupying ourselves. I smoke another cigarette, alone, and remember our conversation last night. I reminisced about the days of drinking. Years spent gazing at Irish whiskey as I sipped at its aroma and strength… years guzzling microbrews, dark brown Guinness. She was not ashamed of me in the least. She just said, "Don't forget to breathe… keep your head above waters… all the suffering you've seen reminds you how far you've fallen… it pushes you further toward being confused… so don't forget to breathe… you're whole life is here…"

***

We hugged each other through part of the night. After she woke to take medicine and drink water, she came back to bed and was close, curled in my embrace. Ania is not one to hide affection; she displays it often and with great passion. At the Farm, where I work and live, people tend not to share their physical touch. I had begun feeling people did not desire to touch me. I have been starved for hugs and kisses. To have physical touch now is comforting.

During the depth of night I was enjoying the sounds of Quincy.

OF NOD

Ania had a window open in the bedroom. The city was quiet; but, there was still traffic noise, occasionally the muffled sound of her neighbors. I heard a newspaper being blown across the parking lot, scraping edges over pavement. At home, in the heart of night, all is quiet except for the creek running in back of my cabin. In a fashion, the various noises of the city are as soothing... and, there was the sound of her cat sharpening claws on the cardboard scratch pad. I believe I fell asleep soon after listening to her cat's ritual.

***

Yesterday, instead of visiting Cambridge, we decided to go out for sushi in Quincy Center, and take a walk on a beach close to Ania's apartment. It was at a restaurant on the main street where we ate. We sat at the bar of an establishment. There were few customers. It was late in the day before we were able to venture out. We arrived after the lunch rush and before the dinner hour. I have always heard good sushi will melt in one's mouth... and, that *was* exactly what this sushi did. It was succulent. Ania compared the experience to having an orgasm.

After sushi, we went to Wollaston Beach. Instead of walking the path by the road, we chose to take our stroll on the sand where scattered was seaweed washed ashore. On the beach we headed northward and could distinctly see Boston in the distance— great buildings, lights in the fading light. The smell of salt water... it was refreshing. Walking hand in hand, conversing, we stopped at one point and kissed— the taste of the sushi yet present.

~ 74 ~

It is two-thirty in the morning. I woke because Ania's cat scratched me on the foot as I was repositioning myself. Ania woke when I let out a cry of pain and scolded the cat, tossing it off the bed. I came into the living room and decided to take some time to myself, listen to music, and write.

It is good to meditate, to record our time together so I will remember the beginnings of what we are experiencing. When we were in New York City, and I was holding Ania in the bed of my parents' second apartment, I said to her that that was a significant time in our lives, that beginnings are extremely important... beginnings never happen again. I feel this relationship holds promise and, want to remember.

I am feeling tired. My back hurts seeing as I have been sitting on a futon couch while typing. Ania's warm sleeping body is waiting for me. Tomorrow, our plan is to go to Provincetown— a two hour drive. The weather is unseasonably warm... and, the sun is supposed to be present in the sky... a perfect time to be on the point of the Cape.

***

Yesterday, Ania called her parents in Poland. She told them about me for the first time. Seeing as Ania tends to feel I deserve her undivided attention, I stayed removed by writing my editor. Of course, I could not understand the conversation; it was spoken in their native tongue. At one point, I heard her mention my name, pronounced differently than she has ever pronounced it... accents in different places, with a rolling "r". The conversation seemed to become heated. Afterward, I realized excitement caused the tone to become loud, intense. When she hung up, she was happy, kissing me, saying her parents are pleased she has met someone.

Ania is divorced. Ten years ago she married an American and soon found herself in an extremely unhappy relationship, lost in a foreign country where she knew neither the language nor the customs. She was young when she first met him, twenty-one. The relationship soon turned into a long distance affair, spanning the ocean, until she married and moved to the States.

She is still embarrassed. After we visited my parents in New York City, then took the train to their home in Croton, we had a wonderful lunch at my dad and stepmother's home. During lunch, my stepmother, Dawn, asked Ania how she first came to the States. Ania was not happy to have to relate the story about the marriage and the subsequent divorce. Dawn was understanding, helping Ania find a way to express to people that she is divorced... a way that might cause her less stress in the future.

My parents seem to be glad I have found someone to spend time with... and, I am hoping they see the potential in this relationship of which I am so keenly aware.

Although my last relationship ended horribly... with me, in the aftermath, falling into despair... I feel I must try with someone again. I must not be afraid, for, as Ania says, "Just because it happened one way before, does not mean it will be the same this time." She is wonderful. She is carefree. She helps me remember my old self.

The friend who helped me during my last fall is a clinician. I lived with Clara for a period when first at Reed Farm, six years ago. We had both arrived at the same time to start our lives anew in the therapeutic community. Back then, we would share a lot, sitting in the living room of the house called Jameson... and, she was very helpful. She has been extremely helpful to me in the present as well. Clara is one of the Farm I can share a tremendous amount with about life. She is good at helping me gain perspective when that perspective has been lost, or clouded. Her friendship is one of the most supportive aspects to my life. She helps me grow.

The sun, present in the sky... I glanced out the window and could see shadows of trees cast. All looks brilliant now the rain and the overcast skies have gone elsewhere. Ania yet sleeps. She is coming down with a cold, so I am careful to type quietly in the living room. There is a siren screaming in the distance. The apartment smells of incense. Cool wind blows through an open window.

***

We are in Provincetown. We drove from Quincy yesterday, not arriving 'til noon. The town is mostly closed because of it being November. It took a long time to find a place to stay, but, with searching, we discovered a wonderful hotel in the museum district. I found it fun to take a room with Ania. For a moment, as we were crossing the threshold to enter the studio, I felt as if we were on a honeymoon.

OF NOD

On first arriving, we parked in the center of town on the main one way thoroughfare. Then, we walked to the end of the pier and drank coffee while placidly sitting on a bench, looking at the current-waves, the boats in the harbor. A seagull joined us, landing close, perching on a pylon. We photographed the gull, the water, the sky, and the boats… as we looked up, we saw three flags billowing in the breeze. One happened to be a Polish flag, exciting Ania to no end. Finally, we went searching for the hotel room where we now stay.

The owner of the hotel is a wonderful man. He talked a lot to us about places where we might eat. In order to get Ania's car, we walked back to the center of town; but, this time— as the hotel owner suggested— traversing the distance on the beach. The sun was setting during the entire walk. The lights of Provincetown we loved seeing. We held hands, and stopped to kiss numerous times.

Later in the evening, we went for another walk, looking for a place to eat. Unfortunately, it was Monday, so many of the restaurants which might have been open during high season, or at least on the weekend of the off season, happened to be closed. We thought about eating at a place called Mews, but the establishment was too formal for our tastes. Eventually, we made our way back to the hotel and ate the yogurt, bread, orange juice, honey, and cheese we had brought with us. It was an ample meal, satisfying our hunger.

***

I rise early so I might have time to write. Our days tend to be full. There have been only sporadic moments when I can stop and record the happenings of this vacation. Besides, I tend to feel Ania needs my undivided attention. We are good together in that respect... we love being with each other, aware of each other's needs.

Last night, before going to bed, Ania and I went out on the deck, smoked our last cigarettes of the day. It was a bit cold; but, seeing as I had just taken a hot shower, the chill did not affect me. The tide was in and lapping against the deck supports. The stairs, before leading down to the sand, descended into high water. Stars were visible. Orion was in the sky, set at an angle. We stayed close while smoking, taking deep inhales and letting the exhales blow into salty air.

I just went outside on the deck. Early dawn is breaking. The water has retreated. I was in awe of the colors— a strip of cadmium yellow pigment over the horizon, tinted with red. After smoking, I knocked off the ember onto the damp sand, extinguished it with my foot.

Ania is dreading the end of our vacation. So, last night, I suggested we make plans for the next time we will spend in each other's company. While holding her in bed, after we shared our bodies, we decided we would meet at my cabin in the Berkshires, the weekend following the vacation. It will be Thanksgiving weekend. She will be visiting her sister in West Springfield. It will not be much further of a drive for her to be at the Farm, just for a night and a morning. On completing our plans, Ania's sadness vanished. We continued to hold each other.

~ 79 ~

OF NOD

Gold has flooded this land and water. Gulls swim close to the shoreline and fly through early air currents. There are many a gull's footprints close to the deck. As they swim, each draws a V in the shallows. I am alive to this morning. I am waiting for Ania to wake but will let her sleep; let her enjoy the dreams that visit her.

***

The first shards of light are beginning to show. It is five-thirty in the morning. This is our last day to spend in P-town. We will check out of the hotel by eleven, then walk the Breakwater— a last event before heading to Quincy.

Yesterday, we spent a good part of the day sitting on the deck: drinking coffee, smoking cigarettes, looking at the ocean, conversing, and eating lunch. I enjoy the fact Ania and I do not need to be constantly busy— being in each other's company is enough. We did end up hiking the dunes, walking out into that desert-environment, and then sitting on a sand-hill, drinking water, taking pictures; our bodies close so to stay warm.

We seem to be friends as well as lovers. There is no end to our conversations and to the closeness we feel.

Me: "Before you, the days would get so long…"

Ania: "I know it is hard."

Me: "I am trying to put it right."

~ 80 ~

Ania: "Maybe that's a starting place."

Me: "You've been hiding from the hurt too... I see you hiding your face in your hands."

Ania: "No one will understand. I am so tired. Maybe I should cry."

Yesterday was not an easy day, emotionally. There were things which needed talking about for us to continue. One cannot live pretend. You see, we both struggle with our own illnesses... I have schizophrenia, she has depression. Until last evening, we had not let each other know about our internal workings. It seemed we were doomed unless I was honest and told her about my struggles. Then, was very surprised about her response— that she has her own lions which she is trying to tame.

Everything changed. We went outside on the deck to smoke. I noticed we had suddenly become human, our humanity was showing... and, there was more comfort... we were able to stand there talking, looking at each other with love... real love in our eyes... unconditional love.

"I don't see you in any other girl's face," I let her know... and she then pulled me close to her, wanting my arms to hold her...

I, the lonesome warrior... toss me into the bay, toss me into the retreating water... a shell, a stone thrown from your hand... then, I will be carried, carried by the water to other shores, to other shores... whoever grasps me to her chest, "Let my heart free," I say... let my heart be tossed into the bay, into the retreating water. Dreams, I have dreams of women... but they are merely ghosts— smoke exhaled, floating on the calm breeze, floating over the tide that retreats. I thought nothing could be forced, and now I realize the heart is a commodity: it is bought; it is sold, by friends, by lovers, by family. The soul is more that which is given away, that takes years to return to its original owner, a dove released off the stern of the Ark. Perhaps I was the one who tossed that white bird into the salt spray air, perhaps I am who now waits for her return, waits, waits, waits for your return.

The ocean is gray and calm, the air cold. This hotel room though is warm. Ania and I have made this place cozy. I will be sorry to leave today, and wish we had a week to spend here... but, she has a cat at home... and, I must start thinking about heading to the Farm. Ania has said she would like me to drive her to the Farm later in the week. We'll stay at the cabin for a couple of days before she'll head back to her old-life.

I told her that if, on her returning to Quincy, she feels she cannot live as a long distance couple, we would begin to change our lives so as to be together. We agreed though we would try the long distance, at least initially. I love this woman... and, I told her so yesterday. The look on her face, when I said those words...

While on the dunes, sitting, looking over the environment, I took some sand in my hand and let it fall into Ania's open hand. Ania said "Let it fall quietly," as if she did not want me to ruin the moment with words. That moment seemed to signify the mingling of our lives. The sand fell through her fingers... but, much of it was held in her palm. I am sharing this time with her... and, this is only the beginning.

***

We woke late, lingering 'til well after checkout time. Ania talked to the owner and he did not mind. Again, we sat on the deck drinking coffee, smoking cigarettes, and watching gulls. To our surprise, a cat from a house across the street took a liking to us. We discovered his name was Wrangler from someone staying at the hotel. Wrangler lounged, in the sunshine, by our deck chairs, sometimes jumping on the porch table to be closer.

We spent the afternoon driving, deciding not to stop at the Breakwater... I felt that might be too emotional. It had been such a wonderful vacation... and, during the time spent in Provincetown, I grew closer to Ania. I did not want to leave and, did not want to have such a closing. I did, in somewhat of a playful fashion, thank the hotel room as we crossed the threshold, locking the door... saying it had been good to us, saying I was grateful for the time we spent there.

Last night, while sleeping, we held hands, fingers entwined. Then, this afternoon, after arriving to her apartment, I needed to take a nap, tired from drive. She came and lay beside me, coursing fingers through my hair as I fell into deep sleep. When I woke, it was dark in the room. The light in the sky had gone out. I had no idea what time it might have been. I felt drugged. I stumbled into the living room to find Ania entertaining herself on her computer. She quickly put the computer aside and began showering attention on me... but, a sad look was in her eyes. She was concerned about the Sunday that will come. Regardless how we try to enjoy ourselves, I believe, at this point in the vacation, she and I will have to keep in mind our time together will have a hiatus.

***

I am here, in Quincy, by Ania's side. She is comforting, beautiful. The window is open. Cool night air flows into the apartment. Music plays on the stereo. There is peace and calm in the room.

This vacation continues. We might not be standing by the Cape's ocean at present, but, Ania is an ocean unto herself... and, I wade in her waters... I swim out into depths, fearless. She holds me safe from the world. She allows me to be youthful. Her salt water cleanses. When she takes me into her, the secrets of life are shared. I understand now, the tide is retreating, but it will return. Pylons are visible. A gull floats close at hand, eying me as I wade further into dark water. There are lights on the horizon, a lighthouse on the point. If I swim far enough, perhaps I will drown, and, in drowning, find my soul, there hidden, in dark, dreaming waters.

***

Last night, we lay in bed and talked about visions we see when closing eyes before falling asleep. Ania imagines entire events... while, on first settling into bed, I tend to have such psychedelic imaginings course through my mind— last night a woman I do not know, bright star upon her face.

"Tell me, Love, what you see when you pull the curtains aside," I posed.

"I see birds stealing bread from homeless men; I see you when you arrive from a place I have never visited... such as now... you are present... how did that happen?"

"Tell me, Love, does my company make light of this day?" I asked.

"I've been thinking lately about all that we don't share... what we don't say, that we don't hug or kiss enough," was her answer. She was testing.

"I mostly think of this mystery... how I am so like my father... how you are a prayer that grows inside," I responded, pointing to my chest... changing the course.

"Do you see me how I see you?" Ania wondered...

Ania takes an active role in shaping her future. She has been through so much, but continues to have hope, faith. I tend to let my visions occur randomly, not trying to shape them... they are pleasing to me, but I do not understand most of my mind's creations... they don't seem to relate to waking life, merely fragments; perhaps formed from the days of drug use, perhaps not.

OF NOD

***

It is early morning, dark outside. I am eating nuts and fruit. We are planning on taking the T to Cambridge today. Ania is dreaming. I am slowly waking, typing. A cigarette dangles from my lips. Smoke wafts into my eyes causing them to tear, reminding me: I was with Ania in the Provincetown hotel room. We were gazing at each other more than we were conversing, lying on the couch. I wanted to tell her I felt I loved her... but, instead chose to look at her and tell her with my eyes, my face... then it dawned. I am almost forty. I have searched my entire life. Pain when relationships did not work... lonely months and years. She, though, was there, in my vision. I watched her watch me. I cried in her company. Belief does play a factor. One might feel emotion, but not believe in its reality... then I knew.

Sunset soon forgotten... yesterday was difficult... and truly, I do not remember your sunset at this moment, when the morning is brilliant... a new day. This might break your heart, that I love... that is probably the worst I could do, correct? To love... but, I will share with you: my feelings are my truth. Some would attempt to quell the heart's pang, but, when I attempt such, then I am less of a man, then I am more of what is not human. Love is imperfect for me. I tend to love what I cannot have, I tend to love what is out of reach, and I tend to love that which lives only in imagination. Make a hole in the sky for me, my Love. Open for me! Let me soar, a bird of night... not from tree to tree, not in the fashion of the common owl. I would soar through the opening; I would rear my head in the dark of tonight's heavens if only to touch your soul.

✿✿✿

After writing in the early, predawn morning, I was about to go to bed... but, realized— I had been smoking during the writing process. Incense needed to be lit. Ania is not supposed to be smoking cigarettes in her apartment and, maintenance people have been in the building since we arrived home. So, I lit incense, and proceeded to fall asleep on the couch.

While sleeping, smoke and haze filled the room. I had a very odd dream... imagined: a woman was leaning over my prone body. She blew scented air from her lungs into my open mouth. I inhaled, taking that perfume into my lungs. This dream, mirage, or hallucination occurred three times, then, I woke. Light was pouring through windows, it was morning. The bedroom door was open. Ania was not in bed. She had never woken before me, but, I was not worried. I figured she was outside smoking. If anything, I was anxious she had seen me sleeping on the couch. She would be worried I did not desire to sleep in her bed. Ania did return. She came back to the apartment while I was making coffee and was indeed worried I did not sleep part of the night in her bed. I explained I did not want to leave the incense burning unattended and, by accident, had fallen asleep.

I just made eggs with cheese and toast. The cheese and bread were what remained from food we purchased while in P-town. Ania washed dishes while I prepared breakfast. She is a different person, awake early... this is not an Ania I have seen.

OF NOD

It is sunny, but the chill of early winter has arrived. When Ania goes outside to smoke, her kisses are cold when she returns. We kiss often. She loves my attention and I love hers. We have been planning how I might be able to secure a job for her. I think and tell her that would definitely be possible... and, I think further— I would love for her to live with me, at the Farm, working by my side.

***

I sit, smoking a tobacco pipe. Ania bought the pipe for me while we were in Harvard Square. We took the Red Line into Central Square, walked the Commons and the Boston Gardens, found ourselves at a quaint coffee shop in Beacon Hill. There, we sat drinking our coffee and latte, eating pastries at the outside tables, watching people who walked past, and conversing, always conversing. The tobacco has a rich flavor.

I used to smoke pipes through my twenties. Not until I started working at the boat building factory, at age of twenty-seven, in the town of Rockland, Maine, did I begin smoking cigarettes. When we walked into the tobacconist shop, I knew I had to pick up such a fashion of smoking again. I have many pipes at home, but, seeing as I smoked marijuana from most of them in my misspent twenties, I wanted a pipe that was free of that history and, one which was bought during this vacation.

Ania is asleep in the bedroom... I would think so, seeing as we walked a tremendous amount yesterday. Instead of taking the T into Cambridge, we chose to traverse the four miles or so from Beacon Hill by foot. At one point we passed through a seedy neighborhood... but, we held close and all was fine. It was good to see that part of Boston, to see the city's reality. One of my favorite moments— we stood on the bridge crossing Charles River. The architecture of the bridge was ornate, river wide. We paused at a place that was made for sightseers, a platform cut-out in the side wall, for people to stop and take pictures of the panorama. I took a picture of Ania. A lobster boat was docked in the distance. Further in the distance one could see Beacon Hill, red brick buildings.

Also while in Harvard Square, we browsed at a bookstore. In the basement, we found a large selection of secondhand books. I chose Camus' *The Plague.* I had tried reading that book a long time ago. It may have not been a good translation, seeing as the novel didn't hold my interest. I am hoping this will be an engaging version.

The Harvard University campus was awe inspiring, a great library presiding. We walked slowly, holding each other close, holding hands, and kissing numerous times.

When first arriving in Harvard Square, I was thirsty for coffee. Ania sat outside while I bought my drink, saving a table for us that would be perfect for watching walking traffic. Later in the evening, when we were walking hand-in-hand on the campus, she told me there had been someone at the coffee shop patio approaching women, giving them a difficult time... that, just when he was beginning to approach her, I came out and sat next to her. The shady character had then decided it would not be a good idea to continue his advance.

OF NOD

I am a large man. I believe I hold myself with strength. I used
to be a lobsterman, so, there still is a lot of the salty character
inherent in my mannerisms.   I am tall, and weigh a good
amount, thick in shoulders and legs. Sometimes I believe my
presence intimidates people. I suppose that can be good or bad,
depending on the situation.

***

*If you walk within my rooms, while I lie listening, then might I
hear your quiet breathing as you notice a picture, a trinket, a
box that holds keys… and, if I were to hold my breath, then
might I hear all the more your breathing? The world is full of
deceptions, but, one thing I can discern— the breath that you
are… for, I am slowly dying… my breath is becoming short…
and, there, I can hear it even now with a quiet sigh. Sometimes
I imagine… can I tell you while there are only the two of us
here? You, as a bird of grace and beauty, but, not caged… oh,
not caged. Maybe it is the fluttering of your wings that I listen
to, the sound so breath-like. Some people search the world for
truth… but I have found it here, on this farm… a breathing
love, a fluttering love. When I look through the window, there
is darkness, darkness. If there might be a time that you would
want… (and in wanting, want more of what I desire… because,
oh I do desire— a never ending yearning…) to walk in these
rooms, then I hope you might visit, visit my home and breathe
the air that is my life.*

***

At the Farm… it was not a long drive.   The conversation

~ 90 ~

between us made time pass quickly. The people of the community are happy to see me and, they keep mentioning I look good. I think, *"This vacation must have done wonders... and, to be in love, to be sharing my body, heart, and mind with Ania must be healthy. I feel good."*

Ania sleeps. The cabin is warm, wood stove burning all night. I slept well... wonderful to be home and in my own bed, with Ania. I woke to feed the stove, but easily fell back asleep.

Ania and I talked through the evening. She liked sitting by the open door of the stove, fire blazing, warming her. She enjoyed lounging in my rocking chair. I sat close to her, held her hand, and caressed her shoulders.

Ania told me about her youth. I love the stories concerning when she was a young girl. Part of her childhood took place on her grandparents' farm. She would, at times, help with the moving of their cows from pasture to pasture. It is good to hear about her young years... I am not sure why... the mystique of her having grown up in a foreign country? I do know I enjoy when she opens about her past. When she shares those experiences, I feel closer.

***

Windy and overcast... after Ania wakes and readies herself, we'll go to Great Barrington, hopefully arrive at the bank before it closes. There, I will open my security deposit box and check that my passport has not expired. While driving yesterday, she asked if I would go to Poland with her and visit her family during the summer. I said, "Yes."

Last night, we made love into the early morning hours. Afterward, we sat in the living room, by the wood stove, smoking. She had my heavy bathrobe draped over her. The cabin was warm, almost a sauna... and, she had such a smile on her face. She was radiant. While watching her, I began to fade, the day having begun to weigh heavily. After cigarettes, we went into the bedroom. I opened the window, letting in cool air. We drifted asleep, close, listening to the coursing stream.

***

The cabin quiet, cats sleeping, Ania creaming. Yesterday we went to Great Barrington. While in town, we drank coffee at a popular spot on Main Street, and then made reservations at the Japanese restaurant. We also had lunch at the Co-Op. The day overcast, a chill to the air. While holding Ania's hand, I noticed she slightly trembled.

Last night, on driving back after having sushi, we took Hearts' Lane toward the Farm, pulling off the dirt road, into a field, looking to see if there were deer. There were no deer, but we stayed parked for a time, lights off, gazing at the moon. The night was beautiful, stars present, sky lit by the crescent. I held and kissed Ania. Dashboard lights reflected off her face. I have been here at the Farm for a long time, but have never brought a woman to Hearts' Lane, until last night.

Outside, the sky glows, morning is here. Pine trees are silhouetted. Ania will be leaving today, but this dawn will not be my last, sitting, writing in the next room while she sleeps. I have fallen into the depths. Her waters are all encompassing; they flow through and over this cabin, over my sinking body. I do not fight from lack of air. I am taken. Perhaps I will wash up on a distant shore someday, my body swollen and blue from the death of my soul... but, no, now I live, breathing, taking her waters into my lungs, finding the ocean is easy to breathe, like the air of the world. The crescent moon lights this scene. If I begin to fail, if water begins to exhaust my endurance, I will reach up, grab hold, and pull myself into the night sky.

I am walking. The path is overgrown. Eventually I will attain the hill where the laurels flower. They will be in bloom next summer. I will find Ania, meditating in the midst of white petals. She will spread arms, accept me into her heart. I will let myself flow, a brook, into the river of her blood. I will not deviate. This path has purpose, meaning... it is less traveled. The trail might be in darkness yet, but the sun *is* rising and will flow through the forest's canopy, lighting the brush, the fallen leaves, and the lonely coursing stream. We will rest then, after loving each other, with light gleaming off our sweat. There will be a multitude of birds chirping. We will listen, just listen.

The firewood in the stove just flashed into flame. On waking, there were coals left, scattered in ashes. I carefully stirred the coals and set seasoned, split logs on top, closing the door and opening the draft.

Yellow is in the sky, close to the horizon... the cats are awake, making noise as they wander about, jumping on the kitchenette's counters and onto the living room couch, sharpening nails on woodwork. The light of this moment…. We slept well, the strong current of the stream lulling us quickly into unconsciousness. I am being carried further out; there is no way to reach shore even if I try. It is too far to swim. I must flow, with the current, I must let the sea carry me to where it desires.

PERCEIVING

Ania is showering. We have taken our time, lots of hugging, kissing, holding each other. I've enjoyed the day's gradual course. Afternoon... light hazy, windows cracked, air cool. The sun holds promises, glinting off the coffee table, off kitchen counters. We talk sweet nothings. She wears an engagement ring... it has caught light as well, glittering into my vision.

There is a significant open space beneath the bedroom's closed door. Now I see her shadow, where light washes through, flowing from the eastern window. Drawers are opened, they are closed.

The seagulls have been scuawking through early morning. They must be pleased about the warmth, a January thaw. Early in the morning, the heart is at rest. It is only after life's burdens present themselves, gradually, we begin to feel the pain that is living.

Her hair drier is running, making the stereo seem quiet. Ania is still in the bedroom, door slightly agar. In that bedroom we slept, though the early part of morning, entwined... and, I dreamt and heard strange voices... nothing I can relate— it was disconcerting. It was disturbed sleep.

Awake before dawn so as to finish editing a book. I drank coffee, black, with honey... numerous cups. Once the manuscript was complete, I snuck back to the bedroom to hold her, to be tortured by random fear-thoughts, to breathe in the scent of her sleeping, to hear her breathe like a sleeping child... there, curled with face against my breast, my arms wrapped around her, as if protecting her from the day. It was more I who needed protection— from the disturbing nature of my mind. Then, after we crawled toward light— out of bed, I almost choked on granola, famished. When that had been digested, and day began to unfold, my mind focused. The sun's glare pouring through windows... burnt away all hurt and madness, left over from a youth which will never be different, regardless how long I live.

***

I was the first born. Long after I was pushed onto that sterile table, into the doctor's waiting hands, my mother held me in her womb through motherly affection; through being "a momma's boy"— I was saved from the darkness of the world, until I was a young adult. With that first taste of a drug, I was released and, the walls of that spirit-womb, the boundaries of my consciousness, those gifts given, crumbled. The wasteland showed itself, I was taken. That which was offered by some beauty named Melanie, took me from all safety I had known (in some fashion I willingly offered myself to the Nothingness). *Yes, Mel, I did then begin to see the world differently. Yes, Mel, the shadows became prominent... for, maybe you took me into your young womb, then traced your fingers up and down my arm, over my hand, limply holding your hand... like a mother would do with her newborn.*

***

No, I have not forgotten: the apartment I left behind in Iowa City, that life I was living, like a corncob just husked. Something had to change. I was wandering down a road leading nowhere. I was treading a path through woods, its end a deception. I was young, naïve. I was a heart broken. I was not finding myself; I was losing myself in rooms filled with marijuana smoke. I was lost, and have been finding parts, pieces, ever since; no, I have not forgotten.

***

There are clouds over my sixteenth year. The moon, in spots, shines upon Wilmington, Delaware, land of memories. There is no stream running through the woods, close to home; but there are woods. During one night when the blanket of darkness hovered still and calm overhead, almost as if some great being held breath, I wandered into the trees and brush, found there burning a small campfire— crackling and hissing as flames consumed pockets of moisture contained in kindling. The event was deep enough into the trees that its light could not be noticed by drivers of cars on the little road that crossed close. I sat, there in the cusp of autumn, and, nervous as I was, when offered I grasped hold with hands that had not yet matured. The other young men, or grown boys, surrounding lurked in shadows. Quiet laughs and sordid conversation in my awareness as I sipped gently... someone said "He has no time to sink into this life. He will drift." Or, maybe I misunderstood, took what they said out of context... then, as no one was paying attention, I laid to rest the beer in the leaves and moss at my feet, my first offering to the gods that were in the darkness, and smiled, but felt deeply the trust and faith which had been broken.

Soon after the university courses ended, I made my way to Amsterdam. In a bar below street level people playing billiards, someone announced their birthday and began passing around a clay cylinder. It was about six inches long, one end wider, packed with herb from Thailand. The owner of the pipe was proud about his marijuana. It seemed I should not be shy about the inhale and, after the smoke had been held, then exhaled, the room disappeared. All went dark. Blinc, I searched for a chair to sit upon.

I do see clearly this world of light and shadows... and, am keenly aware of the insanity, aware of the fragility of my mind, aware of the drug world that I chose to become involved with. I was an addict. Temptations were too great. I had wanted to experiment with my mind. It was after the car accident, on a road close to my university— there, my life changed. There, I first understood how fragile life is, but had yet no idea how fragile the mind can be. I thought I needed to "live." I thought I needed to taste all the "life" I had been frightened to partake in up until that devastating moment. The driver of the vehicle ran a red light. Another vehicle struck my door. I had no seat-belt on. That moment could have been my last, but was not... for, a few years later, I stood in the Red Light District of Amsterdam, high, contemplating three women who danced naked behind glass. That sin of the flesh I yet hesitated to engage. It was more the mind, my mind that had begun to interest me... how I could change its manners of perceiving— the world.

OF NOD

Many factors must fall into place for one to recover from drug addiction simply because most of the world's culture revolves around drug use. I started finding I could go nowhere, could visit no one, and be safe from being offered one substance or another. I suppose one can go to A.A. / N.A. meetings, but one cannot live in a continual A.A. / N.A. meeting. I though decided to dedicate myself to working with people whom have mental illness and whom also struggle with addictive natures. I became a residential counselor at a therapeutic farm in the Berkshires of Massachusetts. Then, realized I could no longer indulge... for, at heart, I am an honest man... and, I quickly noticed— once when I began this employment— that I would be a hypocrite otherwise. But, it was a long process, starting many years before my employment at Reed Farm... with many people I have to thank for support... mostly the ones who quietly urged me to toward sobriety .. who never told me in words that I had to change, who spoke through the language of love and friendship.

Like wings upon my back, my shoulders were gifted to me by my father, whose hand I held one summer on the coast of North Carolina, frightened by the suck of the tide (it was my first time experiencing such force in nature)... and, later, when we snorkeled together in Maui, how I became stranded, clutching to the coral hilltops that rose out of the crashing, churning current... how he pried my arms— cut and bleeding— from living rock and bid me swim back to safety. He is a great swimmer. His shoulders tell stories of the thousand miles he has traversed through clear water, salt and spray. But, he was not gifted in matters of people... so, my mother taught me the smile I now wear... told me— even during my darkest period— to force a look of happiness upon my face... to create an image that was not natural... to forsake my father's downward bent lips, and then, she said I might find contentment even when I seemed to be too far gone. She was a nurse, and I'm sure convinced many a dying man he was worthwhile in the world. I am Marc, the tall, the wide... the smiling one. I am Marc... yet holding my father's hand, smiling at the froth of ocean, at the mishaps of time.

***

Ania's hair is long, red, a deep amber-red. Her eyes are dark. She is not a tall woman, but has a strong back, thick shoulders. She is passionate... she though feels she overwhelms me... but, I keep telling her, *"For one to hide ther passion, and not feel it, or not express it, that that will drive a person mad over time."* What I have not told her is, I feel my passion— contained most my life— is what has brought upon my own strangeness, what causes the voices. Madness is a strange art... to be mad, but to focus such passion seems now my purpose— to convey thoughts and feelings through spoken as well as written language. Ania helps me exhume emotions... helps unearth them, bringing them into light, to let them grimace— at God and his sun.

Ania curled up beside me, hugging me from the back... a needing, long lasting hug... we just finished having shared our bodies, and now, she is tired, while I feel lively, wanting to relate impressions. Blinds are drawn. Two candles burn. Cold coffee is in the red mug I use when visiting. Presently, she has given up hugging me, and lies curled at the other end of the couch, falling asleep.

I heard the slight inflection of your
voice, signifying there was reason I
posed the question not adverse to your
ears.

Screaming came from the distance...
an old woman's voice bouncing off
great boulders on the shoreline... as
her, you are screaming in the depth of
your mind, realizing you're growing
old... forgetting to take into account I
would enjoy growing old with you,
only you.

The radiator, at this moment, sounds
like a squeaking tin whistle a child is
learning to play— his mother in the
other room hesitating to stop her
ears...

I am just learning to love... please don't
stop your ears...

The fighting of the cats woke me...
oh, but they were just playing... a
sound that then was music, like and
unlike when I lie awake and listen to
one of them— as he relaxes by the

> wood stove, or just under the radiating
> iron box of heat— breathe heavily,
> dreaming…
>
> I listened to your labored breath— you
> lay beside me, in bed, in the process of
> a nightmare— even that is beautiful!

***

Ania eats bread and cheese. I smoke another cigarette. I am trying to quit, finding it difficult to smoke less than ten per day… each one tasted is giving in to the addiction that has affected me for ten years. Ania drapes her leg over my lap. I reach over her shin to type. She sighs, resting head on fist. The night has a threatening aspect to it… but, we are safe, in her apartment. I am not sure why I feel fear. Maybe it is because tonight I became vulnerable, I opened to Ania like never before, telling her how much I care, that I love, trying to help her realize this is genuine, this relationship is determined by forces greater than her or me. She talks of me as her soul-mate— she must understand.

Ania asked I pass her the ashtray. She lit a cigarette. She was readying to call her sister and, now they are talking, in their Polish tongue. There is beauty to that language, foreign. I am no longer anxious. Regardless of sirens, regardless of the occasional scream or yell I hear in middle of night, we are safe. We will hold each other through darkness and wake tomorrow to another day.

***

I am yet in the womb. My thoughts are sleepy. It has been raining. Ania left a window open in the bedroom. Through part of the night, I listened to rain and wind. Inclement weather always bodes for good sleep, so it chanced I slept well; but, now am struggling.

In the dimly lit room, behind the reality I know, there is another, other reality occurring. I see movement, as if spirits are here. There is a dancing of light and shadows. I squint, peering into darkness.

A few months ago, on talking with my editor, Erika, I told her it seems there are spirits influencing us. I tend, lately, to gravitate to those which are part of the depths of Earth. Light *and* darkness are essentia... without one a person cannot have the other. I try to maintain balance. I have explored heights, now I attempt to delve into depths. The heights can be so reeling, dizzy-like, floating on a cloud... when the depths seem to ground. I sink my roots deeper when I write about darkness and that grounding is comforting.

I believe there are many types of inspiration, beyond and in-between the clouds and Earth's center. There is the matter of Nature and, there are the songs of the cosmos that one can relate. All writing must draw from a source of imagination and, I find, when I am drawing from a certain place, be that the space of the cosmos or the that of Earth's core, I am changed, and would hope the reader might go through similar shifts of consciousness in experiencing my writings.

Also, one must consider the muses, which certainly take part in creation... and in appreciating art. So, the question might be: *if, when I am speaking of, and drawing from the places of darkness, am I calling forth deep spirits to take part in my reality, in my creative process?* I would say that yes, I am (in a fashion)... but, Earth's matter... that which dwells in deep caverns— or in the place of ocean where no light reaches— is not evil... or morbid. Those creatures and spirits are vital to our struggles just as the blessed ones of a perceived Heaven. Those subterranean spirits are ones which, I believe should be explored and called to aid. They are not evil and they are not good, they just are.

For now, I must maintain momentum. Rt. 90 stretches into the distance, the road home a long one... but there is one day and one night left. Ania seems warm under the comforter. Her cat, Lalunia, lies by her head, purring as if to wake her. I do not want to leave, but have obligations at home, which include a job and two cats. I must get back to the rest of my life, eventually.

In the early morning, tea is better than coffee... it is soothing, yet wakes me. I set the hot cup of water, with tea bag, steeping, on a used cutting board and mixed in milk and honey, stirring the concoction while I contemplated bread crumbs. I drank the tea as if I was dying and, it seems to have quenched thirst for a time. I am waking slowly. Tea is medicine, Ania is medicine, the vacation is medicine... to have four days away from work and all stresses... to be, instead, here in Quincy, writing... eating at restaurants... reading... love making... the lonely poet's soul has found peace. The heart of the matter is I am not mad. I am extremely sane, but sanity is fragile and I must take good care not to slip into the other place, swallow life's beauty, and be willing to fight through points of turmoil. One's existence is a long endeavor and I am merely midway through the journey, journey of the wounded soul... but, I have found a mate and her ring dispels future nightmares. She will be at my side throughout the coming storm. Life is one raging storm, with a few calm moments where one might swim to the surface; take deep breath, then to be pulled back into the sucking of the mother. She is unmerciful, this life. She will drown a man as easily as let another have fair winds, calm waters. In all honesty, I am thriving. The world is kind to me. I have struggled, but, now I have a good job, a good woman. There is no more I could ask for. Thank you god of the seas, you have been over kind, for you have held me safe in storm, you have let me take breath.

***

There was a voice that spoke, woke me during night. It was Ania's voice. She was sleeping beside me. We were in her bed. I had been comfortable, but, then I heard her. While I slept, I heard her speak... not to me but as if making statement to all her known relations. She was not talking in sleep... for, when I woke, she was in a state of peaceful rest. In dream, she said, *"God did this to me."* I wonder... but, do not spend much time wondering. The voice was a figment of my mind's depths, I realize.

The snow... it *is* snowing... falls at an angle because of wind. A scented candle burning, the air smells of vanilla. The sound

OF NOD

of the wind is audible. I must remember this time here, the moments… each an eternity. There are four weeks 'til she'll make way to the Farm, to live with me, in my humble cabin… there in the woods, as one walks downhill toward the sauna.

I was in love all night long, held in a state of love, there by Ania's side. When I went back to the comfort of bed, she and I hugged, staying close to each other. We guarded each other from reality, there, curled under covers, sleeping, letting the world of dreams succor us against the coming day and, I slept for a while that way, holding to her while she held to me.

Under the nightmare world, I hold you, there in Earth's depths. We are such when asleep; we are in the heart of this planet. We are striving to unite in the realm of love… and, on waking, a host of doves fly from our minds, from the reservoir of our souls, flying upwards, into the gray of the day-lit heavens. It was not a host of crows that flew forth this morning, it was the flapping, the disappearing of doves. It was potential sent forth, dreams that will transpire through waking moments. Prayers, unconscious though they are, are not less potent. We must have been praying all night and, in the flock's midst were not only hopes for today… there were also those white wings soaring for the distant future. You have granted me life. You have sung your prayers even though you do not believe in any god… but, he is listening to your heart nonetheless, as he is listening to mine, his great ear pressed to my chest throughout dark night.

***

At the Farm, we live in a vibrant community… so many people

striving for similar goals, binding us. I rarely feel loneliness, especially now I have Ania to visit during weekends. She has changed me. I am self-confident. I am excited about life.

So many people surrounding... but, when in this apartment, it seems we are removed from all traffic and the business of the area. One can hear cars— people going to and fro... heading to work, going to buy this or that... going out to lunch, sitting in crowded restaurants where they don't know the people whom sit at the next table. I cannot wait for Ania to be part of our community. She will love such experience. She will find people are connected there. On the five-hundred acre plot of land, where lives one-hundred-and-fifteen people, I know all... and, I know their extended families. I am familiar with the young and old, with the infants and great grandmothers... and we are well aware of each other. We help each other when one is in need... when one must be driven to the doctor, when one has car trouble, when one experiences a death in the family, etc.... Life is good at the Farm and we desire, as a community, for Ania to be with us. It was announced during Staff Meeting she would begin working on the Residential Team within four weeks. There was applause.

Ania is busy, going through a photo album, sorting through pictures, tearing discarded ones into little pieces. Maybe the process is beginning. She is starting to sort all her life she has stored in this apartment, and is throwing out parts of her past she would be happy to be rid of. I am not asking her what pictures she is destroying. Maybe they are pictures of her ex-husband... maybe not... I feel I should not ask.

***

Outside, there is a plow truck making a bit of noise, pushing fallen snow to the sides of the drive, so it will not impede those living here. The snow will melt, when we have another thaw, it will become part of coursing underground streams. Strange to think there are perhaps rivers flowing beneath this city. There is a coursing, moving current beneath Earth's surface. In the same respect, there is a coursing, moving current inherent in the depths of humans. I have moved from location to location many times throughout life and, sometimes it was the oddest scrap of note or old movie ticket that I happened upon which brought all sorts of emotions and memories to surface, those I had forgotten during the hectic course of daily life. I feel for Ania. I know this move— sorting and throwing away, the packing of her belongings, then unpacking— will not be easy… and, now, she is at the drawer beneath the stereo, thumbing through more of her old, soon to be remembered, life.

***

Back at the Farm… yesterday was a warmish day… sun brilliant, it shed light over mountains, pastures. I took a long walk to the main road, Tyringham Road, and then made my way back, slowly to the Lodge, hoping to arrive before dinner; but, as I was at the lower part of the Farm, I decided to stop at the gravel pit… to watch the ending of day. There I stood, on the sand ridge, looking over a snow covered field. Colors of setting sun were magical. The forest, beginning on the field's edges, reached outward from the Farm's boundaries. My eyes followed curves and dips in the top of the unbroken canopy, to the horizon. All this beauty, this serenity; but, in my heart, I felt a sense of loss, as if a great friend had been left, forgotten. The memory of that lost friend seemed to lap into my consciousness, like waves against a pylon... the retreating tide... the empty boat that has become unsecured, now floats free of the dock, into the majestic ocean, carrying a ghost of my past. Then, I was suddenly aware— off in the field roamed a lone coyote, sniffing at the snow, perhaps looking for some mouse or vole to nip its teeth into, to swallow down its hungry gullet. The coyote hadn't noticed me... until I took steps away from the edge of the pit, heading to the pig house. As I tread, my feet heavy on snow, the coyote stopped its course, stopped its searching, halted, and looked up to see me.

***

Soon, the melting of snow, ice— green lush growth will become apparent. Now is a good time for Ania to move, for she will have opportunity to see harsh winter change to beauty of spring. It is a time for awakening, for gathering one's energies, for soaking in light.

In the middle-winter, all is bleak, harsh. Cabin fever sets in and a feeling of anxiety pervades... but, there is also a gathering, a closeness we feel while we are closed within the warmth of houses. We read poetry, play board games, have dances, or just sit and talk.   Meals are time for lingering, contemplating coursing ideas, sharing thoughts, digesting musings as we chew and swallow good food. Eventually, we'll be hard pressed to stay indoors. Soon, we'll walk the muddy roads, trails, searching for new growth: the first grass blade protruding from earth's clay; the first bud upon an awoken sapling; the sound of water released; the rushing current of a stream thawed; and, the wildflower.

Three hours and I will meet Ania in a town by the exit from Rt. 90. She will follow me back. She is learning the roads, some of which tend to be closed during winter, for they are not plowed. The Farm is located in a rural portion of the state, the most rural area I have lived in for any significant part of my life. I am biding time, waiting for early afternoon, when I'll drive to Lee to meet Ania and bring her back to my, soon to be our, cabin.

***

The moon full and large... a Wolf Moon— the closest that magical sphere will be in its orbit to Earth this year. She is the symbol of womanhood. She is the current of Ania's blood— that moon pulls Ania's emotional currents as she pulls at the oceans. I believe I am infatuated by the present moon; but, it is more the sight of that object by which I am hypnotized. When I stand under the great lamp, partly shrouded in cloud, worries dissipate. That globe pulls at consciousness, she holds sway. I am an ocean; my tides are greatly influenced by her closeness. I feel at ease. So much pent up— frustrations of daily life, undercurrents, and resentments— always present regardless of where one works or lives; but, I am free... freed from the failures of this past week, disappointments. All is new. Thank you, moon, for shedding grace. Ania touched me; let me feel the excitement of her flesh. There was little confusion, trepidation. We were one... sighs, bonding, and emotions. The look in her eyes— that is what I truly love— looking in her

OF NOD

eyes.

The desk lamp has a little cobweb on its glass shade. The cabin is clean; but, I must have missed dusting. Ania is not a fan of cobwebs, so, I will have to take a rag to the lamp. I made her a sandwich this afternoon— goat cheese, green pepper, and onion— on the Farm's homemade bread.

No moon showing through these windows. I must go outside to witness her again. The dance will soon occur, or is already in full phase... moon dancing in clouds. I must leave the cabin. I must go see how the evening is for Ania.

***

A conversation occurred while Ania was readying herself to have another night shadowing.

"You've been taking too much on... you have yet to come back... but I look at your picture... you sitting there, on that deck... remember Provincetown?"

I replied, "There I go... the voices are present again, as I rub my eyes... it seems my preconceptions are what should have been destroyed. Nothing's changed but the surrounding confusion has started to make me laugh... I am distracted, for I know what is going to happen next..."

She was pleasant to talk with. Her thoughts were running quick and deep, but not disturbingly deep. In a manner, it seems I have delved too far... all has become muddled. Thus, I've decided to instead focus on the moment, and live wholly therein.

I continued, "To stay centered is a chore… but, I am more than willing to meet the challenge. If I forget, I will one day remember." And I thought, *"I will keep feet planted. I will not lose balance. I will live through this day— and many more. Nothing can make a tree fall if its root system is deep, vast… not a wind-storm, not freezing rain… only if the earth were torn open by earthquake, or a tornado descended, would a healthy tree fall from grace— a long life of reaching toward light is not easily disturbed."*

Ania and I will drive to Quincy tomorrow. I will stay with her for a couple days, and return to the Farm by week's end. I am looking forward to the drive. It's good to travel distances with Ania. We listen to music and have wonderful conversation. I filled a large clay bowl with food for the cats and made the bed for our last night in the cabin. The sheets and covers were in disorder, left from the nap we took midmorning. During the nap, Ania had nightmares she would not describe on waking. She was quite upset. I should have woken her.

***

Ania has gone to buy groceries. It was a wonderful afternoon. Although cold, the sun was bright, brilliant. She needed to wear sunglasses through the drive. She has trouble on bright-lit days. The sun affects her eyes.

When I asked if she was alright, her squinting even from behind the dark shades, she had replied "Into the sun, into the sun… keep driving. You know, I couldn't find a better man than you even if I tried. You *are* my better half, my Love…"

Traversing the state, we talked about Farm life. She was curious concerning many of the staff, and wanted me to tell her about them— what they do to help the Farm run, whom is married to whom, which kids belong to which set of couples… and, she wanted to know what the various work teams accomplish. She is very excited to eventually be living and working at the Farm, and I am excited for her. The job she has been doing for the past seven years sounds challenging— in a school program, as a teacher for behaviorally challenged teens with Autism. She gets bitten, kicked, and hit regularly when children she works with have needed to be restrained. I am thinking her time at the Farm will be less physical— we never restrain… and I am hoping she will enjoy the break from her present field.

It is good to have arrived early, that we have the day to enjoy each other's company. I feel rested. There was little traffic. The afternoon was and is pleasant. It is strange— now Ania is beginning to move, I suddenly feel this apartment is another home to me and, am sad it will not be ours much longer.

***

Ania and I stayed awake, talking about the mishaps of childhood… how she at one point, when seven, found a copper wire and proceeded to push its split end into an electric socket… how she saved her sister at another point, seeing as Kasia fell through a glass door, and Ania, just in time, pulled her

~ 113 ~

from where she had fallen, as glass crashed downwards… and I told her about the dog attack… about my brother falling from a tree… about how I jumped off a seventy foot quarry cliff and tore my shoulders to shreds.

This morning, Ania's alarm did not ring, so I went to the bedroom and quietly crawled into bed, rubbing her shoulder, saying her name… calling into her dream, hoping she would wake gently, "Ania, Ania… it's time to wake… you're back from the world of dreams now."

Ania left for work. She wanted to stay, but could not. She has good work ethic, which will serve her well at the Farm. I will be alone here today, with the only company being her cat, Lalunia. There will be plenty of time to rest, catch up on lost sleep from this past weekend, plenty of time to contemplate. It is lonely here. This will be an adjustment, learning how to find comfort in this apartment. I will be spending more time here, when she is at work, during the week she'll be moving, so I can support her.

Someone outside drags a metal trash barrel over pavement. I don't know how she has lived here so long. I have needed to spend time with people or to have the peace and quiet of the forest surrounding my solitude. At home, the forest and the stream running behind my cabin are company. Just hearing the wind press its face against the cabin's windows, during storm, is enough to make me feel close to a presence, close to nature. Nature is a force, has a consciousness… it tends to awe me— I feel a mindfulness inherent in the sounds of the trees creaking, and even in the quiet of a winter day… when snow falls as large crystals glittering white. It is as if I have forged a space for myself in the universe, when I sit by the stove, tending fire.

***

I took a few seconds to look at photos posted on the refrigerator. There is a picture of me, sitting on a deck of a hotel in Provincetown. What a wonderful moment— standing there, now, long since our first vacation, gazing at that picture... memories: the ocean, the salty air, the gulls that hovered in the breeze, Ania and I taking our morning slow, sitting on the deck together, quietly conversing, drinking coffee... watching the distance of ocean as if peering toward the rest of our lives.

***

The light of day— streaming through windows— grew dim. I was not wearing glasses, so the combination of both the fading day and the blur of my vision made the moment quite mysterious... as if we were spirits, lounging in bed; paint on canvas. Ania, in particular, was more spirit than flesh. She was beautiful in such light, at such moment. I was in awe. When I explained to her what I perceived, she did not understand, but then, as I elaborated that she looked like a Monet painting, she grasped my meaning. There *is* something quite beautiful about that time of day, noticed when one does not turn on an electric light. Perhaps we are more spirit than flesh. Perhaps, at dusk, we take true form. When I wake in the middle of night, the experience is very different. As I orient myself to where I am, many times I peer through darkness to look at Ania. The vision I see is not one that amazes me. It is frightening, disturbing. In the almost black, on just waking, when peering through the leftover darkness of my dreaming mind, I discern a phantom beside me... a creature with little to no human qualities... something that has crawled out of Earth's depths (or from the sea), to lie by my side and breathe the same air as I... but, I do not scream... I wait for the moment to pass, and, when my eyes adjust to the blackness— as if I have stopped the nightmare— then, I see clearly: the Ania I have loved, asleep beside me... with lengths of hair curling, strewn about her face. Beauty manifests, the sight is one of magic. I find myself wondering— having so quickly forgotten the previous vision— how I came to have such a beautiful woman in bed with me... how she loves me with much of her fragile heart.

***

I woke Ania gently from deep sleep, so she could ready for the day. Work calling... but, her not wanting to leave the quiet of the apartment, the security of bed. We held each other for a time, there in dawn's light. She fell in and out of sleep, rising like a wave, in the ocean of dreams, and then crashing on the shore of wakefulness. The eddying currents, the dreams briefly recognized, before they finally swam to distant waters... forgotten, forgotten. I held Ania for that brief spans. I witnessed her eyes that opened briefly, then closed, only to open again so they could focus on light and its waiting responsibilities. The tide was in, but, now it retreats... the waters silver in the breaking morning... gulls feed on fish swimming in shallows... the lighthouse, on the Breakwater... a ship, from unknown shores, sails out beyond... its captain navigating waters, hoping instruments are accurate... hoping to steer clear of shoals.

A bird flies high, reaching another plateau, in overcast heavens. The flight of that creature is majestic as well as tragic. Those are the emotions conjured within as I watch it soar, from here, in this apartment, gazing out the north window. Ania has left for work. The day sprawls out before me. In her absence, many moments will need to be filled. That bird, it has now flown to a region of sky which lies outside the window's frame. From where I sit I can only imagine the soaring, wondering what it might be searching for, with its keen sight, up in gray-blue.

I can hear the traffic, as if a light turned green, and the cars which were stopped before— engines purring— now race down the busy thoroughfare of Quincy.. drivers rushing to arrive to work on time… to take the early T to Boston. I think I will be staying here, not planning on heading to the city. When I do make my way into Boston, I prefer to have Ania's company. I am yet of the Berkshires, not used to fighting crowds, comfortable biding time in Ania's apartment.

The little jewelry box I used to present Ania her engagement ring sits on the tabletop, to my right, by a picture of her nephew, Lee. It was about two months ago I presented her the ring. I can yet remember Ania's reaction, one of not believing and pure happiness. Since that night, she has not taken the ring off. I inherited the ring from my grandmother when she passed. Amazingly, the diamond laden band fits Ania's ring-finger perfectly, not needing to be resized. Ania and I joke, saying it is like Cinderella's slipper.

OF NOD

I was experiencing a tension in my head and neck, probably from the strong, black coffee I drank when traveling. I do not do well with black coffee and continually forget, because I love such rich brew. After eating a good meal and napping, with my head resting on Ania's lap, I woke, a half-hour later, feeling better... we then decided to go to bed early.

Medication is a struggle. I hesitate to take it, even when I am sure it will help. In the end, I usually decide the meds will be the lesser of the evils, so I swallow the pills. I might go a while with feeling stress, or with little sleep, before I can come to the point of doing what needs to be done. I, though, do take some medication on a daily basis to maintain sanity. I take those pills on first waking, and do not belabor the point. I was once hospitalized because of my struggles, and am quite sure I never want to return. I have too much to lose.

I sit here, reading Bukowski. He is lewd, but an engaging author. I am finding his sparse use of vocabulary refreshing. His simplicity and his commitment to the vile aspects of life... all are more than interesting. Ania gifted two of his books to me at Christmas. She is reading one of the books while I am reading the other... and, she remarks that the Polish version of the same book (which she read some time ago) is tame compared to the English copy. It fascinates me that a translator would take such liberties.

I keep looking at the clock, remember being a child, having to lie down to nap for an hour each day... how I would watch the clock... how it meticulously counted time.

***

I drove from the Berkshires yesterday, excited— it is the moving-weekend. I left early and didn't see traffic. On arriving to Ania's apartment, I let myself in and stayed occupied— reading, writing, listening to music, through the afternoon and early evening. Ania was at work and, then, needed to have dinner with her supervisors— it being her final week at the school. There was not much to eat in her refrigerator, but I was able to survive on a couple fried eggs with cheese, a bagel with cream cheese, and a V8— expiration date past.

Yesterday evening, we spent time on the couch, close, talking about various matters. Ania looked good. She was though anxious about how much weight I'd lost. I explained I'd only been hungry for greens during the week. She kept asking if I was healthy. We ordered out so I might eat well and, once the feta and spinach calzones arrived I feasted as if there was no filling my stomach, feeling much better after doing so.

Some moments are charged. This day and the days following will be filled with periods of significance: Ania's last day at work, an outing with her friends and co-workers tonight, and the ending of her time here in Quincy. By Monday we will have moved all we can to the Farm. On Tuesday, she will begin her new employment. The light of this day is bright, as if we are being spot-lit, so the camera— that records momentous occasions, played back when the last breath is taken— might focus.

I fell in a shaft of sunlight which splashed on the bed, and slept.

OF NOD

The week was long, at the Farm, readying for Ania's arrival. The cabin has new furniture. Ania will need storage space, so I moved in two dressers and a bookshelf. There's not much room; but, it has yet to feel cluttered.

***

I slept well, going to bed earlier than Ania. I partly remember when she arrived to bed. Ania curled next to me, repositioned my arms so they wrapped around her. I woke around two in the morning, unable to move because she was using my arm as a pillow. I escaped without waking her and came into the apartment's living room to smoke. All of this seems to be happening in dream, perhaps because I have lived long as a single man. I'll turn forty in a couple weeks. When one is used to a way of being, anything else seems dreamlike.

***

Ania practically ripped her and my clothes off when she returned from work. We had sex, but it was pressured, as if she had something to prove... not to me, but to her inner demons, all that haunts her from her past. Then, within an hour we readied ourselves for the night at The Half Door— a bar in Quincy Center. On arriving, many of her friends were there already, immediately greeting her. The drinking started. I didn't know what to expect, for it had been long since I'd spent considerable time at a bar... and, we were going to be at that establishment for five hours. During part of the evening, Ania had two, sometimes three Coronas in her hands, guzzling them down, uninhibited. I was worried she would pass out, or get sick, but she is truly from Eastern Europe. She could hold down more drink than many men present. She reminded me of myself when I was her age regarding the amount she consumed. I would sit nightly, with a twelve pack… finishing off two-thirds of that brew during the course of an evening. Ania danced and danced… with women, with men. I rarely experienced jealousy. Only when she went off to a different corner of the bar and sat with someone, hugging him, did I feel jealousy rise. I did not confront her. I simply approached and began talking with the two of them expressing to Ania I was frustrated with how long the evening was, there in company of a bar full of drinkers… me, not drinking. She thought I was angry. I said, "No, I am not… I just feel uncomfortable." So, I *was* able to not let jealousy hamper her socializing… for, she was, in fact, spending time with an old friend… someone she'd worked closely with during her time at the school. I forgave myself. The feelings of jealousy were natural enough, seeing as I was out of my element, with all her close friends drinking to their hearts' content, while I was sober and, although talking to them individually, from time to time, not enjoying the situation. By the end of night, though, I was happy I'd been at the gathering. As lights turned on, music stopped, and the bar began to close, many of Ania's friends made a point to approach the table I was sitting at, expressing congratulations— saying I was fortunate to have met Ania. According to them, Ania was also fortunate. She seemed happy. Ever since I came into her life, she had been "glowing." I was able to witness the beautiful ways people loved her. She is well liked in this community. Many of the women cried on parting.

I worried Ania would become sick. She did not though… and,

before long we were in the comfort of her bed, her falling asleep in my arms, talking nonsense as she drifted into the realm of dreamless sleep— perhaps saying goodbyes to the phantoms that visited. I lay there peering into darkness.

***

Before going to bed last night, Ania opened a pack of clove cigarettes which I had bought earlier in the morning. We sat there, on her futon, in quiet, smoking. Perfume filled the air.

***

Ania probably will rest soundly 'til ten o'clock... or later, considering she was not feeling great, after celebrating so fervently Friday evening. I am happy to be awake, writing, and composing myself. This afternoon, we'll enjoy a lunch with the woman from the Czech Republic, and her husband. I met both of them at Ania's party. They are wonderful people. The husband— who's name I forget— is from the Midwest. He loves to hunt pheasants. His dream is to have a hunting dog and live in an area of the world not like Boston. He noted to me he felt a pang when he heard Ania and I will be living in the Berkshires. He then asked about the hunting that occurs there, eyes lighting up when I spoke about deer, about many lakes and ponds.

***

Most everything is in boxes, suitcases, or backpacks. The trunk of the car is full. Now we have only the back seat left, leaving room for her cat... and, the cleaning of the apartment... the leaving behind odds and ends— back next weekend to gather the last of her belongings.

It would be good to arrive at the Farm for dinner, maybe earlier. Yesterday was good, with some rough parts though. Ania not wanting to face the endeavor of the move... feeling ill in the morning, not talking to me 'til noon... then a bit of an argument when we returned from having lunch. Regardless, it was a good lunch. We lingered at the restaurant long after finishing our meal, afterward finding an Irish pub, to have drinks and coffee for another couple hours. I enjoyed examining the stone masonry in the basement-bar, for I used to be a stone mason tender and still appreciate the detail that goes into making walls. I had the feeling Ania was intentionally lingering, but I did not mind because the company was good, the food was good, and Ania was radiant.

We stayed up 'til midnight, going through her belongings, tossing all we could, boxing and bagging all Ania wanted to bring with her. At points, Ania happened upon photos or notes that brought back memories. I sat by her, listening to her reminisce as she sorted. At one point she found her old diary, written in Polish.

***

Ania woke from a nightmare. Just at that moment I was having a wonderful dream about her and me being at the Farm picking spring wildflowers. I shared with her my dream, as she was so upset from hers— she had called out in her sleep that she did not want to leave. After I told her about the wildflowers, she smiled and we held each other. They were of various colors. Most memorable were the little purple ones... they are still vivid in my waking mind.

***

Now, in Tyringham, the day will unfold as a hatching butterfly, unfettering wings, to waft and stretch in morning light. It is yet dark. I don't know why I have woken early. If it were my choice, I would still be asleep.

Last night Ania remarked that, for her, it feels the stress of the city is left behind. She was sitting on the couch here in the cabin, the night young. We listened to music, watched cats, made sure they did not fight. Lalunia found a safe perch on the cabinets in the bathroom. My cats were well behaved, giving Lalunia distance, allowing her to become used to them, slowly. Whenever they approached, she hissed and spit... but they were no danger. They seemed inquisitive, not angry or aggravated.

The tiger cat rubs his side against my shins. Lalunia might be sleeping under the bed. Ania sleeps on that bed, peacefully, resting after living in cities for some thirteen years. This is the country. No sirens screaming in the middle of night... quiet... the quiet of the natural world. Everything is dark outside. I feel as if I am the center of creation. The universe revolves. A silver heart sits on the desk, a gift from my stepmother and father at Christmas. The paperweight shimmers in light of the lamp.

NATURE

Flight of a blackbird... over the field... pushing its body toward the forest... sun brilliant... spring colors... green of new grass... leaves, each turning... ecstasy as wind blows... a dragonfly— close at hand— flies straight.... Spring: flowers... long walks... listening to sounds of birds— fluttering wings... chirping, calling, singing... they are pleased... they are the voice reverberating... there is also the quiet, almost inaudible sound of water flowing— the babbling brook... thinking nature... and she ponders, in quiet manner, courses and means of men... flight of the blackbird— its shadow darting over field's growth— passing of its shadow... deer that think— quieter than the brook— wander, seeming lost, through depth of wood, over hills, through long grass... looking for place to bed. The sun... a god— to the brook, blackbird, deer, and dragonfly... the sun creates, destroys... all life depends... all shadows. In distance is seen, in shade of evergreens... a man and woman... they love, roll over, listening.... The humans can remember, vaguely, last spring and the spring before... how the current of the brook has changed, delved... they understand the blackbird, as if both once were blackbirds... they almost feel... but yet they do not completely... and so cannot be one with woods, sun. They have forgotten how to pray, no longer understanding the importance... instead they've created an abstract god— in their own image. Birds... the sounds of birds— but now bird songs represent weather's turning... dark clouds, laden with moisture, ride the horizon... the clouds roll as ocean waves, seeming spirits— they plume, burst, flow, rebel... threatening daylight... lovers hold, watching... birds flying close, no longer mirrored by shadows... the dragonfly has found a mate and two fly as one, united, across the field. Clouds blanket sky... no pure light seen... a rendering in charcoal... melancholia... faces of the lovers seem to have lost purity... a snake crawls from under a rock, begins slithering... through grass... tongue flitting, tasting weather, tasting beauty. Then... the snake feels it... the beginning, the first tear... shed on distant mountain... the cry... even here, in this valley, far from that mountain, the snake is aware... because the earth is aware... and the snake's belly is pressed to the earth... the raindrop that hits a distant hill is as a pebble being thrown into a pond, sending ripples through forest and all forest creatures... the cloven hoof of the deer no less sensitive... the tear is felt... the deer understands.... Where have the lovers gone... no longer beneath the evergreens? They have discerned... they have made their way home and are now curled... under blankets, caressing, comforting... the man lets his fingers course over the contours of the woman's body— and she becomes significant. A cat cleans himself... gray light flows through two windows... love moans... then the clouds release... and wind grows... and trees— seen from windows— bend, sway... leafy branches a tumult.

***

We moved into this house a month ago. Ania and I have been happy. There is more room, and the place has been recently constructed... so, it is new, like our relationship, like the beginning of this day. Outside can be heard one of the cats leaping from the porch railing onto the floor of the porch. His front paws thumping first, then his hind paws landing after.

Ania is at work. She is doing an overnight at one of the Resident houses. We have not seen much of each other this past week, for she has been training to begin working elsewhere— off Farm— at a place in Lee which serves people who have Autism. It is more of what she is accustomed to, similar to the work she was doing in Quincy before moving to the Berkshires... except— thank God— she will not be needing to restrain her clients— she will be more of what might be called a Behavioral Specialist.

Sun rises... dawn... birds chirping, singing... and, I, on the front porch just now, listening to blissful beginnings. Then, coming inside, filling the cat dish with food, placing it outside by the front door. Now the little black cat leaps from his perch on the railing. I can hear such from where I sit— on the couch, while I type... his landing subtle, gentle.

I have a bit of money in an account, but am saving it for vacation to Poland, to visit Ania's parents. Seeing as we have only recently moved, I am happy to stay here, sleeping much, watching movies, reading, and writing. Sometimes I prefer the comforts of home instead of rushing about, staying in a hotel room, and spending money on food, entertainment. This vacation, I would rather rest, enjoy being home, and be with Ania when I am able, especially since she will be going to Boston for the weekend.

***

On walking up the hill towards the cabin, I spoke with Clara. She asked how my vacation is and I was happy to say all is

~ 127 ~

good, that I am resting and enjoying the time away. She was walking her dog, Guss. He was sniffing at grass, trying to search-out what cat had been that way. He is a hunter of cats. He tends to go completely mad when he sees a cat, wanting with all of his being to chase it.

The cabin tends to cool a great deal during night and, because it is in the shade and is well insulated, if the windows are kept closed, the cabin tends to stay comfortable all day. At least this is what I have noticed is happening, it being our first warm season.

Today, went to meals at Lodge, also went for a walk on the roads. I saved the walk for late afternoon seeing as midday the sun was strong. While walking, I stopped at the pig pen, which is on a hill at the lower end of the Farm, and called Ania in Boston. It was good to say hello and, she seemed happy to hear from me. The turkey was loose. It was walking around the pigpen with a few chickens following. He put on a display when I came near, ruffling feathers, gobbling.

Flies buzz. Birds chirp. I can hear an owl hoo-hooting. I feel at ease and think how Ania is presently in Boston, how she must be listening to a plethora of different sounds. Our life together— since her arrival five months ago— has been wonderful. I have fallen in love with her day after day, each time more intensely. It is like hearing the birds chirp this evening, when they have sung their songs so many nights... but, with age, I have begun noticing the subtitles of nature.

❈❈❈

Last night, I had dreams about women. Now, being alone I find I am remembering what it is to be single. It is not that I wish to be single. The chase took most my life, was tiring, disappointing. Always kicking, struggling to hold my head above surf, treading water— rarely movement. I am content... more than content, feeling life is all that could be wished for. I count blessings. Dreams are but dreams... night is night... dawn dawn... I have survived the night to live another day.

I think how Ania must be asleep, peacefully... in a bed, in an apartment in Boston... how I wish she was asleep in our bed... now... quietly snoring... how I would let her sleep throughout morning, waking her sometime in the near future... whispering her name, kissing her shoulder, caressing her forearm... but no, she is in Boston... visiting. She has not been back to her old home in five months. I am sure she's enjoying time spent there, and I am happy for her.

I stretch... my soul growing. It curled itself within the tiny shell when I slept, there to witness the dreams of mind— where it would be safe from storm, from turbulent waters. Now, at dawn, the soul crawls fourth, swells... finding the boundaries of flesh once again... needing to wear this body throughout day, it must find equilibrium. The freedom of flesh, and the imprisonment... every morning is invitation... one must live, but, every night, one must die, letting the dreaming mind hold sway... until another morning dawns _ and the birthing, the finding, the discovering... orange-gold glistens the line of trees to the east...

OF NOD

***

The world of flesh, bone, rock, and water... night visions quickly forgotten. I wonder if birds dream... dream of the songs they'll sing... brains the size of peas; minds unfathomable.

A boat, engine purring— leaves shoreline... disturbing placid surface, carrying witnesses— my perceptions— of new dawn. The catch will be large, no time for sleeping... time for heading into the lost silver. No anchor will be tossed. Once when we arrive to the fishing spot, let the boat drift. The mind's fishermen... the ones compelling the vessel to continue... the drivers, the searchers, the quiet... watch with eyes of wonder... steer this vessel to a place where life's dreams might be captured.

***

Under an old oak I buried one of my toys. I was a child, thinking I would return again the next summer. A farmer woman of the church watched me through the upstairs window, digging into earth, extracting from my pocket the childhood memory, placing it in the grave I had delved between roots, and then covering it with dirt and a bit of moss. The item buried is long forgotten... but, I do remember the event... and, I remember the old woman's great black dog... the size of a small bear... that dog would sleep all day, every day I visited... there, by the stairs to the cellar... he was a Newfoundland. My brother and I would play board games with the little girl of the family... and I would cheat like hell, pocketing Monopoly money when they were not looking. I don't remember the little girl's name. I remember her happiness though.

✷✷✷

The tiger cat has gone outside, or maybe he spent most the night outside... regardless, he is there, on the porch, curled on the cushioned chair. Birds are singing morning songs. Ania will be returning home. I look forward to holding her in my arms. When we spoke last evening, she was groggy, having just woken from a nap. I can remember the sleepy inflections of her speech... the huskiness to her voice, she having had beer and cigarettes the night previous. The day overcast, no gold showing in trees across the dirt road, only gray sky behind bluish-green leaves. Clothes, newly washed, draped over the porch chairs and porch railing.

✷✷✷

When I was young, every summer we would rent a house on the Delaware shore, always within walking distance to the beach. I spent my days playing in surf and sand... building castles that would be devoured by waves when tide rose... and, I would swim, ducking my head under water when horseflies began to land upon my scalp— their bites deep, drawing blood. I played, on the beach, with my brother and cousins. We would throw wet sand at each other... the sting as it hit our sensitive flesh, sun burnt. We would fish and crab with our uncle, either renting boats, or finding a pier, casting our lines and traps into the depths. At night, when we returned home, our mothers would tend to our sunburn and bread and fry or steam the shark or crab we had caught. We then would feast. Our little fingers would hurt— the sharp points to the crab legs piercing flesh, the spice seeping into fresh wounds.

***

Cape Cod is not far, but too far nonetheless. Perhaps Ania and I should move. Work has begun to become repetitive. I need to hear the breaking surf outside my window. Bird songs are not enough.

***

Ania is home. Now I am awake and cannot sleep. The night has been exciting. It was good to spend time away from each other. Not that we were having trouble, it is just that sometimes I need to allow the fire of the soul to kindle and catch, then burn like a bonfire once when in her company again. Darkness blankets windows... but, it is a quiet and thoughtful darkness, unlike the morning, before sun rises. Predawn tends to seem as if there is a storm brewing, the day preparing. I awake before the curtain is opened. At midnight, it is as if I have watched the entire play, that it has been good and that there is some bliss which has taken place in the last act.

While sitting at the kitchen table after she arrived, Ania ate a tuna sandwich which I made for her. Between bites, she told me she had a wonderful time while in Boston... she visited with old friends, she went out to eat at numerous restaurants, and saw a bit of Boston nightlife. Later, while we were sitting on the porch, she described more about how she had spent her time. She seemed tired, but happy... as if the time away was good... also, as if she was content being home.

***

A long time ago, my father's father and I found a garter snake, dead, in the tarn water that had collected within the confines of the community pool. It was my childhood. Later that summer he would build me a sandbox that I would paint bright red. The yellow and black patterned snake had quite an appetite, seemingly, before it passed, for its body bulged at one place, as if it had consumed a frog or mouse. Maybe it was so hungry that it slithered over the lip of the pool's edge, falling, falling to the bottom, then clutching hold of its victim with jaws, swallowing with relish that last meal .. not knowing that it would be unable to find a way out. And, my grandfather, yet one of the living, before cancer clutched at his throat and began to choke... was kind enough to preserve that well fed garter for me, in a pickle jar... the vinegar being as good for keeping the snake from decay as it was for keeping pickles crisp to bite into. My grandfather now does the Dead March to who knows where; or, maybe after all these years, he has arrived at some end to his journey... I do not know, only wonder... between here and there, must be an answer on the road.

***

As an older child, I would stand in front of the honeysuckle bush growing by the fence on the edge of the Hell's Angels' property. Picking those blossoms, one by one, I pulled the stamens by the green bulbs at the flowers' bases... drawing those delicate nodules slowly out so as to pull the nectar from the flowers' wombs. Then, I would lift each droplet toward my

~ 133 ~

mouth— catching a last glimpse of the glittering in sunlight, letting each king's treasure finally be tasted... *oh God... to be young again...*

***

My mother's mother... I never knew her. She committed suicide long before I was born... asphyxiation. As was described to me at a young age— Aunt Ann came home from school to find her in the garage, dead, car running. My grandfather, Adam, remarried sometime later. A marriage he called "financially logical." Claire— his second wife— died a couple years ago, Grandpa dead many years previous. Claire... I still remember her at my cousin's wedding. She had Altimeters. She asked me to dance and, it was as if she was eighteen... and I was not her grandson... and that she loved me... as if we were the only two people alive on Earth. I never saw her again after that night, and I was unaware of her death until well after it had occurred... but, she was graceful during our dance and, if I remember right, she kissed me numerous times... on the lips. Perhaps she knew we would never see each other again.

***

Over time, we forget... and then, without warning, memories of a lost childhood, of a grandmother's last dance, will dawn— it is like being hit in the head with a baseball bat— the inexperienced batter letting bat fly from his or her hands after the contact is made— I, not paying attention— standing in the wrong place at the wrong time— and, *crack*, the second contact is made unmercifully. The world goes black. I fall from a

~ 134 ~

height, landing on soft grass… the field of madness…

***

Now I watch: in the window frame is a moth stuck in spider web, flailing, fluttering body and wings, needing to find freedom, the memory of which is yet present in a pinhead mind… an unquestionable, although brief, experience. A small spider upon web, hesitates to crawl down and force venom into the black and gray patterned beast it has caught.

Caught in the web of another's design, needing to feel, I attempted the impossible, grasping hold of the Jacob-ladder, climbing a rung or two, only to slip and fall, then, eventually, climbing to a height where a fall would be my demise… this is the way of celebrating young adulthood— being invincible, god-driven.

So my hold weakened, so I lost footing, like all men of action do eventually, and me, flailing in the aftermath, as I fell, flapping arms as if they would turn to wings, to land, to land in the webs of innuendo, of the sordid friendships. Being possessed by the spirit, risking everything, brought me toward a painful— too painful to relate— end, and the marking of a beast— symbol that, in the end, all men and women carry as burden— was scrawled on my forehead by the outstretched finger of a so called friend, one dark and stormy, one ceremonious night, on the coast of Connecticut, where water and sand met, as I lay in an acid dream, in the land of Nod.

***

The flowers we picked are slowly dying, in vases… petals limp, lifeless… but, our love survives… its own flower. Not long ago… sun shining… you noticed purple blooms by the abandoned cabin close to our home. I held the stems in hand, while you cut more from the little patch of purple hidden in long grass and weeds. I was worried you might be stung. The cats lay in the gravel drive, rolling on their backs, bathing in dust.

***

My grandfather showed me how a nail might be reused… how, after it was pried from a two-by-four, and, because it was bent, he placed it in the jaws of a vise, gently tapped this way and that, until it took on the semblance of being straight— straight enough so as to handle the downward force of a swing, and sink deep. The prying and sinking… the depth of man measured according to his sensitivity regarding iron, steel, and wood. The hammer must have been wielded by a skilled carpenter in order to have fashioned this reality— we see things as they are meant to be seen, not as we might envision if our eyes had been born other than from tools of necessity. I am a man who won't be bent by another, fashioned how they might choose… and that fighting is what we call spirit. So, when I stand on the beach, holding your hand, my Love… and let water course through, I feel the sinking— the semblance of this life becoming apparent... as if, at this juncture, I have been made to feel the beginnings… the grandfather, how, in that poorly lit garage— Winston-Salem, North Carolina... a lifetime ago, attempted to teach— and I learned, somewhat, what existence meant to him.

He was the first of my teachers, the one who reused what others might discard... then there is the prying forth of that child-dream... that I would become something of worth someday. Days later, the building of my fortress, there in the backyard... hidden in brush and bramble... that first nail which was straightened by his old hand and knowledge— gentle manners— taken in the grip of my little paw, the great Hephaestus hammer held in the other... the eying of the first two-by-four— it would hold the structure sound... with its scars— nail holes apparent... the clumsy swing, downward force of all the forefathers... and so, after long afternoons of such endeavor, I have, in the end, built a place to hide my child, the dreams and lions of his temperament... the structure rickety, but serving undeniable purpose.

***

While a youth, thumbing through Bibles— huge and small... paper, black covers, bindings brittle— heirlooms... I found a lock of blond hair... I wonder if one of my ribs went missing when I began to love all of who you are... and so God causes the man to sleep, and creates a woman from his rib. The man names her "Woman", "for this one was taken from a man". "On account of this a man leaves his father and his mother and clings to his woman." Morning... I brought coffee to you, my Love, in bed... and, there was the smile. . a blessing... we held to each other, forgetting ourselves, becoming one... later, you helped cut my hair... the gray shavings that fell to the sink.

***

OF NOD

Now, where I live— in the cabin of my dreams, here in Tyringham, Massachusetts... I think how spacecraft— missions to The Nothingness, have exploded as they lift off— all passengers sent into True Oblivion. I watched— one day sick and home from school such disaster— live— I found the channel just at the right, or wrong instant, lying there, on the living room floor, in the Fairway Falls home. The moon— its pocked-marked visage seems to revel as it bears witness to the mishaps of humanity. We are neither here nor there— halfway between, leaning toward destruction— I leaned toward the TV in such a manner... hungry-eyed, swooning, a child, in Wilmington, Delaware, knowing something of great import had occurred; something had gone wrong. Our Aunt's and Uncle's backyard... the anthills, by the above-ground swimming pool... many hot afternoons, rain fell... daubing the granular, intrinsically small, mounds. I yet stand there— watching— mystified while my brother dives from the platform, splashing into the waters of childhood... how it was a boulder crashing into the sea of memory— or a great meteorite colliding with Earth— falling from that precipitous cliff... when my father brought the shotgun into the Chalet Drive home, and had intention to end someone's life— maybe his own— but, instead, was wrestled to the garage floor by my mother and uncle before he had opportunity to succeed... then, in my twenties, maybe misspent— I, a lonesome spirit, paddled the canoe out into North Pond, Waterville, Maine... brought that vessel to land on a rocky jut— where no eyes could witness except mine— high in the rain... the mystic, slow pausing, as the million droplets of God's tears became part of the body, adding minimally to the depth— each impact vivid— etched in an older man's memory... such as explosions, the bombing of an already wounded land, appearing to the innocent and removed as crime and punishment.

***

We made love just ten minutes ago... countless people in the world surly doing the same. I am not so tired any more, the aching abated. A memory of you— the moisture still on me... the kisses I yet taste... and, I released in you all of what I have been holding for years— those worries and wishes, hardships, and blissful moments. Swimming in you must be thousands of warriors... pushing toward the ultimate goal. You sit beside me, thinking insecurities... and I comfort you, now, in your time of need, as you have comforted me t me and again during this past year. Thirst drives bear to seek the dark water... I wear the bear mask and have drunk, now wading in the shallows of your river. Outside the bedroom, when we were engaged in the act, our mastiff scratched at the door, wanting in... and then, as he must have heard our love cries, he became quiet, resigned to being left out of the play. He sleeps presently; on the couch... quietly barking... as a man or woman who talks while slumbering. When you talk in sleep, you tend to speak three languages— Polish, English, and the third being the mumble language of all who speak when in dream.

***

Grandfather— the other night, I remembered when you would smoke outside, in the drive, by the garage door. It is as if you'll always be standing on the crest, taking those Camels into your lungs. . and, each cigarette I inhale, now, I imagine you take a part in the love-consuming.

Over many days now I have been recalling how my lovely bride-to-be, accepted the diamond laden band sometime around Christmas over a year ago... there in her Quincy apartment, in the middle of night, after she and I loved for a second time that day. The other afternoon, I dreamed about the child that might be born from Ania's and my desire... the boy would have blond hair, and would be tightly wound— like a rubber band twisted to the point of breaking... his spirit would fight, through constant momentum, the unraveling of tension.

When one dies, perhaps he or she falls toward another reality. Mother, I yet jump from the pool's lip, into your waiting arms, requiring time and again to feel the determined wanting, that culminated in the leap— knowing you would catch me... how I consumed drugs, so lost a great part of myself... and had to have you save what was left of me from the grip of the hospital Psych ward. You brought me to Kemah, and nursed me back to this life. I suppose the losing of my identity was a fall, so I would be caught, yet in air, as I died... as I leapt into the waters of childhood.

Grandfather, when you passed, on the morning after standing over your open casket... I asked Pearl, my grandmother, if I might have one of your pocketknives... you had left a collection about the basement rooms where you and she lived the last years... and she gave me two of the knives— I then keeping one and giving the other to James— he who you loved so, for he was the younger... and would, as you guessed, be taller and wider than me someday. The little that I know about the world of darkness, I believe is delivered to my dreams through your ghost, somehow remembering me, dreaming me as you strive yet in the afterlife, planting and growing your rhubarb— that Grandmother would, and maybe yet— long dead now too— bake into her pies.

***

I woke at one this morning and could not fall back toward sleep... my mother, out at sea... down off the coast of Florida— a storm that has been affecting them... the ocean, turbulent, that surrounds their vessel. How they must feel lost, out there, how she almost cried at the end of our conversation yesterday. "Slowly, slowly I am sailing... but I have no time to think... it is time for me to sink into the beauty...," as if she knew she had gone too far. It was a dream of theirs, to retire and sail coastal waters until the end of their days. Last night, while in bed, awake, I imagined their plight, and how unforgiving the sea is... I saw them, a speck on the horizon of my mind... following the sun's reflection, toward lands that none of us venture to touch unless it is the only, last choice. *Quiet now, and you'll hear the waves lapping against the hull... close your eyes and you'll see the long stretch of water-horizon on all sides... and the dip and bob of the boat... unforgettable, how you ride on the surface, buoyant, but oh how easily capsized.* All this while I lay in the warm bed of my making, trusting... where the eye of the storm lies, in my heart, I might feel some reprieve, I might fill with other emotion so not to fear. And, when I realized that I could not sleep in any other fashion, like one condemned, I opened the door to the refrigerator, reached in and took hold of the last dark bitter beer, cracked open the bottle, and suckled, as if I was yet a newborn, nestled to my mother's breast, finding the nourishment that would fill me complete. After drinking the waters of Lethe, I went back to the bedroom where my Love slept sound, nestled against her— even put my arm out so I could rest my hand on her soft belly— that region of the womb… imagined, falling to sleep, that our first child therein floated on the great red sea of Ania's center.

***

Parakeets will sometimes sit on one's lower lip, sticking their head in your mouth, and sing songs to the echoing, moist darkness… as if she had lived another life, my mother would recline and allow the yellow feathered family pet to lull her, toward a distant adulthood… as if that little bird taught her the ways of the tamed wild, chirping and whistling into the depths of my child-mother's soul. She has lived long, and now sails waters toward the haven where I will soon be wed… the waters carry her, now, like the bird's song once did in her youth. Maybe the parakeet imparted more than song to her dreaming mind… spoke, in its way, to her heart of hearts about a boy-child that would, one day, grow into a man.

I was thinking the other day about how I nursed my grandfather towards his last stand, that final day of his life hopefully made more comfortable by my presence and compassion. As if he needed to know me before he died, she asked that I make the trek to his home in Florida. I am grateful for that time spent helping in the only ways that I knew how, me struggling with my own, emerging sickness. There are pictures of my grandfather and me hidden in this Massachusetts cabin, in some drawer, that I will discover again sometime in the near or distant future. How thin I was at that juncture, in a way mimicking how he looked while passing towards the next birth. It is his wedding ring that will be placed upon my finger... and I will be proud to wear such shimmering gold.

Parakeets sing songs when pleased about their existence... balanced upon your lower lip, mother will always be that creature of delight, imparting its songs so you might sing back to the world your love of life, as you so often do when I have been in your presence, so little over the passing years...

Birds are a metaphor for flight and, ultimately freedom— we are born, we learn to walk, so that we might travel over this globe— the sense of adventure the driving force of our forefathers, it having determined how the scientific Adam and the scientific Eve eventually met, and united— perhaps they were in search for some sense of meaning, that which you seemed to have found, when, in your childhood, you trusted the bird's song.

***

I cannot discern what reality is and what is of my creation. I do know that emotions are swelling. I feel, now like never before. To be alive is to feel. I feel all of who I am... and all of who Ania is. Our feelings... that is what I must honor, protect, what I must tend. The moon is an entity. It would have us feel its pull at times... so we must let that be. That others influence us should not be considered a trespass... merely part of nature.

OF NOD

That bodies of light— the sun, the moon, the stars— make their impressions... that people are no different... that we are true to our own emotions, that we see when we are influenced and give and take at those times... that I love her might not be all which matters, but that we love each other... paramount... and that we are true to each other... that the Earth is in orbit around the sun, and that the moon is in orbit around the Earth— that time never, never stands still.

POLAND

I am in Warsaw... meeting, for the first time, my future in-laws. Ania's father drove us from the airport.. a very nice man... kind, gentle. It was a long time on the plane. Night is brilliant over the city's center. The second largest cemetery in Europe sprawls directly across the street. From where we stand on the little patio, we watch the evening birds circle and hear them cry. Everything is small here, except the cemetery. Even though the apartment has numerous rooms, we must step carefully not to trod on each other's feet, or stub toes on furniture.

I type with one hand. Ania just woke and now is holding to my right side and arm, falling back to sleep. It is eleven o'clock... night. I had gone to bed early... so tired. The movement when she crawled into bed interrupted my sleep. Not that I am complaining... I am glad to be awake, listening to traffic and trolleys. Ania quietly snores She is happy. It was a year since she'd been home. She is here now, and radiant in the company of her father and mother. We sleep in the bedroom at the end of the hall, on a couch that unfolds. Before going to bed, she showed me her old room from when she was a college student— the center room of the condo.

A fan is blowing. The day was hot and night yet holds heat. At this moment, all traffic has ceased. . so quiet... no sound, except the fan.

***

OF NOD

The sun rises over Warsaw, over this humble complex. I slept well. Glow of the new day... moon sets, having spent its allotted time in the Europe sky.

God, this sunrise is beautiful... and, the sky vast. No hills to block sight of the horizon. Ania's shoulder though is a hill, a mound with light of new day breaking upon it— the ocean wave of pinks, blues, and greens. I touch her foot with my foot. She rolls over and faces me, not waking.

***

Rain falls on Warsaw. The roaming clouds... I watch them move across the wide horizon, hover over the city's center. This afternoon, we went back to the airport to gather Ania's sister, Asia. She is here now and, the parents are glad to have another of their daughters visit.

We took the trolley and bus to and from the airport. There is no air conditioning in much of Poland and there certainly was none on the trolley or bus— sweating and uncomfortable, about an hour each way. I looked out the windows to see the city. Ania oriented me. Yesterday, on the drive from the airport, she was engaged, talking with her father in their native tongue.

I sit in the living room... the sounds of traffic... the sounds of the pouring rain. We just went across the street to a local German grocery and bought beer, juice, and water. Now, the women of the family are in the kitchen talking. Ania's father just returned. He sits down in the living room and seems happy. There are fresh flowers... carnations in a vase by the television.

We were hoping to visit the Old Town of Warsaw this evening, but, weather is not agreeable. It is just good to be here... to ride a trolley... to go to a German grocery... to drink the homemade wine Ania's parents shared with me last evening... wonderful. It was strong, like Port, and sweet. One glass and the bed was calling, especially after traveling for the previous twenty-four hours. Ania's parents were pleased I enjoyed their wine. Her mother said it was made from fresh grapes and wild berries.

***

Rain has ceased. Dawn will begin momentarily. Daylight begins early, and it does not grow dark until after nine. Apparently, I wake when sun rises no matter where I am in the world.

Ania was snoring— now she breathes quietly, absorbed in dreams. On falling asleep last night, she talked in sleep... both languages at different times. She was tired on settling down... a night of good food, watching European football, drinking beer and vodka. I brought her father a bottle of Kettle-One for him to enjoy at his leisure. After last night, the bottle is mostly empty... but it was enjoyed. On sitting down to dinner we toasted to each other's health.

I also had a couple beers that we bought from the German grocery. They both were of a different variety. Each tasted of the unique bitterness one finds in the beer of Europe. I, though, after having a mere three drinks, was quite disoriented when stepping out on the little patio. I did not enjoy such sensation, being slightly drunk— the vertigo that was caused by looking over the railing, nine stories up.

***

Ania is waking, but still in bed. I just went to the bedroom and lay with her, rubbing her lower back and shoulders. I am hoping we'll have a chance to go to the Old Town today. It would be good to see that section; but, rain might not allow such discovery... at least not today.

I step outside to smoke my pipe, and look upon the city— how beautiful, this overcast day. The water in the teapot is readying to boil. Ania is out of bed.

***

I lay down for a nap, and when I woke, Ania was ready to go to Old Town. We left around eleven in the morning and just returned to have dinner. While in Old Town, we took pictures, had Polish beer in the center, and visited a café that had internet. I had my laptop with me, so we checked e-mail and Ania wrote a few of her friends, hoping they will call.

We walked cobblestone streets, resting briefly a few times. Through much of the day, I had my head tilted upwards so to see the architecture. We also visited two churches, gazing at stained glass and domed ceilings... at statues that lined walls... and at the intricate carved woodwork of confessionals.

While sitting on the veranda at a coffee shop, Ania and I played out our engagement again. For that moment, she gave me back the ring and I asked for her hand in marriage, pretending I'd never asked before. We laughed and kissed.

***

Four or five shots of Polish vodka and I am feeling well. It is late, close to midnight. Ania's family and I spent the evening watching European football. The team we were rooting for was the victor, the Spanish National Team. It has been the final games of the World Cup, taking place in South Africa. Ania's father is a lover of this sport, used to play when young.

Ania's father and mother needed to go to bed, her father especially seeing as he must be at work in the morning. Although I had a few beers during the day, at that time, I had thirst for vodka. Ania's sister was more than happy to join me... but it was more than I was expecting. She brought a half bottle to the kitchen and we closed the door. Ania cracked open a beer and talked to us as we did shots.

Night is cool. There is yet the sound of traffic on the roads. The condo is quiet. I cannot hear Ania and Asia, but they are yet in the kitchen. I feel darkness is young, as if I would like to stay awake 'til dawn. While shooting vodka, I kept looking out the single window at the buildings close at hand, the street lights, and moving vehicles. I had to hold the curtain aside to see.

The clock ticks on the shelf by my ear. Time is flowing, a river

that won't be dammed. I am the curtain being drawn open.
Polish vodka brings a sense of understanding to the moment.

***

Ania and Asia do not feel well. I did not feel great on waking,
but, after espresso I am better. Ania is showering. Asia and her
mother are in the living room watching Polish television. We
just returned from shopping at the grocery and market... lots of
food bought for our time in the country, which is where we
head tomorrow. The family has a county house, close to
Warsaw, that Ania's father built.

I laid down for a nap and slept soundly. Then, on waking, ate
more of the food that Ania's mother had prepared. In the
meantime, Ania's aunt arrived from Germany. After a brief
period at the condo, Ania's parents and aunt left for the country
a day early. We will be on our own tonight— Ania, Asia, and I.

***

We have started drinking Polish beer. I have such a feeling of
vertigo when standing on the patio, but, regardless keep going
out there to talk with and kiss Ania. She was sitting there on a
chair, smoking cigarettes and then came inside, making her way
to the back rooms of the condo. The television is on, in the
Polish language. Asia finished her conversation on the phone
and came into the living room to pour more beer in her glass.
The lights are yet off, but, some light flows from outside. It is
verging on dusk. Ania stands on a footstool and turns on the
ceiling fan's light. The fan is running.

~ 150 ~

***

The crows caw. I slept soundly. I made myself espresso and now sit in the living room, enjoying the morning glow. Perhaps today will be a sober affair. Ania and Asia yet sleep. I will wake Ania at eight and then we'll ready ourselves to go shopping again. Ania is in search of a pair of shoes.

On top of a boxed deck of cards sits the empty espresso cup, Jung's *Modern Man in Search of a Soul* beside, its yellow cover bright in the haze of this new morning. In the distance, on the horizon, the great buildings of Warsaw loom. Last night, the city's lights were brilliant. Before going to bed, Ania and I were on the patio. I remarked to her how I feel comfortable, as if I have been here a long time. It is strange to be away from everything I know but to feel at home. Maybe this is now another home.

***

From the street comes the sound of traffic, trolleys running. People here tend to drive wild. Many times, throughout night, I heard spinning tires and revving engines as people sped down the road. The police seem lax, but I am sure they are concerned about other matters. There are four large bolts on the front door. We have barred ourselves in for the night.

***

I have the feeling few people speak English here in the country.

OF NOD

Ania is my link. Without her, I would be lost in a foreign land. I had the idea on leaving America... that I needed to not worry, trust all would be okay if I was going to travel so far from home. I still feel that way.

Dogs yet bark in the close distance. I can hear the people of this house— Ania's family— snoring. The house needs to have some finishing touches done to it. Ania's father works for a construction company. He built this country home over the past two years. He is very proud of his accomplishment, as he should be.

A moth just landed close by, keeping me company. When smoking my pipe last evening, a huge moth or some other insect hovered close. It seemed attracted to the smell. I am wondering how the people who own the dogs in this neighborhood sleep... incessant barking.

Last evening was spent eating Polish food that Ania's mother prepared, and drinking beer, while sitting on the back porch. I am sharing communication with this family, facilitated by Ania. We were able to convey many different thoughts and impressions to each other... and we laughed. Humor seems the best form of communication.

Although it is good to be in the city, with all of its attractions— Old Town, shopping centers— we have more room here. There are six of us staying at the country house.

***

Ania and I are back in Warsaw. We returned yesterday, early, with her father as he was driving into the city for work. It is good to be back, the condo spacious with only a few of us here. We are taking time to explore. Yesterday we went to an old cemetery about a half hour trolley ride away. Many Polish historic figures are buried in that cemetery. The tombstones were as if in a forest, many trees, lush and large... the ferns and ivy. Many of the headstones were different from what you find in an American cemetery... ornate... some essentially sculptures, modern in style. The ironwork around the burial spaces was intriguing. Numerous candelabras were lit as day was coming to a close. Ania and I stayed for a long while, taking photos and walking slowly the paths that threaded through trees and granite markers.

**

Mid-morning... we are back in the country. Ania and Asia were not awake, so I sat outside, with the older generation and ate pastries, drank coffee, smoked. It is cool weather, refreshing. After eating, drinking, and smoking, the group of family members started working— in the yard, on the house... so I came inside and now sit on the edge of the bed where Ania sleeps.

Yesterday, while in Warsaw, we went shopping at a mall and walked through Old Town. For a long time, in Old Town, we sat in the beer garden, drinking. Later, when we arrived at the country house, Ania's grandmother was here, visiting. She and Ania happily greeted each other. I would say Ania takes after her grandmother in many ways. especially in regard to her looks.

OF NOD

Ania worries about growing old. I do not see why when her grandmother is so Gypsy-like.

Instead of getting back in bed, I decided to return to the backyard. When it became overly hot, I came into the cool house and played flute for Ania's grandmother. The acoustics in the house are incredible. My flute sounded as if I was playing in a church. Ania's grandmother clapped on my completing the first two songs.

Ania is awake and is now in the kitchen with her mother and aunt, preparing breakfast... second breakfast for some of us and a first for others. The day warm... I think we'll not be active today... a lot of sitting, talking, eating, and drinking. It is good to see Ania working in the kitchen, with the women of her family. At home, she rarely cooks. Apparently, she knows a great deal about preparing food, but chooses to not do so except when with close relatives.

I napped for part of the day, in the backyard, under shade of a tree. During that time, Ania was busy working in the kitchen, helping her mother and aunt make dinner. It is four in the afternoon. A storm has begun, the sky shedding water. The day hot, so it is good to get a little rain. Ania and I were outside, and she was smoking, while I was sitting next to her, commenting that, in actuality, we are only half through the vacation.

We are planning on going to Warsaw in the morning... early, with her father... wanting to see more of the city. The country is beautiful, but there is not much to do besides rest, eat, and drink;   although, Ania and I did visit with her uncle who has a home close by. It was a good visit... drinking sparkling lemon water... good conversation about the color of the sky and my brother and family. "I had a dream," I said... "I was standing beneath a stormy sky, with my brother, by the water and waves of an ocean." He speaks English somewhat, which made our time spent with him pleasant. He said "It sounds like a lovely dream." Now that I am in Poland where few people speak English, I find it an odd sensation to be speaking my home-language. I feel as if there is cool, soothing water flowing over me during such conversation... or when listening to music with lyrics sung in the English language... when reading a book from home.

The rain stopped, but might start again, as dark, heavy clouds are roaming over the land My flute lies upon the dining room table. I recall playing for Ania's grandmother this morning. The music is still present in this room, as if it was just played. Now, the sun shows itself. Humidity rises from the sodden earth. There is a slight breeze present. The doors and windows are open.

We were out of beer, so Ania, Asia, and I went for a walk to the closest store. It was hot, the sun burnt my skin. While on a county path that led through a small section of woods, we passed by a river where there was a swimming hole. Some locals were swimming in water I would have been hesitant to wade into. At the store, we each bought six large cans of beer and proceeded to carry them home. Someone stopped us at the swimming hole, asking a question. I am not sure what the person was asking, but Ania and then Asia gave a "No" response and we continued on.

We've been sitting on the porch, drinking and playing cards. Ania's uncle stopped by not long ago with his dog. Now, he has a beer in hand and is enjoying the evening with us. I did get some sun. My face is red and I'm feeling a bit tired and relaxed from the burn.

The skies cleared. During our walk, the dark clouds made their way elsewhere. This night is much cooler when compared to last. We have not heard crickets as of yet. Crickets are endangered in Poland, so when one hears a cricket, then everyone stops, listens. Crickets are so common at home, that one pays them little attention.

***

The sound emitted by crickets is commonly referred to as chirping; the scientific name is stridulation. Only the male crickets chirp. The sound is emitted by the stridulatory organ, a large vein running along the bottom of each wing, covered with "teeth" (serration) much like a comb. The chirping sound is created by running the top of one wing along the teeth at the bottom of the other wing. As he does this, the cricket also holds the wings up and open, so that the wing membranes can act as acoustical sails. It is a popular myth that the cricket chirps by rubbing its legs together.

There are four types of cricket song: The calling song attracts females and repels other males, and is fairly loud. The courting song is used when a female cricket is near, and is a very quiet song. An aggressive song is triggered by chemoreceptors on the antennae that detect the near presence of another male cricket and a copulatory song is produced for a brief period after a successful mating.

Crickets chirp at different rates depending on their species and the temperature of their environment. Most species chirp at higher rates the higher the temperature is (approximately 62 chirps a minute at 13°C in one common species; each species has its own rate). The relationship between temperature and the rate of chirping is known as Dolbear's Law. Using this law it is possible to calculate the temperature in Fahrenheit by adding 40 to the number of chirps produced in 14 seconds by the snowy tree cricket common in the United States.

Crickets, like all other insects, are cold-blooded. They take on the temperature of their surroundings. Many characteristics of cold-blooded animals, like the rate at which crickets chirp, or the speed at which ants walk, follow an equation called Arrhenius equation. This equation describes the activation energy or threshold energy required to induce a chemical reaction. For instance, crickets, like all other organisms, have many chemical reactions occurring within their bodies. As temperature rises, it becomes easier to reach a certain activation or threshold energy, and chemical reactions, like those that occur during the muscle contractions used to produce chirping, happen more rapidly. As the temperature falls, the rate of chemical reactions inside the crickets' bodies slow down, causing characteristics, such as chirping, to also slow down.

Crickets have tympanic membranes located just below the

middle joint of each front leg (or knee). This enables them to hear another cricket's song.

(Wikipedia: Cricket— insect)

***

Ania's mother came indoors to check the food. The stove is small, there is not much counter space... but, she creates one wonderful feast after another, in a seemingly effortless manner.

***

We drove into the city with Ania's father, leaving the country house at five-fifteen in the morning. Everyone is tired. I do not want to sleep though. I would rather go to the market and buy pastries, but will wait until Ania is ready for that excursion. Ania is on the porch, smoking with her aunt and, drinking coffee. Outside the kitchen window, birds are flying in circles. I can see their shadows in this kitchen from one moment to the next. Asia has gone back to sleep. Sun is shining through the window, light made soft by a lace curtain.

When Ania's father was driving us home, I looked closely at Ania, as she was sitting next to me. She was not happy about being woken early. Her eyes were closed, head resting against the back of the seat. She wore a skirt, her hand resting on her knee. I could see clearly the engagement ring on her finger, reflecting the sun's glow in early morning brilliance.

The electricity turned off for a few minutes. I looked outside and saw one of the trolleys stopped, standing still. It must have been horrible for the passengers; the sun beating down with full force this morning. Ania and Asia yet sleep. I took a nap. I am not sure how long I slept, but, when the room's temperature became unbearable, I woke, sweaty, and made my way into the living room. At this moment, Ania's aunt has just returned from shopping. Another good meal will occur in the near future. There are potatoes soaking on the stovetop, and some dill, chopped, on the cutting board. When she returned, my unlocking and opening the door woke Ania.

✿✿✿

After shopping for shoes, we came home because of how hot the afternoon was. Inside, we are at least in the shade. We ate Ania's aunt's pickle soup and I drank a dark beer. Ania's father just arrived home from work.

My head is spinning from heat, and drinking a beer during the height of afternoon... then napping, waking in a sweat. My lips are chapped. I just made a soda water with grapefruit juice. The drink has begun to clear away the mind's clouds. Power went off three times today. According to Ania's father, many parts of Warsaw are without water.

We head back to the country tomorrow, late afternoon. Ania's mother called, saying she is missing our company.

✿✿✿

Tonight has been a night celebrating the end of Ania's aunt's

~ 159 ~

stay. She will be missed. She has spirit... a lively woman, who loves the company of others. She will be heading back to Germany tomorrow. We have been drinking very good Polish vodka, mixed with apple juice... a traditional drink. I am in a heightened mood, happy but somewhat numb. When I went out on the patio to smoke a bit of a cigar, Ania's father was there. He usually does not sit on the patio. I was surprised to see him. I could not speak a word to him without Ania or Asia present, and so felt anxious in his company, with his dark piercing eyes.

⁂

Awake... my head heavy. It is eight in the morning, everyone asleep, except Ania's father. He was awake before me, and has already gone to work.

Last night I went to bed early, a bit frustrated. Ania and Asia seemed to want to talk their native tongue rather than speak English. I understand and, am glad I went to bed at a reasonable hour.

Espresso slowly drips into the tiny mug, dark morning drips, clarity. I am sitting at the window in the kitchen. On first waking, I smoked a bit of a Djarum, with the door closed, breathing the smoke as best as I could to the outside.

⁂

We have returned to the country, arriving last night around seven. Ania's father drove us at an incredible speed. I have not driven that fast for some time. I went to bed early and am waking early, my normal routine. I am getting used to sleeping here, regardless of the dogs barking and noises of the night. Asia did not come with us. She stayed in Warsaw to meet her boyfriend, who will arrive sometime tonight after driving from Scotland. I miss her company. Ania is the only person here that speaks English at present. She just woke, drank water, and is trying to fall back asleep.

Ania's aunt left for Germany yesterday. Apparently her bus will be traveling through a storm that is affecting western Poland. We are hoping she'll be safe. It seems there is a possibility the storm could come as far east as Warsaw, around the time we are supposed to catch the plane back to the U.S. If we will be unable to fly, we might have to postpone our trip. Ania and I would not mind.

Ania's mother gave me a piece of cheesecake to eat. Delicious... and, I made strong coffee, which I drank thirstily. The sun is bright, hot. I am on the back porch, for a while fighting off biting flies, but now they are not pestering. A white moth floats, flapping wings across the back yard, lands on a red carnation, and pauses before flying away.

Grape vines grow in the backyard. The grapes are not ripe as of yet, bright green. I enjoy cupping clusters in my hands. It is as if I am then holding a part of Eastern Europe. I am holding the fruit of the people in my palm, gazing at the bright, young fruit— a nation.

Ania's father walks across the back yard— the industrious one, working on his house. I feel the sun on my skin and enjoy the last part of our time spent in Poland. The other night, when looking at pictures from the beginning of the week, it brought upon a happy sadness to see the photo of Ania, her parents, and me. I feel I am part of this family and, it helps me understand the meaning of being engaged to Ania... as if I had vaguely comprehended the importance before. I am wondering when Ania will wake, hoping she'll be feeling well. Yesterday, she asked me if I love her, very worried that I do not. I reminded her she is wearing the engagement ring I gave her, that I came all this way to Poland to meet her family... that she means the world to me... and she broke then, crying, saying they were happy tears. She believes in my love now. I know I can be distant much of the time, and do not intend to be, it is just how I am... and can understand how Ania might worry.

The leaves of the trees are moving in soft wind. The ferns in the backyard are alive. Another moth floats across my vision, goes to play above the grass. Now, a butterfly flies overhead, turns corner, and disappears around the side of the house. I sit with elbows resting on the tabletop and watch Ania's mother as she contemplates the plants she tends diligently; but, the plants are dying... too much heat... not enough rain. The day is wearing on and the heat becoming more intense. We sit in the back corner of the yard, where there is a bench and table under trees. The warmth is unbearable there too. While sitting and smoking my pipe, another butterfly flew close... flew from behind me, swerved over my pipe, and off into the yard. Ania's mother commented that it is not tobacco I am smoking, but butterflies. We all laughed and that made us forget...

***

Ania and her mother are preparing food. I woke from a nap, in the shade, under the trees. We all ate a tub of ice cream. Now I am sitting inside. The TV is on. I am wet from having sprayed myself with water earlier... not soaking, but very damp... the damp shirt is keeping me cool.

***

I indulged again. While we were sitting under the trees, in the corner of the back yard, Ania offered and I could not refuse. Now I feel better... thoughtful, more at ease. It is strange... after taking a break from drinking for the past few years, now to be enjoying drink again. Everything is surreal— the vodka and beer allow me to relax, enjoy... as if to do otherwise would be imperfect, us being in Poland.

It looks as if there may be storm clouds moving this direction. I am hoping it is not the storm that affected the west of Poland, damaging houses. The clouds heading this direction are heavy, layer upon layer rising upwards, dark shadow to their bases.

***

Last night, in the middle of night, I lay in bed... not tired... the rest of the house asleep. All was dark except for moonlight which drifted through the open window. Even the dogs had stopped barking. It was hot. I was sweating. I was anxious... thinking of all the ways things could go wrong while I am in this country... worried that my passport could become separated from me in some way... worried that I could get sick and would need to use the public health care system that is so fraught with problems. Then, I thought to myself that I just needed to enjoy that specific moment... the lying in the dark... the quiet... the heat— that I needed to just breathe, breathe in the air of this time, and so, it was as if I took my first breath since being here... as if I had been holding my breath up until that moment out of fear. I breathed in and tasted the moment... the darkness, the risk, the beauty... and exhaled it back into the night air... soon afterward, I fell into a deep sleep, still breathing in and out— all that this means to me, this visit to Poland.

***

We had a wonderful breakfast and have since been sitting in the back corner of the yard, in shade, talking. I am feeling well, not having drunk myself into oblivion last night, having been moderate in my consumption. Sleeping well and taking the morning slow... drinking coffee and water, and eating well... I am new.

Regionally, there have been storms last night and this morning, but rain has not affected us. I suppose that is for the best, because… even though rain might cool us, the heat would only return with a humid vengeance. Early tomorrow, we'll be heading to Warsaw... to ready ourselves for flying home the next day. It will be difficult to say goodbye to Ania's family... but, I will see them again within a year's time... when Ania and I marry, they will be visiting the States, so as to be present at the ceremony.

I just put on a shirt— one which I'd worn during morning. As I was placing it upon my torso, I could smell the clove scent from the Djarum smoked upon waking. Then, I doused myself with water so to feel comfortable in the heat. Ania and her sister sunbathe. Now, dark clouds gather. A storm is upon us. The two sisters are unaware of the sky. They lie in the last shards of the day's brilliance.

AWAKE BEFORE THE SUN

I sit, listening to music, wondering what the day holds... and, you... generally asleep during this hour. After the thinking has settled, I usually return— this morning listening to you and our mastiff snore. Then, I fell asleep as well, just before the alarm.

***

I look at pictures from the Cape... my Love, you were beautiful, walking our mastiff in the late day, on the deserted beach... running with him where sand and surf met... and the sunlight was radiant as it glistened in your lengths of red. The tide was out... there was no telling what had become of our past selves, the wounded parts of us that had drowned in the churning waters of our love's dawning... of dawn, that time when I wake, then wait for you. The more one's innocence has been shattered, the longer it seems one needs sleep, for sleep heals all wounds. So I let you sleep, deep in dream and, ran with you and our mastiff during the setting of sun.

***

Our mastiff is tired from the long walks we have taken today... resting, and calm on the couch. We await your arrival. You have been at work and now the day has begun to feel as if it is passing slowly.

After you left, I shut the bedroom door, closing off that part of us that woke holding each other, forgiving the night previous...

leaving me... wounded, my heart growing arms and hands... hands as crows flying... shadows reaching into the Berkshire Hills, hoping to remain in flight. That is painful— the growing, the beautiful aching. Without you I might be lost— passing through Earth's caverns without you to guide, to walk with. Yes, I am blind, requiring your elbow (or hand) to clutch. The closed door— I might make my way into that space to change shirt... to find a pair of socks; but, morning ended... you are in your car... driving toward the making of money. Our mastiff lies on the bed in the other room. He lets out a sigh... long, heartfelt— missing you my lady of morning... we love you before you arrive to this night.

Early autumn... there is a chill, but it has not become cold. The leaves are falling, trees shedding summer finery. A window is open in the kitchen, without screen— the cats broke the screen... but, there are no flies entering though that passage. The dishes from the weekend are clean, drying.

This past weekend was wonderful.. as if we searched for our bodies through darkness— a rose that I found during the depth of night.

We play with our mastiff. All over the house we play. We are happy... and he is happy. We are the love birds now. The moon lights this country. Below a planet is glowing, hue different from that of the stars. I drink wine. Now, with each sip... life. Our mastiff is excited we are home. I have been practicing Polish words with you.

***

Last night, when I woke, I went outside and, while smoking... more than a rustle in the forest. There was the close heckling of coyotes as they made a kill. Just moments before, Tug, the tiger cat came running down the rock path, making his way up the porch steps, and, when I opened the door, he bolted indoors.

The tomatoes in the Farm's garden must be ruined and, there were thousands of them. It is unfortunate... soon, though, I will be lighting a fire in the stove. There are promises of warm nights in the dark of this frosty morning. Ania and the mastiff sleep soundly, the bedroom door closed. Tug meows, wanting out.

***

Last night I had a couple of beers and a tequila shot. Ania convinced me that Patron was a good idea, now I am regretting. Our mastiff sleeps. Ania is away for work, traveling across the state. I woke late and then went to Great Barrington, to run errands... came home and went back to sleep. I just ate lunch, and am yet feeling the weather of this day.

Ania's sister and nephew visited this weekend. I am beginning to feel as if Kasia is part of my family— a comfortable, casual dialogue between us. She is a good person... and, her son I love spending time with. He is five, but acts as if he is ten.

***

Autumn leaves... the trees are on fire. This morning I looked out the window and witnessed the sunrise... pinks and cadmiums... subtle blues, and mists of white clouds. Then, petting our mastiff... he looked sad, thoughtful... upset I had woken early. He loves to sleep late most mornings, happiest when Ania is home, for she loves waking late as well.

Ania was in West Springfield last night, sitting for her nephew. Kasia needed to work at the restaurant. Ania and I talked for a time. I told her I was missing her. The day was long yesterday without her company. I slept an awful amount and, was thinking this morning how much I need her in my life. We do not always get along perfectly, but *what life is not mostly imperfect?*

Leo is looking at me with sad, puppy eyes. Ania is his playmate. They run all over the house together, playing fetch and keep-away. It is good Leo likes taking naps, for I nap often, perhaps too much... when I am feeling uninspired.

My black cat keeps pushing his nose against my hand, asking me to pet him. I place him on my lap, hoping that will be enough. Many leaves are fallen yet they hold their colors— ochres, umbers, oranges, yellows. I rub the cat's neck and head. He lies on his back on my lap and rests there until I might pet him again.

�֍✖✗

The night is a black tide, pressing against the breakwater. So long ago— Provincetown... waves lapping... memories... and then, how blissful that I have built a store of memories during this past year to be gathered, caught in nets and brought upon the fishing vessel's deck, hauled from the depths.

She was beautiful, that night... no, I will not begin in that manner... she was the rising tide... the bridge... she is whom all seafarers fear... she is all encompassing, the soul, the silhouette of a tree, the shadow of a bird... the sun and stars... she is my wife-to-be... she is the woman I've wooed... and am wooing... she is all women whom I come into contact with... she holds out a thousand hands, letting the sand fall into my thousand hands... she is the subconscious, the soul... she hearkens to my call, and I hearken to her... the morning is young, this relationship drags me into the pit, but, once I have fallen, instead of landing on hard rock, another world opens... where the islands scattering the sea are ours, where the languages of the people are for us to understand.

Last night, Leo was running through the house, tossing his chew toy into the air, catching it in midstride. We watched in awe his athleticism and, talked about all the trouble he causes. He is the center now, our language and our bodies hover about him.

Recently, a man that I know fell from his tractor. His neck vertebrae were seriously injured... and, just two weeks previous, his dog died... an old, wolf-mother dog... beautiful and strong. Alfred went nowhere without his dog. Then, she passes and he has an accident which will affect his health for some time... no riding tractors... no throwing hay bales... no loving the work that makes him what he is. I am older than I once was... and am swimming... through the moments, which are tied together with fisherman's knots. If I untie even one cord then I am lost, then the vertebrae of time are broken, and I will spend a lifetime wondering what it is that I did to unravel my thoughts, to cause the thoughts to dream of other thoughts... to dream the many layered dreams... and all that is beautiful, because that is what I accomplished a long time ago.

***

I am trying on the forms of the dead, seeing what pieces of armor fit, fortifying myself for the day. We must don armor... construct the castle, that has mote, retracting bridge, and great layers of walls, in the early morning... so our inner kingdom will not be sieged during daytime.

I believe I will learn the Polish language this winter... I will read a few books, and finish the few books that are half complete. I will nap through afternoons, and wander through the white wooded land with the mastiff on days when the cold is not severe.

The other day, Ania had a severe fall. She slipped when going down a flight of steps, leading from the second floor, outside, to the ground of the backyard. Last night, while watching a film, I massaged her thigh and knee. I could feel the knot that existed above her right knee and, am worried about her heath. She has an appointment at the doctor's for this morning. Ania is precious to me. I cannot believe that she fell that distance and happens to be merely battered and bruised. She is lucky in that she did not break any bones.

Just now, on the front porch, smoking, looking at dark woods.

OF NOD

Within my vision, I remembered the beginnings of my adulthood... saw that time, in my early twenties, when I lived in Iowa City, pursuing the poetic life... chasing after the dreams of youth... and it was as if I could never actualize the wants that I had at that age... wanting so, feeling as if this life would be short, that I needed to make a name for myself while alive... and the stone vase that held the cut flower broke, causing the healing process to begin. Thus, I have spent the past ten years healing myself from the damage done... the heart fragile... the mind even more so.

I yet remember my youth... the other pressure, that was forced on me since the age of seven... that I needed to somehow be the responsible one after my father was no longer part of our lives, me being the eldest son. It was then I adopted the mentality which has plagued me... but, I have seen over time life needs to be enjoyed. Ania is good for me in that she helps me to see— life is more for play than for work and enduring. Most of the dead leaves have fallen because of wind and rain, leaving the forests green again. Shed emotions litter the ground.

What are these dreams of catastrophe? The end of the world seems so near on waking from the floods and the nuclear wars. I would think it should be otherwise... that, on waking, I would feel the comfort of this life and say, *"Life on this globe will continue. These dreams are not portending an eminent end. There is safety to my existence and I will live 'til when old age will take me to her breast."* In general I do not focus thoughts on the pressing forces. One must not pay attention. Maybe these visions of endings are metaphors for the ending of summer... or the passing of youth... or the destructive nature of age... or even for the sun that never forgets to set and the darkness that always takes its turn. There are so many endings to this life. So, I dream of endings... not of beginnings... and wake, bedclothes wet from sweat... stumble outdoors to witness the beginnings of another day— darkness, wind, rain, and then there is the light... light I turned on, moths flying about its warmth and glow, when wind and rain subside, casting grotesque fluttering shadows upon the porch planks and dewy grass. In the gray light of morning, while walking the mastiff— how he finds bear scat close to the cabin... and sticks his nose in the dark feces, smelling wild berry remnants, smelling dumpster refuse which has been digested and shat onto the ground. I pull at his leash, saying "Ew" and "Come," then he proceeds to leave his own pile on the earth, nearby.

***

Night... two months later... it has been a cold, damp weekend. The sun has not shown through clouds except in a gray, unfocused hew. All seems misty— an impressionist's work of art. The trees of autumn still have color and leaves fall daily, marking the passage of this season.

Our mastiff, Leo, is still the center of our lives. We focus our attention on him, as if he were our child. He is just eleven months old, and is growing every day— not taller, but wider— and has become affectionate lately, cuddling with Ania on a regular basis. We had to lock him out of the bedroom during our love session this evening, and, when I opened the door, he was lying there, with his nose to the crack beneath the barrier. Sometimes we do have him in the bedroom, but not this time...

for, he was riled and would have been hard to settle.

The autumn leaves are lost in darkness. Lamps within this cottage are reflected back in the window glass. The cottage is warm, no draft. There is quiet here. I can hear every breath that Ania takes and exhales in the deep night. I can hear the cats jump from off of the kitchen counter after eating. I can hear them walk and pace about. I can hear the mastiff snoring. Leo lies by Ania's feet, sleeping with eyes partly open, ears aware.

***

I remember Poland… sitting in her parent's Warsaw condo, smoking cigars on the back porch of their country house. I wish that we could visit on a whim. It, though, takes money and planning to be in Poland, even for a matter of two weeks. I am glad we visited this summer. It was so hot. The sun beat down on my exposed flesh, burning memories of that vacation into me. I came back to the States with a tan; but that darker skin has faded back to the pale mien. I miss the beer. I miss looking into Ania's mother's eyes. She held me close to her heart with her gaze.

I taste the beer of Poland on my tongue. That bitterness enlivens me. Walking the path from their country house, past the river's swimming hole, to the little store on the town's street corner. Then, with Ania and Asia, carrying the beer back home. The setting of the Polish sun… the rising of the Polish night, as if it was a creature crawling from the rabbit hole, carrying with it, on its back, promise of rest. The holding, the sleeping next to each other, Ania and I on the little futon, sweating, breathing softly… coughing from time to time… and the creaking of the wooden platform, the memory of America becoming like a fading moon… and the rising to a new day, before the sun even then… and the watching of the sky's emerging colors.

***

Leo is on his bed, chewing one of his toys. He and I took a couple walks today. He was well behaved… and, loved saying hello to people… tail wagging, mouthing hands… trying to jump up and lick faces.

The sun has been behind cloud, and is still hidden, as it makes its descent. It has been a gray day. Emotions stunted, heart pounding its coffee rhythm. I am hungry for more life… and so is Ania. We have not grasped hands all day, reaching and clutching at the nothingness, hoping we might hold on to something meaningful and purposeful. She is playing cards at present. The afternoon was warm. I was outside in a t-shirt and jeans. While walking on the lower farm, we saw two people at their work… Jenifer and Jarred… Leo found apple remnants by where Jenifer was making cider. He tasted, and then ate the mashed apple with relish.

My black cat sleeps on the sofa by where I sit. He keeps stretching. Just a moment ago, Leo climbed on the sofa and lay down practically on top of Wookie. *"Pour Wookie,"* Ania exclaims, and goes on playing her solitaire. Wookie goes to the other end of the sofa and makes himself comfortable.

OF NOD

Dusk— it claws at windows. It has come again to this land and seems to revel in its accomplishment. Perhaps now the shift will happen. We will see this world with other eyes... see both the physical and the spiritual, and so be able to appreciate more of this life. Ania is walking Leo. We are going to go to dinner at the Lodge. Sometimes just being around others helps. We are *all* flailing about in this existence, reaching for the dangling rope that is merely part of imagination... as if we could pull ourselves upwards at will... as if we could climb to the moon and hope that there, things will be different.

***

Ania woke early because she was unable to sleep. I was snoring, loudly. I woke a few times last night, but, on returning to bed, was able to fall quickly back into dreams. They were sordid, disturbed dreams, frightful dreams... but, thankfully, none can be recalled except the last... something about being lost, driving around in my old pickup... then being in a restaurant... with a Resident from the Farm. We went into a back room where a meeting of men was occurring. They all suddenly donned hooded masks. We had to force our way through the exit in order to be safe. I woke... Ania was already out of bed, petting her cat.

Leo rests on his bed, by the cold stove. All is the brown and yellow of late fall. Yesterday I sent out save the date cards to friends and family: June twenty fourth, two thousand and eleven.

***

I am lost, walking the path that leads from the actual, where I have never tread. I diverged, somewhere in the black night, and so am meandering through leaf and bow, amidst the trunks, feeling my way. In the distance I can see a porch light... wondering if it is my home, but I do not run... I feel slowly, sure footed upon this shadow-ground. I remember the direction of where might be home— at least where might be people who could give me guidance. The coffee cup, full, sits upon the table in front of me. Night blankets windows, presses like an ocean against my vision of the future. The dreams last night were laced. An angel visited and scattered the dust of the stars on my makeshift grave. I rose, a flower toward heaven. It is raining... I just accidentally sat on my tiger cat. He was asleep on one of the front porch chairs. I thought I saw a wild turkey cantering about in the front yard. Darkness... my Love asleep, the mastiff asleep... both in the king size bed. She is quietly breathing the air of this new day, yet to bloom. The flowers of evil, cut, litter the front yard, left there by some crafty gnome— he who thought it prudent to play his joke, when our relationship is flourishing. Ania taught me some of her native language last night. While I was drifting in and out of sleep, she taught me the words for "sleep" and "bed," for "light," for "dog," and "what." I forget all now except for "sleep." She was beautiful, shedding her beauty— loose rose petals— on my prone body.

***

I am running toward the rising sun. There are wings secured to my heels and, when I reach out with arms, holding the sun, I would hold my Love 'til the everlasting night descends. First

OF NOD

there is the blink of eternity's eye— my life snaking out before me... a river running through the forest of autumn... the trees bare. This is the cusp of winter. I am living every moment as if it is my last, and have been doing so for some time. Ania is by my side. She looks over my shoulder at the flowing waters... smiles, knowing. Our rivers merged, sometime ago. She is well aware that the waters we gaze upon are of both of us; but, we, in this moment are detached. We stand separate from the current and listen to the wind in the river grasses, hear our dog barking in the distance— we have let him run free through the nearby forest... he is chasing the squirrels no doubt, until he tires and comes back to us, to rest and roll around in the brown earth at our feet.

JUNE

June first... this is the month our marriage will occur. I have been lost in dream for the past seven months, drifting with the current. The spring has been unseasonably warm, some days ranging in the mid to high eighties. Ania is home sleeping. I am at work, an overnight at a Resident house. There is humidity to the outside air and the sun is strong already at this early hour. I stand outside and smoke my first cig of the day, blinking my eyes, trying to wake and perceive all that surrounds me: the green, lush forest; the clear blue of sky; the black pavement of the road that runs through the center of this Farm; the sounds of the multitude of birds chirping and singing to the morning light.

Much has gone into the planning of that looming day... and money has been constantly on our minds, as well as the looking forward, the questioning, and now the realizing that this is going to happen, that we are ready for it to happen. The morning brilliance is not oppressive, it is enlightening. I am the river, I am the current. I am singing within my heart— the love that I feel, for Ania and for this, my Life, this, my existence, this, my sun.

☆☆☆

The process of tying up loose ends, making sure all will transpire with little stress. Yesterday, on coming home to walk the dog, just before dinner, I found a large, pink magnolia at our front door, a gift from an unknown admirer? Or from someone that merely wanted to express their friendship? Regardless, it is a beautiful flower, and now is in a glass of water in the center of our kitchen table.

Leo is sleeping on the little fold out bed this morning, by the south window of the cabin. Ania is asleep in the bedroom, her cat watching over her dreaming form. I can see traces of clear sky through the waving mass of green leaves that surround the cabin. A slight breeze... I can feel the chill of the morning air on stepping outside.

My legs are sore. Yesterday was a comfortable, cool, and windy day. The mastiff and I took advantage of the weather and walked for two miles over this farm's country, eventually making our way to the hay field off Hearts' Lane at the lower end of the property. The hay had been recently cut, and lay in long rows. I let Leo loose. He ran and played, while I walked between the rows of hay, back and forth across the field. Up until yesterday, the field's growth had been too high to make walking there possible. I was grateful to the farmers for having cut the hay. There is a little hill in that field. As we walked, I whooped and hollered numerous times to scare away any deer or bear that might be on the other side of the hill.

We do not walk in the forest now, for that is deer tick country, and it is annoying to pick them off of us on returning to the cabin. Ania was at work during the day yesterday. I wished she could have been with us on our walk. She would have enjoyed seeing Leo play under the blue sky, with wind blowing, and the sun beating down.

It was a long winter and we are blessed now to have warm weather. It snowed a significant amount, with many days of subzero temperature. The winter was not easy for me... and, it seemed to be more difficult for Ania as she had lived so long on the coast in Boston, where winter weather is mild because of the sea.

We have rented a beach house, in East Haven, C.T., for the week before the wedding and the week after. We are looking forward to that vacation. It will be a time for the meeting of our closest relatives. The house sleeps sixteen, and we will have at least eleven to thirteen people staying there during our entire stay. Leo will not be coming. We are going to have a few people from the Farm take turns feeding him, letting him out, and taking him for walks or runs. We will miss him, but it just seems impossible to bring him along, for we are planning to spend time in New York City and in New Haven during our time away.

A white, bright light is breaking through windows, falling on the floor here in the living room, and in the kitchen. Ania is showering, letting hot water soothe her. Outside, the leaves of the trees wave slightly in the breeze. There is still a cool quality to the air. Leo now sleeps curled at my back on the couch where I sit. The Berkshires are beautiful— flowers blooming, the lush forest, and the green lawns. Ania is happy living here for now, but we are hoping to relocate before the next harsh winter, wanting to be closer to Boston, or in Boston. We have explored other options, including moving close to my brother, in Wilmington, North Carolina.. or to work and live at another therapeutic farm in Ashville, six hours west of my brother, in the mountains. We are putting off making definite plans until after the wedding and beach vacation, wanting and needing to concentrate on the planning and the time with her and my family. We'll begin to consider the move seriously once the visiting families return to their homes.

***

I have been sleeping for the past two hours. The windows are cracked, letting in fresh air. Lalunia and Leo have been sleeping through the afternoon as well. Farm life agrees with us... but it will not last forever, I know. Ania is more a city person. She needs to be around the stimulation that only a city can offer. The animals and I will have to one day make the sacrifice for Ania, giving up our country life, and move to where all is a rush, where there are no fields to run and play in, where there is no front porch and cushioned chairs for the cats to rest and cat-nap in. I am willing to make such sacrifice and, am actually looking forward to the prospect of living in a place such as Boston. I have lived in the Berkshires for over seven years, and the comfort I feel tends to verge on boredom. To be in a city would offer other challenges, would force me to grow in ways I am not accustomed... and I do believe that if one does not challenge one's self, then he or she becomes stunted.

I am looking forward to seeing Ania's parents and sister, Asia, in a couple of weeks. The three of them will be staying at the beach house, along with Kasia's family, my mother and stepfather, my father and stepmother, my brother, and my friend and roommate from college, John. The house will be partly full, even with so many of us there, which is for the better, seeing as it will give people space and privacy during the time at the beach.

I would like to walk Leo, but he is yet napping— most likely tired from the stress of being at the vet this morning. He usually has so much energy, pesters me constantly to take him for walks. There are a couple hours before I have to go to work. I am sure he will eventually wake and we will then head to the field... and he will run, chasing geese, trying to catch the gofers that live under the farm machinery.

*

Vultures circled overhead, there in the field. Much of the hay had been collected into large wheels, sitting heavily on the ground, remnants of what had not been collected scattered about. One large vulture sat on top of a particular wheel, in the haze sunshine, watching us in a sinister manner— Leo running, me walking slowly, zigzagging through the field. The Farm puts its compost in a pile by the entrance to the field, on the side of the dirt road. It reeks of sour vegetables and rotting meat. On arriving to the field's entrance, between the hedges and trees that line Hearts' Lane, we disturbed a host of crows and vultures from their feast. There was the sound of flapping wings before we turned the corner. Then, the few that had taken their time in deciding to take to the air, saw us... the black wings of the crows and the great, far-reaching wings of the vultures, spread and lifted. Once airborne, those creatures stayed circling above or landed on the hay wheels, watching our passage, seeming to guard the field, as if we were trespassers to their country. Leo dove into some thickly piled hay. Then, he seemed to want my attention and began biting and pulling at the cuffs of my pants. I had to grab him by his collar, saying "No," dragging him along, until he shifted focus. I picked up a stick and he was happy to run and find the stick that I threw through the air, it flipping over and over until landing in the distance— and he ran with such speed, was there almost before the sun and rain bleached stick landed, picking it up in his jaws, biting and gnawing, crushing it easily into small shards of soft wood, a crazed look in his eyes.

✳✳✳

Ania ordered a margarita. I drank St. Pauli's Girl Non Alcoholic beer, seeing as I was driving. We sat on the front porch of a Mexican restaurant in Great Barrington, sipping our drinks, eating the spicy nachos and burritos, talking easily about the wedding and the vacation, making vague plans for the first week at the beach, and enjoying each other's company after a long morning of being at odds. Before shopping, Ania had been easily angered and frustrated. That is how she exhibits her stress about the wedding… everything under the sun bothers her when she feels pressured… and I was fighting back. When at the restaurant, morning drifted away and we loved being with each other, as if there had been nothing different, our love a blooming garden, or a field of wild flowers that wafts in the breeze of a new day. On returning home, she put on some perfume and we were close, physically, touching each other in the comfort of our bedroom, with the dog outside the closed door, wanting in, maybe worried for us. We were making the sex sounds of two that have found passion in the failing daylight— made soft by the paper blinds, shadows allowing us to unite again and purge the loneliness which is such a part of being human.

***

The sky is a bit dark now, and was so while we were at a coffee shop... but, it has not started raining... only threatening. In the distance, I can hear a dog barking, reminding me of when we were in Poland, at Ania's family's country house, how the dogs barking would keep me awake through nights, only settling when sun rose in the early morning hours. Leo rarely barks. One of the characteristics of the Corsos is that they infrequently bark.

***

It is Monday, less than two weeks before we leave for vacation. The weekend transpired quickly, but a number of things were accomplished in regards to preparation. Ania revamped the guest and seating list for the reception. I am grateful that she spent the time to do that, and am happy she is taking more initiative in the planning and organizing of the event. I think, by doing so, she'll not feel so stressed, for she will know then that everything is in order, no detail left half finished, and she'll be able to relax come the day of, and just enjoy. Furthermore, we did some figuring about costs versus how much money we have saved. All looks good. There are some things that still need paying for, but, we seem to have quite a bit extra for spending on food and other expenses while her parents and sister visit from Europe for the month.

OF NOD

I can hear a plane flying… a small propeller driven, four-seater. I wonder if it is Alfred, the farmer. He has a pilot license. Many times when he takes to the air, he steers course so as to fly over our five-hundred acre farm. Alfred had an accident last year and injured his neck. He has seemed to heal, for he is out of his neck brace… back to farming and flying. When Leo and I walk through the farm, Alfred generally gives Leo a treat or two, and pets him, saying "There, there."

A doe just walked through our front yard, paused as it was entering the forest, and urinated there, in the trees, just outside the boundary of our lawn. It stepped lightly and walked slowly. I seem to be attuned to nature this morning, in awe as a little gray moth fluttered around me. Then, down the road, I looked and saw a crow flapping wings, heard it as it scraped the tips of its wings on tree leaves. Now, back in the cabin, I can hear Ania breathing peacefully, and I see the cast sunlight by the front windows of the cabin, falling on the floor and little bench.

I sleep less during nights and more during the days— a sign of stress. I can hear the hissing of the kettle, water heating. The dreams last night were odd, confusing visions. The water comes to a boil, and the kettle whistles— the call, time to wake, to watch sun rise… and, there is the sun's light, breaking through the dark forest canopy, spots of gray-blue… something besides the black that held nightmare and fitful rest. The gift of another day now presents itself, and I am free, awake, and shedding the skin of the snake— sitting on the porch and peeling the lace-like fragility away from the creature that slithers at my feet… it is a garter snake this morning… other mornings it has been a rat snake when in Maryland working at a camp, or a water moccasin in my youth, in North Carolina, where I grew to be the boy with white-blond hair that my mother loved so, that my father could not understand. The serpent slithers into the woods, leaving me a spirit of light— for it had crawled from my soul on waking, and I played with that creature, cleaning its long body of the shed emotions until it might pass into the darkness of brush and long grass, until it might leave me, in my loneliness, to open my eyes again and wish the day into being.

☆☆☆

We have not been able to let Leo run the last couple of days... but, yesterday there was a break in the heat, just before a storm. I quickly drove him to the field by the gravel pit, and we walked together, him mostly running, glad to be free from the confines of the cabin. Although it was only four o'clock, the sky had grown dark, and was becoming even more so as the storm brewed— thunder, long, and rolling in the depth of the gray heavens. Even the crows and vultures had disappeared, looking for shelter, or having already found some safe haven in which to wait out the turmoil of ripping wind and cold rain that was to begin. Leo tired quicker than I expected and made his way back to the car, me following. We drove home, and soon after we arrived to the safety of the cabin, the storm broke like a tempest— wind, rain, and lightening. A tree was downed close to the cabin. I could hear it break at the base and then tear and rip the forest canopy as it fell swiftly to land, in the dense undergrowth of the woods. The cabin's lights pulsed through the hour and half the storm raged. Then, all was calm, sky clearing, and I breathed easy.

OF NOD

The wedding day draws near. We are on a course that has as its end a beginning, and though there is some stress at this point, for the most part we are just looking forward to having two weeks at the beach and the party that night midway through the vacation. It is difficult to grasp the impending moment when we'll become husband and wife... that, truthfully, seems as if it will be more dreamlike, it being so unfamiliar to our daily existence.

✿✿✿

During evening, Ania and I took Leo to the hay field. The storm had long ceased, leaving cool air in its wake. During our walk, he found a piece of a tractor tire that made a great toy. He ran and ran, hair bristling on his back, making circles around us. We were glad for him, and would try and take the tire sliver from him when he sprinted close. This only excited him more and he would not let us have the toy, playing keep-away from both of us. The grass was wet. My leather shoes were soaked, and Ania's feet— she was wearing flip-flops— had grass on them on arriving back to the car. The sky with wisps of white clouds... the great hay wheels, scattered throughout the field, were sodden after the storm. Still no sign of crow or vulture, we had won the freedom of the field, of the long stretch of sky, of the rim of forest that surrounded. Before turning back to make way to the car, we kissed, there in that field, at the far end. No one was witness. The field then faded from consciousness... as if it was a temporary vision, a fleeting stage. What became

~ 188 ~

obvious to me was that I was walking with my wife-to-be, and that we would have many adventures. We were walking together, regardless of surroundings and ground, and we could touch each other, visit the depths of each other's eyes through gazing into the waters of the other's soul. There was hope in her eyes, finally. She had given up a great deal to come live with me over a year ago. Soon, we would make a life together near the waters of the ocean... that constant reminder, that lapping of the waves, foam and spray.

✿ ✿ ✿

It rained all night, but instead of lulling me into a peaceful rest, the downpour brought me nightmare after nightmare. There are no bird calls this morning, for there is no sun. I am walking through this cabin, trying to shed the long nightmare.

This is what is amazing the waking, how every day is another chance for us to understand this mystery, or just live it, just experience the great beauty. That is why I like mornings. It is only in the early morning one realizes the altering of consciousness. When one wakes late, then he or she sleeps through the most precious part of day. Then, on waking, the day is already in full swing, and there is a racing to catch up, to be productive before the end comes and bed calls.

✿ ✿ ✿

There is a light brushing of dawn outside these windows. I stretch, arching my back and lifting my arms above my head. At one time, on waking from a confusing dream, I went outside on

~ 189 ~

the porch to smoke. There was rustling in the woods. Something was hunting— a stick broke, and some creature let out a cry of pain… a whimpering almost… paused, and then let out another what seemed loud painful cry in the dark quiet of night. Inside the cabin, the mastiff was alarmed… he woke and began his deep throated barking, jumping out of bed, roaming the cabin… checking that all was okay in our home… sneezing from time to time in the excitement and aggravation of the moment. When I heard something was close in the woods, making a kill, I quickly knocked off the ember of the cig I was smoking, grabbed the little black cat that was sleeping on a porch chair, and came inside, saying "It's okay, Leo… it's okay…", trying to calm him before he woke Ania. My heart was racing, but I was able to fall back to sleep quickly, into dreams, where all is a strange drama.

Sometimes, there is the thought that occurs, is occurring this morning, which is a wondering, which creeps in and says, *"This is for forever, for the rest of your life, Marc. You must be sure. You must know this beyond anything that you have ever known. This is not something that should be taken lightly, for so much depends on this decision."* And then, I shake off that anxiety, saying to myself that one cannot know anything about life for certain, especially when it concerns others in matters of importance… that people are apt to change… that life is unpredictable… that I am sure as I can be, that one can never be completely non-questioning about anything in life. That I know and love Ania I am well aware of, and that I need to have faith in us… faith in her… and faith in myself… and believe, deep inside, that we will be happy together— then, only then, does that creeping voice of worry quiet… so I am able to find myself back in the moment, loving this process.

***

The past couple of days have been exhausting— readying to leave, needing details of the vacation and wedding to be settled, and packing everything that needs to go. You would think we are moving to East Haven considering all that we are taking with us.

Last night I woke at two, and found Ania was just then readying for bed. She frightened me. Initially, when I woke I thought she was on the other side of the bed. I came into the living room, heading to the front door to go outside and smoke, and found her in the dark kitchen. It seemed she had just turned out the lights… must have been Leo snoring on the other side of the bed. I was startled, we laughed, and she joked about how tired I looked, teasing me by reaching for me and inviting me. Now, I am wondering if she had finished the bottle of wine that we had opened the other day, for she had that look in her eyes— crafty and nymph-like. She was having fun on our last night here at the Farm… good for her.

***

We arrived at the beach house during the day. Now, it is deep in the night. I had been sleeping, but woke, and went outside to ponder the large, dreamy moon. It was in the eastern sky, lighting the fog, making all seem mysterious and milky.

***

The house might be old and dusty, but it has character and is located right on Long Island Sound. The views are amazing. Also, there is the constant lapping sound as waves reach the shoreline. Early in the evening, Ania and I went out back and watched the dark shadow waves roll in, then quietly break and foam when they had found the end to their journey. In the distance, lightening would flash, illuminating sections of the distant horizon. We held each other, telling each other how happy we are. It had been so hectic during the past few days. While standing out back of the house, where water met land, I could feel the stress dissipate. I loved life again... and I loved Ania again, there under the scattered stars. When hugging her, I could feel the goose bumps that were forming on the backs of her arms.

***

I have woken and already sat out by the foggy Sound, listening to the gulls. On returning back indoors, I left the sliding glass door to the porch open, to let the fresh, damp, salty air into the house.

Ania and I had to push the two single beds in our room together, to make one large bed. Our room is on the back, south side of the house. One can see a great view of the water from our windows. The room is on the second floor of the three story house.

We are looking forward to when Ania's mother and father arrive on Sunday. Today, besides my old roommate, John, and my brother, James, arriving, Ania's sister, Kasia will be bringing her husband, Rainey, and their son, Lee, to the beach house. To experience some peace and calm before the families begin arriving was absolutely necessary for our sanity. We were rushing and busy throughout the past week, and really for the past month. I feel that this is the first easy time we have experienced for a while and, for me, to have this morning to sit by the rolling water, to drink my coffee in the quiet of this house, on the quiet of the back lawn... the seagulls and my thoughts my only company... all the rushing and business has become worthwhile.

***

Ania is sunbathing in the small yard out back, by the calm water. The sun broke through the early morning haze, and all is a brilliant flash of water, green, beach houses, shoreline rocks. Ania is finally resting, after going through this house like a typhoon— cleaning bathrooms, making beds, and moving furniture. The house still needs a lot of attention. I have been washing dishes throughout the morning, and unpacking.

My brother just called. His plane landed at J.F.K. He will be taking a train to Grand Central Station and another to the New Haven station, where I will pick him up. He was stuck in Charlotte overnight, because of the weather. It will be good to see James. He is my only brother. He is the younger. I feel grateful that he is making this journey to visit before and during the wedding, and am hoping he will find being here relaxing, rejuvenating.

~ 193 ~

OF NOD

***

Soft waves are rolling to the shore. My mind is as the ocean, thoughts moving slow, ebbing and flowing. Movement is occurring, but is hindered by the residue of beer which yet courses through my being. Last night was the bachelor-outing, spent with James and John. We visited a bar in New Haven, where we drank micro-brews and foreign beers, ate seafood. Throughout the day yesterday I was drinking, since a late lunch... so, I was unable to have much at the bar. Good to see both John and my brother. Now, I wish that I did not feel so foggy this morning. There is no fog though over the Sound. One can see clearly the distant islands. I keep going outside to smoke, wanting to cut through this mind-haze. Everyone is asleep in the house except me.

Kasia, Rainey, and Lee are here too. They drove from Springfield. Was good to see them on arriving home last evening. Ania's parents arrive today. I have been caught... a whole flock of geese caught in a great wind, as it brings us toward our destination. That is how we are... the families. We are being brought together. We are finding the destination is the Taft Inn in East Haven.... or at the beach house where we now stay.

***

Yesterday evening, Ania's father and I went down on the beach to skip stones. The beach is entirely stone. I picked one rock and put it in my pocket as a remembrance. When I look at it, holding it in my palm, in the future, I will know that on the day

I called that piece of Earth my own, I also went to the Town Hall of East Haven and signed the marriage license with Ania... and kissed her afterward, there in the Town Clerk's Office... then we walked hand in hand across the Green, back to our car.

I am in the living room, gazing out the bay windows at the great Sound. I am sleeping later during this vacation, and can only attribute that to the vodka I am drinking. Sharing such passion with Ania's family seems not only necessary, but agrees with me completely. Now, I tend to not be hung-over on waking. I tend to feel alive and well at such an early hour. Last night we grilled sausage and kielbasa, ate out on the little porch in back of the house. We talked, and laughed, feeling free, enjoying each other... the water close, calm and lulling. Afterward, we came inside... for there was a chill to the evening air. Ania's father, Ania, and I played cards until we tired; we then all went to our rooms. In Ania's and my room, when crawling into bed, we could hear soft waves... and we held each other, falling into a dreaming sleep... whispering and kissing.

Even though it is good to spend time with Ania's family, I need time to organize my thoughts. Waking early, before everyone else, I am alone, walking quietly around the first floor, careful not to make much noise... going outside, gazing at the ocean, at the boats that course.

Yesterday I went swimming for the first time since we arrived. The water was cold, refreshing. It surrounded me, held me like a mother would do with her newborn. I waded first, then walked out further, eventually submerged myself in the healing Sound... and, on rising from the deep waters, while swimming back to where my feet could touch, I thought, *"I have become other than I was before."*

***

I just finished going swimming with Ania's father. It is late afternoon… three days before the wedding. After swimming, I went upstairs, showered, and tried on my suit. The white collared shirt that I had not worn for a year is slightly tight around the neck, but should be okay. The suit itself is perfect. My father and Dawn recently bought the suit for me during the weekend of my birthday, in March. Ania's family is out back, sunning… except little Lee, who is watching cartoons in the living room. The sun outside is bright, blinding… and, hot… so hot that I feel uncomfortable being outdoors very long. The swim was nice though. Jan and I swam out to where we could stand on sand, past bottom stone.

Ania's father just came inside and shook his head at me. I suppose he wonders why I don't spend much time outdoors with everyone. I am fair skinned and burn easily. I am not trying to be distant… and, they are all becoming burnt… which would be uncomfortable for me. It was good swimming with him though. He is a good man. We do like drinking with each other at night over dinners. I like having shots of vodka with him especially. Last night, at dinner, during one round, I poured the shots for everyone at the table. I am not adept at such task. Kasia, on the other hand, works at a bar and, when she pours, usually the shots are of equal amount. Then, when she has had a bit too much, some vodka tends find its way onto the table during the process… and everyone laughs… and we say *na zdrowie*, downing the vodka with smiles on our faces.

Outside by the water... I took a minute to put suntan lotion on Ania's legs. I am at ease, looking forward to when my father and Dawn arrive tonight. Asia should be arriving around the same time. Ania's mother, Helena, is in the kitchen preparing food. Lee is still watching cartoons, and Kasia is out back, smoking, and talking with Ania. An empty Corona bottle sits on the table to my left, the lime within a bright green, a little remnant of golden beer at the bottom of the bottle. Ania's father has taken the kayak out for a paddle, staying close to the shore, making way to the east, where a point of rocks juts out.

***

Last night was the first time my father and Dawn and Ania's parents met. Ania's mother and sister, Kasia, were good enough to prepare a meal throughout the day, which was no easy task seeing as meat is such a Polish staple, and my father and Dawn mostly are vegetarians. Surprising to me, my father and Dawn were more than happy to try all of Helena's and Kasia's cooking, even the breaded pork. Dawn and my father brought with them a case of Polish vodka and, throughout the course of dinner we drank an entire seven hundred and fifty milliliter bottle. My father and Dawn mostly drink wine, so the Zubrowka was not something they are accustomed to... but, they enjoyed drinking it nonetheless, and a good time was had by all... laughing, joking, telling stories... with Ania doing most of the translation work, the only tense part of the evening being when the subject of family trees came to the forefront. Dawn shared with the table that she thinks I have a good

~ 197 ~

portion of German heritage as part of my bloodline. I let her know, and the rest of the table, that we should not emphasize that part of me, that in essence, I have a mixture of different nationalities as part of my makeup. She though continued emphasizing the German in me, for she has German in her and is proud about that fact... but, said that I am a fifth generation German, dating those relatives to having arrived in America well before the war that affected Poland in recent history.

Excitement is carrying me on towards the wedding day, and, I expect I will rest more soundly afterward. This day is young. The house has yet to wake. Morning called, and so I woke, walking gently into the future with each step. When I was young, I would need less sleep, especially when summer arrived and I was working in camps. I seem to be recapturing part of my youth. I am more as I was before age and complacency took hold.

Jan just came into the living room, wanting to turn out the lamp. He looked at me like I was odd. I think he is not one to wake at dawn. I cannot help that I feel most alive when sun rises, and wish I could explain to him why I feel such in the early morning. Most people sleep well past first light, and he would probably not understand even if I could speak to him about this in his language. I try to be quiet, but this house is old, with creaking floors and, I am a heavy man. I hope he did not wake because of me, and if he has then I am sorry… but I cannot change this about myself.

***

Helena and I sat out back and smoked, sipping our coffee, watching the gulls at play over the water. The morning is hazy, like most mornings here. As was the case yesterday, it seems it might rain again today. That would be unfortunate because today is the rehearsal and rehearsal dinner. I will hope we at least get a break in the weather around the time of the rehearsal. Yesterday it was pouring at various times. In the morning we took Jan and Helena over to the Taft Inn to show them the establishment. They said it is a very nice location, were impressed with the view, and seemed to be impressed with the inn itself. After returning, sometime during the early afternoon, the rain had ceased. My father took a long vigorous swim. He asked that I watch him during his swim. I was happy to do so, sitting out by the wall that holds back the tide, observing him kick and paddle back and forth, in a meandering sort of way… fighting the current when he swam eastward, and going quicker, with the current, when his long arms and legs brought him westward. Then, after his swim, it was time to be busy. Dawn, my father, and I dropped off items at the Taft Inn for the reception, and we went to New Haven to pick up a friend of our family— Pierce, a Frenchman. Pierce is from Paris. He has a bit of money and spends a good portion of each year traveling the world. He has been to Africa numerous times and has visited Prague. While driving back from New Haven, he told us about his time in Russia… apparently though, he has never been to Poland.

Later in the day, soon after we arrived home from picking up Pierce, I received an e-mail from my mother and stepfather, relating that they had a horrible time leaving from France. They had been visiting Paris so as to be at their grandson's naming ceremony— they are Jewish… and, when flying home, not long into their flight, the plane they were on experienced difficulties... had to dump fuel, turn around, and try to get back to the Paris airport. In their e-mail, my mother said it was frightening, but she was glad they had landed okay and were catching another plane to Boston. Then, around eleven o'clock at night, they called the house, speaking to Ania, letting us know they had arrived safely in Boston, were going to get a hotel room for the night, and make their way to East Haven sometime during today.

Most everyone in the house is still asleep, except for Helena, Jan, and I. Jan just woke and walked through the living room saying good morning to me in English. It is nice that both he and Helena are learning English, at about the same rate as I am learning Polish. This morning though, while Helena and I sat outside drinking coffee, little needed to be said. The quiet was appropriate, with sounds of the gulls off in the distance, or closer, when they swooped and played by the shore.

✳✳✳

It is Sunday. There is a ring on my finger, which feels comfortable, comforting. The wedding occurred on Friday. This morning I woke, looked at pictures from the ceremony, and cried. I could not hold back the tears. Everything was so hectic leading up… and then, I found myself at the Taft Inn, making final arrangements with the minister, and the hostess for the evening. Family and friends started to arrive… and there was the forgetting of names, but the knowing of faces. I felt as if I was rushing forward, not feeling or thinking, just trying to

keep my mind from spinning. Then the minister— Uncle
Goline from L.A.— took me outside and talked to me calmly...
about things unrelated, such as lobster fishing. I was looking
out at the chop and surf of the ocean. There was a storm
brewing, in actuality and in my mind. Suddenly, there was a
dawning. I felt completely the importance of my life, could
grasp hold of the significance of that day. Much rose up to
press against my awareness .. while looking out at the waves,
and feeling the wind press against my face, I was again on a
distant beach— a long time in my drug-induced past— and I at
that moment got confused... a beauteous, swimming, heart
racing, expansion of life pervaded my awareness. Only
afterward can I understand, that the combination of endorphins,
nerves, and excitement was what caused the feeling of
euphoria... but, again, one could say that then it was I had to
face my greatest fears, standing there, talking to the minister,
moments before the actual marriage. I had to look, at that
moment, about where I had been... and, I knew that I had
overcome so much up until that point. I forced the feeling of
euphoria down, left that part of me to walk into the night of the
distant beach. I was then completely at the Taft Inn. When I
turned away from the water and waves, still hearing my uncle
talking about how we all feel so indestructible when young, but
then we begin to understand that we are truly fragile creatures, I
was present. The hostess came up to me and asked questions
about how the evening was to run... my logic returned... and I,
although having just moments before left a huge part of myself
in the past, spoke as best as I could about how such an
unconventional wedding/reception should be organized...
about when the introductions would be, and the toast, and the
first dance, and the cutting of the cake. No longer on that

psychedelic shore, I was free of the burden. I knew this was right, that beyond everything, I wanted, within the deepest part of my heart to marry Ania… that she is my love, my life, that all which came before had lead up to that day, and I was ready. I was the lobsterman; I had survived many rough storms on the sea… I had not failed in any manner… for I was standing there… the lions' roaring, the breaking of waves becoming almost imperceptible. I had planned and organized my own wedding… with some help from family members, but I had done it mostly alone in the end… and I was turning away from that part of me that could only find happiness in sordid manners during my youth. I was then a man, sensitive to where I had been and to where I am heading. I was with direction and course. I made the arrangements with the hostess, and then my brother came out the doors, and hugged me and stood by side.

When I stood in front of Ania's family and my own, and Ania was walked by her mother and father to stand with me… I kissed her mother, and hugged her father… then we were there alone, with only the minister leading us through what we needed to say… making the promises at once to each other and to the families… and to God. Ania was strong and sure. She did not falter… but, I became emotional, going first… it was so much… I felt suddenly that I was a little boy again, and that the little girl I had always wanted to hold hands with was there holding my hands. I felt that it was a fairytale we had found ourselves in… that we were magical at that moment I know for sure… and we smiled into each other's eyes and said "Yes, I do…" and then I dipped her and kissed her long and true, while the little kids that were present, namely my nephew Ross, held their breaths, and there was whooping and hollering, clapping of hands.

OF NOD

LABYRINTHS

OF NOD

I

SONG

Where lions den and lovers roam—
Caverns hid within the heart;
Mired in dank recesses of the catacomb...

Where lions pace and lovers groan—
Labyrinth mind, no end no start;
Where lions den and lovers roam...

Where lions roar and lovers moan—
Souls' waters part;
Mired in dank recesses of the catacomb...

Where lions tame and lovers' lays grow—
Dreaming Earth, beating heart;
Where lions den and lovers roam...

Where lions guard and knots are sewn—
Heaven's gate, embroidered by hand of Art;
Mired in dank recesses of the catacomb...

Where lions lay slayed and lovers' faces hewn—
For days long, death's diminishing part,
Where lions den and lovers roam—
Mired in dark recesses of the catacomb.

OF NOD
Part I

Perhaps it was during my twenty-fourth year... things had not been going well for me. I was working at a camp on the Leelanau Peninsula of Michigan. The camp season ended, and I had nowhere to go... so, for a weekend I went to a campground that was right on the shore of Lake Michigan, at the point of the peninsula, and there set up a tent.

I was alone, but sometime during that evening— well after dark— a couple men drove onto the campsite next to mine in their truck, and proceeded to set up camp for themselves, as best as they could with flashlights only to see by. While they haphazardly set up their tents, I sat by the campfire that I had built and wished my peace had not been disturbed.

I do not remember their names, but I do remember later that evening sitting at my campfire with the two of them and being offered some smoke. As was so like me at that age, I was happy to partake.

I am not sure what went wrong. Perhaps it was because I had been searching for so long to find someplace in the world I would be happy... roaming from state to state... working as a counselor at camps during the summers, but jumping from job to job through the winters, rarely living in one state longer than three months. I had lost my grounding... I had lost my footing... something became displaced within me. In essence, I was a drifter, with no place to call home, and with no friends who were stable forces in my life... all of a sudden, that night, I was sitting with two complete strangers and smoking an herb that brings upon moments of clarity as much as it brings upon moments of insanity. I would say that I partook of the insane nature that night.

I saw visions in the campfire... it was as if I was looking into a doorway to the nether world... through the cross-work of burning log and kindling, there were spirits on fire staring... and what was being said by the older two men was unintelligible to my ears. My heart raced... anxiety built layer upon layer...

Around us there was the sound of crashing waves. There must have been a storm brewing, for there was wind present, and the great lake was loud and alive. There was a lighthouse on the point... its beam of white roamed over the land, revolving— an eye that searches.

I don't remember saying anything to the other two men... I believe I just stood up and walked off into the dark night, hoping to find some quiet, to be away from their garbled speech, to walk upon the coastline, and to find some peace, away from the fire.

I found myself eventually standing in a field, gazing at the lighthouse, watching its blinding light, quietly roaming over the land and water... then I turned around, faced away from the light and for some reason put my arms out from my sides, parallel to the ground... as the light pulsed behind, as it strove searching, searching, round and round, as it blanketed the field where I stood... on each of its passes, there, splayed was my shadow for me to gaze upon... an immense, grotesque image.

OF NOD

The next thing I remember is finding a log on the shore...
sitting down and looking out at the waves which were breaking
on the rocky coast... wanting my heart to stop racing, but then
worried it would suddenly cease beating altogether... and, there
was a horrible ringing in my ears, that not even the loud wind or
breaking waves could drown-out... so I closed my eyes and
sunk into myself.

I am not sure how much time passed... I believe I lost
consciousness. When I opened my eyes, I stood up unsteadily,
and made my way back to the campsite. The two men were not
at the fire... I assumed they were in their tents, sleeping... I
crawled into my tent as if it was a cocoon, and drifted into a
dreamless, drugged sleep.

Part 2

I have looked through windows of old glass, how all is distorted from the rippled surface toward the windows' bases... mostly in churches does one find this phenomenon... or, in old homes from the early 1800's. There are gardens outside both types of windows. I have rarely seen such a distorted image when I think back... the peering, the looking into the burning place of memories. Now, being an older man, somewhat wiser, I wonder— have I found a sense of spirit? Albeit frightening at the time, then seeing— we are much more than simple and pure... we have great regions of lurking, seething waters within, which can only be witnessed at odd moments. The wise say one must walk through the dark passage before he or she can find light...

My name is Marc. I am forty-one years old. I am sitting, during this shadow morning, tracing trails of memory while I wake slowly. Outside, the remnants of hurricane Lee has been dropping an exceedingly large amount of rain on this farm's land. I have lived so long I have begun to realize all is not as it appears.

Sometimes lucid moments pervade my awareness... happening when least expected... I might be sitting at home with my wife, enjoying a movie, or playing cards, and the next I know I begin feeling that this life I am living is more of my imagination, that it is more a dream, or a mirage.

My youth and early adult years were strewn with traumatic events... most memorable— the car accident at age of twenty.

OF NOD

Somewhere in this log cabin is tucked away the pictures of what was left of the car that I was in... close ups of the door that held, my door, smashed in a foot and a half... and I was not wearing a seatbelt... I was asleep, in the back seat, awoken suddenly, feeling as if the driver hit a curb, me bumping my head on the window... only to come-to and find that both cars were totaled... and I crawled out of the other door, wandering around in the dark, on the side of the road, realizing that something was not right with the flesh around my right eye... but I could see, out of both eyes I could see... and I cursed and kicked the car, knowing I would carry the scars from that accident the rest of my life... but, I was not prepared for the darkness that would ensue during the next year. Yes, I could see fine, but what I saw was no longer a world with little care that affected me... what I saw was a world with deep set concerns... I saw the meaninglessness, the futility of all actions... I saw the blink of an eye, how life is brief and can be taken from us in a split second... that there is no reason to one's death... and, if that was the case, my mind conjectured, then there was no reason to one's life... that we live and die and that nothing of nothing would remain; but, I have been shown differently over time.

Near death experiences tend to make one wonder. How do we have so many near misses, brushes with death... what decides when the deer will cross the road at the instant I am driving that way... what decides when that deer's life will be ended, or mine for that matter? I made the decision a long time ago that I would never swerve into a tree, or into oncoming traffic, to save a deer's life... but who's to tell if the car driving on the other side of the yellow line, if that driver has made a similar decision?

I cannot count how many times, in cars, there have been close
calls... the deer, the trucks running me off the road when
switching lanes, the metal fallen off the back of a pick-up, left in
the middle of the highway... and the car in front of me
swerving... and me seeing the mess in the middle of my lane
just in time... and there luckily not being another car on either
side at that instant so I could swerve to the right or left... and,
maybe that is why all this seems so dreamlike... for, logically, it
doesn't make sense.

It is raining and windy outside. These early morning hours are
so dark, as if the darkness is harnessed and held to hover over
this land as a blanket. I must be the only person on this farm
awake. This being alone is something I crave, and so wake
before first light most days, pacing quietly around this cottage,
while my Love and the cats and dog sleep soundly, while this
farm sleeps. The wind and rain are as spirits keeping me
company. I sing to the darkness...

OF NOD
Part 3

The autumn weather reminds me of the university... how, in September, the school year would begin. My friends and I would sneak into the church's cemetery by our dorm and sit, by the obelisk tombstone of the town's founders, looking up at the stars or occasional planet that hovered in dark reaches. We were awed by the heavens; we were riding the dream that is youth, gazing into the blackness, each star a pinprick of inspiration. The quiet magnitude of domed night held mysteries we would spend our lives discovering in our own, separate ways. There was no void— we tasted the ever-reaching, never looking back.

There are few times during life one is able to recognize his or her own potential. Visions must be scattered through the wilderness of the soul so we may forever search... and, over time we forget to hold on to the light of youth... over time, subtleties tend to be of more import when compared to the overwhelming, awesome points of turn. I have spent many days and nights wondering; then, have become resigned to the fact that perhaps this metaphor should not be about the full moon, or the sun at zenith... maybe it is more about the crescent or the eclipse... maybe it is about the loosing of innocence, or how a leaf will tumble through the naked air to land gently on soft grass.

> The dirt road that leads
> To where I know—
> Because I have been there—
> I have walked this way...

And, when the time came,
And the sun shown in a shaft
Through the forest canopy,
I stood there in the shard
Of summer's last light, warm—
As summer passes.

And there were moments when the void presented itself so I would be forced to recognize the depth of my struggle, the heart of the matter being that I am a creature of little concern— that I might be living... that I might exist, but that existence is a fleeting experience, transitory in nature.

So much depends on the ocean: its turbulent waters, the froth and brine as waves came to rest on shore's strand. My wife and I would love to live on the beach, someday... maybe then we will watch the sea creatures and sky's stars to forsake the humans' world. The salamander that crawled forth from ocean waves or tidal pool did not think about the consequences of concrete, small, trying to swim because that was all it knew. When in the womb, humans yet have tails. How many swings of the pendulum and soundings of the clock before the salamander became fashioned into man? How many suns rose and moons set until a man could bend down to the ground, almost in prayer or obedience, and, with gentle fingers, pick up the neon orange creature that strives to cross the blacktop? Then, looking in its eyes for a split moment (two black, piercing planets), he, or I, we realize deep within lies the origins— and so all of the parts of us place that simple creature slithering on its belly in the long grass growing by roadside, where it will be safe from harm.

It is only by the ocean where I will be able to find rest, peace. There have been times in life I have lived on the coast, each seeming brief now. Outside it is overcast, rainy. My wife's cat, Lalunia, is busy catching some grasshopper or cricket in the long grass of the front lawn. Ania stands up from her seat, calls Lalunia indoors. Lalunia runs inside and goes to the food dish.

The rain is falling, but lightly. On the cushioned chair, is Leo, our mastiff... he lets out a big dog-sigh, and sits watching as Lalunia rubs the sides of her face on the corner to the coffee table... my feet are resting on that table. I spend my time gazing out the bay window in this living room, wondering if the weather will turn. Although, at times, I feel removed from my origins, there are moments... these occurrences are brief, partly coherent; but, what is not lost and what is vivid are times when I see... the remembering... or the flashes of the past... they tend to well up and burst, each a pocket of air in the molten sea, allowing me to re-live, re-experience... and understand a-fresh.

I just lit a candle. Soft light fills the room. Ania asks if I love her and I say, "Yes, especially tonight...," when she has been so loving and caring... we are happy together, at this point our relationship is easy.

What floods into consciousness at present is the full moon that hovers over this land... the sky a deep blue, moonlight filtering through the forest canopy, to fall, fall, to land as wings of the lunar moth— thousands— on the ground. There are no stars present in the heavens... there are though the wisps of white clouds lingering over the forest. An owl lets out a warning note, more a scream than a hoot. Leo stops chewing his bone and looks— ready for anything— into the woods from where the owl's call came.

Part 4

I look in the mirror... sometimes I do not recognize myself. I have looked in mirrors so infrequently over the years, and we change so over just as little as a week interval, that it is no wonder I do not recognize my own appearance. What's more, it seems to me, that one should not give this matter much attention... one should not stand looking at his or her reflection in the mirror, otherwise he or she will become confused and say, "This is not me." Appearance is a fleeting experience... that we sometimes resemble our sibling, or our mother, or our father... well, that is the nature of man... to don different masks, almost from one moment to the next... it is a mystery and a great beauty that we change... it is a part of who we are.

When a child, I walked into the thickness of woods, there found the slow moving river, bending, and knelt by the waterside, perched on the twisted mass of a tree's root system... that which had been uncovered from the coursing high waters which affected the river edge for years past... then, peering into the shadows, I was able to discern my reflection, staring back... and therein witnessed my life... saw myself young and middle aged and old... saw even my grandfather peering out of the dark depths... saw myself as timeless... and, I shook off that vision... tossed a stone or two at the visage in still waters, then soon forgot all I was to become and so became only the little child digging in the dirt that between roots had collected, left that part of the woods, went to school, and learned the names of friends, learned that I had ten fingers which to count by, learned how to scrawl words on the blank page, learned how to read the scrawlings of others, learned the science of the sun, moon, and stars, but forgot much in the process. Perhaps someday I will peace together the rippling waters, the broken mirror, and so see myself in entirety again— the scars fading, the limits to my gaze, the shadow-minnows that swam through, the peaceful one, deep in the woods, who loved life, so much that he turned away.

Part 5

I just stood outside on the porch in the predawn, smoking, flicking ashes into a clay bowl that sits on top of the little table, cobwebs catching the ashes. I have woken to morning, chest bare, wearing a coat so to stay warm, front open. Ania and the animals sleep, dreaming peaceful dreams, hopefully…

Although all might not be as I would hope, for we do not yet live on the coast… for work is grueling at times… for, I only slept six hours and must be at work early… life is good, I can taste it on my lips with each sip of coffee this morning… I have made an existence for myself here in the Berkshires, at this farm; inside now, the windows are yet dark, not showing the little light cresting on the horizon.

Soon after I recovered from being in the hospital, at the age of twenty-seven, I made my way to Maine to lead a quiet and peaceful life in the Midcoast region, living in Camden, then Appleton, surrounded by tree covered mountains, immense lakes that would ice and thaw as seasons permitted, and by the sea… its rolling surface always a force in my mind. The friends I made were usually of the earthy, hippy type… and, most were first encountered at the Seadog restaurant / bar in the center of Camden… for work I fished, built boats, and constructed stone walls… lately, memories resurface of the times at the boat building factory, my first work I held for any significant portion of my life… and, it was a living hell in that factory… the heat of resin as it kicked off, the fumes, the glass shards that floated in the air we breathed, all added to the poor working environment… but, I was climbing out of many years of abusing drugs and being lost in general... I had to find work, some work... and keep that work for a period of time so I could find other, more agreeable work, in the future... so it was that I ended up building the fiberglass boats for a period of one and a half years, eventually leaving that employment in order to begin working as a stern-man on a one captain, one crew, boat that fished out of Port Clyde... then it was as if I was saved, and capturing my dreams... to be on the surface of the ocean for two years was a dream realized. . and, I was good at that work... I could weather the storms. . it also did not take long for me to get my sea legs... I was nauseous for the first month or so, but was determined, and so was able to find grounding where there was no ground. In the end, after fishing in Maine for two years, and then fishing out of Gloucester, Massachusetts for a winter, it seemed I was more comfortable being on the sea than I was being on land. I would experience the reverse of sea sickness; something called by those who sail or fish as land sickness... the solid ground would sway and rock as if I was yet on the ocean for long periods of time after I had come in from a fishing trip. This land sickness tended to last two or three days, especially if I had been out on the boat for longer than a week and if the water had been particularly rough.

One friend I met while in Maine made a particular impression... she was a mother of three... it was a brief relationship, for I was hesitant to become involved for one reason or another, just trying to find who I was becoming at that age... and it was such a process, the giving up of the past and the regaining of my life... as if I was recreating myself, needing to find some sense of stability... she was a little older than me and maybe more wise... I am grateful for the time we spent together, which should be evident seeing as it was only a matter of a couple of weeks and yet remembered...

One memorable morning, the breakfast she served me was oyster stew... no crackers to go along with. It had been a good evening the night before, sitting first in the living room of her tiny home, then, when the air cooled, going outdoors and enjoying breathing the night air while sitting, watching the sun set, on the front stoop leading into the house— this house, in Hope— with its yellow and white exterior— even a lot of yellow in the kitchen. While enjoying the stew that next morning, over the fish smell I could sense a hint of yeast— a pancake bowl must have been soaking in the sink— the remnants of batter now soft and floating on the surface. I sat then full, as full as the yellow moon that shown through the bedroom window the night previous, looking out on the farmland that sprawled across the main route in front of her home, also noticing the white door that lay on the side of her yard— wondering if that would be a good place for us to sit some night in the future...

The other night the yellow moon shown again, over this farm's land— it was hovering in the eastern sky, the glowing eye of some god— I have been on such a journey through this life— the beginnings and endings all overlapping in a staggered fashion— the strength of constructing anything of lasting quality depends on such structure... Hope, Maine far away— in distance and time— hope, that region of the heart, so evident...

Part 6

Leo sleeps on the cushioned chair, by the west window of this cottage, his paws twitch as if he is dreaming of chasing, dreaming of hunting. When we walk through the fields of this farm's property, he is always searching for deer, or rabbits, or geese to chase... when there is a flock resting in the marshy section of the field, he will fly on his paws toward them— an arrow shot from the bow— and they will know soon enough to warn each other... then the entire flock, as if one mind, struggles to take to the air, running for a short spans on the ground, honking, honking, flapping great wings, until they gain enough momentum to take to the sky... and they then fly off and circle round so as to head to another resting spot that lies in their memory, just over the next hill, or in a glade off where the thickness of trees will seclude them from such a monster as the mastiff Leo. He must dream now, of finding that flock unawares and, this time, he runs with a strength he has never felt in waking life— the geese honk and run, but before they take to the air, he is in their midst, perhaps growing wings then to take flight with them... I can only imagine what he might dream; there on the cushioned chair... his paws slowly cease twitching.

Part 7

Cold, rainy, windy... even when inside, where heated, there is a subtle chill to the air. The leaves are falling, the wind tearing them from tree branches. I am sleeping less, and I am sad, and yearning more than usual... it is as if the summer was a passing emotion, nothing more... something that came and went, of which I was only half aware. I have heard said that the older one becomes, time passes all the more with speed... it certainly feels so now...

Yesterday I walked Leo a great deal around this farm's property, making our way eventually to the hay field that sprawls off of Hearts' Lane... there, the vultures were wheeling and circling above the cliffs of gravel... the sky was the sheen of steel. The hay had grown to the height of Leo's back; nevertheless, he ran and ran through the golden and white blossoms that adorned the green stalks. Off in the distance, a shotgun blast... we both stopped and looked in the direction of the firing. I was caught unaware, not realizing that the hunting season had begun. There is no hunting allowed on the Farm's property; although, there are few fences and stone walls that delineate the boundaries. Many hunters will unknowingly stray onto the Farm's five-hundred acre forests and fields. It is not a safe time to be walking the woods... hopefully, though there is less danger when in the open... that the hunters will see we are man and dog, and not mistake us for prey or sport.

Last night, the waning gibbous moon glowed in the misty clouds... I looked up at one point, while walking the roads of this farm, and was in awe of her beauty, a spirit of night. Now, at this early hour, the coyotes make a kill… I can hear their howling in the darkness, and hope it is not one of the farm cats being hunted.

At home, Ania's sister and nephew visit… they arrived last night, during a community supper. We ate together, but then I had to work, so they went home to enjoy the evening and play with Leo. Ania's nephew, little Lee, was excited to have the opportunity to play with our mastiff.

Part 8

The day rainy, overcast… it is the beginning of the week. I have been sick for a while, but now am better, feeling the vitality of good health. I have rearranged Ania's and my bedroom and am washing sheets. Ania is at work… she seems to spend the better part of her life at work. I just wrote her and am hoping she replies later in the day when she has time… for I was tired this morning… and did not wake as she was leaving and saying goodbye. Now, I don't remember the kiss which she planted on my cheek as she made her way out of the cabin. She and I always kiss before she leaves for the day, or before I leave for the night.

Leo yet sleeps, on the sofa, next to me… when it rains he is as lazy as a cat, napping all day. When sunny, he stands at the window or door and urges us to take him for walks or runs. I am hoping weather clears so we will have time to take a walk. Now that I am feeling healthy, exercise would be good.

Part 9

I think it was soon after being in Michigan that I decided to make my way to Iowa City, Iowa… I was lost; trying to find my way… my truck had been packed for a week and was sitting in my father's and stepmother's garage… Dawn, my stepmother, said "If you're going to go, just go." So I went, without direction and without purpose, driving across the country, eventually making my destination the Midwest… camping at deserted campgrounds along the way for it was off-season. The owners of the campgrounds were more than interested in having me stay on their land, profiting what little money they could during that autumn.

On arriving in Iowa City, I decided to call an old friend, someone I'd met numerous years previous, when I had worked at a camp in the town of Monticello, not far north of Iowa City. Shamus was glad to hear from me and told me to not stay at the hostel as I had originally planned but to continue on to his farm in Monticello… so I hopped back in my truck, and trekked the forty minutes north, arriving late in the evening.

I remember being greeted by him on that rainy night… I remember entering into that big farmhouse, through the back door, and feeling a sense of accomplishment, for I was on a journey and had reached a temporary resting point. Shamus not only let me stay that night, but within the first week there, he suggested I think about paying a modest rent so to stay longer and eat the food his mother prepared, until I was able to find a place of my own. I thought it very kind of him to offer and was more than happy with the arrangement.

OF NOD

Although Shamus was forty years old, he had an eighteen year old for a girlfriend... and he had other friends, closer to my age, who he introduced me to over time. We would spend our evenings, most evenings, getting high in the second floor rooms of that farmhouse, talking and being generally interested in life. Shamus was an eclectic musician sort... a guitar player, vocalist... in addition he wrote a bit of what might be called poetry, meditations that were somewhat mind bending to me at the time... would scrawl them in black hardbound notebooks, and I would some evenings sit reading his words, trying to figure out what he was trying to explain. Some afternoons I would sit hunched over a typewriter that I had found and purchased from a local second-hand store, trying to create my own poetry, usually struggling with writer's block during that autumn... but, occasionally a good poem crawled out of me onto the page when least expected. Shamus then would record me reading my work, and he would add his electric guitar to the tracks... haunting.

During afternoons, when it was yet warm that fall, we were like kids, discovering the wooded land around his home, or wandering through the cliffs of lime rock that were close by. We were discovering a lot about our friendship during that time. I suppose he was a teacher, in one form or another, to me... he was older, but had a young perspective on the world... was attuned to nature, seemed to think himself somewhat magical...

I suppose that was the first time in my life I began smoking marijuana daily... it was Christmas... he gave me some as a gift... and, then things seemed to change concerning my relationship to that drug... I would spend many evenings alone, in his study, smoking and beginning to read a significant amount of literature. He and I grew apart... eventually I moved out, making my way to Iowa City, where I lived in a historic apartment building, and spent my time walking the roads of Iowa City, reading at a coffee shop in the center of town, discovering the nature that the city's park provided, and eating modestly at the local Co-Op market. I think many days I subsisted on no more than a little fruit and nuts. I was losing weight quickly. I had trouble finding work, and when I would land a job it would be temporary. I only stayed in Iowa City for a matter of a partial winter and a spring, but it was a time in my life that seemed to change me significantly.

Today is September twenty-second... summer has truly past,
and fall begins. The day is overcast, and it rained quite a bit in
the early hours. We, at the Farm, are eating a lot of squash,
tomatoes, and kale... hoping that the first frost will arrive later
rather than earlier, seeing as the tomatoes are just now ripe.
Ania is at work, and I am home with Leo, trying to relax during
this time I have off late in the work week; but, needing to work
this evening. It is early in the afternoon. Leo and I just
returned from a long walk down to the field and back. At the
field we saw Alfred working on his tractor... off in the gravel
pit, the laborers mined the gravel with their equipment. Leo
sleeps... he is at peace, for he has had opportunity to run.

From time to time, I feel my age... although I yet feel young,
there are moments when I realize I am not as I used to be... that
I resemble my father sometimes bothers me, for I want to be my
own person... and do not want to feel as if I am becoming him
in any manner. He is a good man, yet to become like him
means surrendering. But we cannot help this... that we
resemble those who brought us into the world is part of being
human... and so he ages, and so I age, becoming like he was
thirty years previous.

Growing old is also, in a manner, comforting... having
perspective on life, allows me to enjoy this time... there is less
anxiety, more confidence... and to be married now brings with
it a sense of accomplishment and pride... as if I have discovered
a part of myself that before lay dormant. Ania I love with all of
my heart... she, a mooring to a sailboat that has seen many

rough storms, and now I have found a place to be secured close to the shore… it is calm here, in this cove… the slight nudging of the little waves lull me into dreaming… dreaming of all that came before and all that will come hereafter, the journey.

Now I am back in Iowa City… twenty-five years old, losing all sense of Ego… intentionally trying to destroy that part of myself, feeling that there lies enlightenment… and, when I look in the mirror one night, after being high most of the day, I do not recognize the person who I have become… I am a stranger to my own self… then, I go outside, and walk in the frigid cold, making my way through the dark of night, toward the park, where a great river flows… crossing the bridge, then I feel that I am merely a thin filament, or strand of light, or a wisp of smoke… there is not much left of me by this point… I can feel the wind blow me like it would a thread, or a lost strand of a woman's long hair. I have destroyed enough of myself that there is little left to withstand the weather of this night… and I walk then through the scattered trees of the park… and wander, wander, as if lost in the wilderness. My heart has ceased racing… I am calm… I feel as if I am more dead than alive… feeling has left me, taking flight into the dark of this night's heavens… leaving me to linger on the shores of Nod.

I have spent numerous months meditating… and I have given up something in the process… an exchange was made… I bartered not for my soul, but for the losing of it… as if I needed to kill all feeling, because to feel was too painful, too confusing. My thoughts had been racing for a long time… there was no stopping the flow… and then the dam broke, and all went rushing away into the distance… all thought, all feeling, all of me.

I am alive again… I breathe, I sleep, I eat, I pray… I find pleasure in the simple matters of existence… I am in Kemah, Texas… I am twenty-seven… I am writing poetry… through most of my days I write. The medication is doing wonders… I am becoming myself again… with the first pill swallowed, there was a shift of a gear, a cog wheel that had not turned for some time began to slowly turn… the mechanisms are no longer frozen… there is pain and pleasure, there are dreams and there are nightmares… the internal machine is functioning… the kick-start worked… I live, and not knowing it, have begun the long life of being, being one who struggles with a mental illness, being one who will have an effect on the world, be that positive or negative, from moment to moment, but who will accomplish great and small things.

Part II

Although all is dark, I know that somewhere in the heavens is the cinder of moonlight. I have woken early with a bit of a hangover. Last night I came home late from work, drank a modest amount, and then crawled into bed with Ania and we stayed awake late talking to each other. It has been a long week and Ania and I have seen little of each other... she has begun to take time after work to exercise, so she is no longer meeting me at dinners.

Then, there was a time during my stay in Iowa, when I befriended another older man who was an artist-type... he mostly worked with watercolor... I think he thought I was his student regarding life matters.. we would spend long afternoons and late evenings either sitting in my apartment, or walking the roads of the city, conversing... or, should I say that he conversed, and rarely gave me opportunity to say much of anything, as if he was determined to impart as much as he could in the short amount of time we had to spend in each other's company. Now, thinking back, I feel that he was a very odd man. Rarely did I see him when he was sober... he smoked a tremendous amount of marijuana, seeming to need to do so... he had traveled, living in various places and states over the years, and had many experiences to relate. I think maybe I was the first friend he had had in a long time.

I believe I was searching for some sort of guidance... and, maybe looked for it in the wrong people... but, then again, one might argue that because I was able to glean quite a lot of knowledge from these two men, that all was not lost. They were thinkers, both of them... and they had lived their lives discovering their own things in their own ways, and felt the need to share their knowledge with me, so in the end I feel grateful for their friendships. They helped mold me into the man that I am today... for good or for bad... and, although most of the time spent with them was in a drug haze, somehow I was able to see through the clouds of smoke, and understand what it means to be an artist in this present-day world... it is not about the finding of fame and fortune through art... it is more about the daily creative process... and, in the end, being a creator of one's own self and destiny... that was the major "lesson" I learned... other than that, I saw that one needs to have patience, and perseverance... that one will naturally become better at one's art over time... and that the natural world is full and brimming over with beauty— if one only allows oneself to see...

At the age of twenty-seven I ceased using marijuana... had a mental break, ended up in the hospital... now I take medicine daily, needing to maintain sanity and clarity... but, no, I do not regret... for, the world I see is magical... and I am somewhat successful in life regarding career, marriage, and hobbies... I feel fortunate, regardless...

I am sitting at my little desk, here in the cottage... Ania is asleep in the bedroom, so is Leo... outside, the owls of night hoot their calls through the woods. My little black cat sits on the porch, lit by the porch lights, looking out into the surrounding night. The mosquitoes are pestering this morning. I go outside to smoke cigs, and when inside, I drink my coffee, trying to wake to this new morning.. I will though, once when the inspiration is spent, crawl back into bed and sleep…

Part 12

I slept well last night... the slight amount of whiskey I had in the evening was as medicine, helping me slumber... now, I am awake, riding the wave of dark morning toward sunrise... Ania and I have had a good weekend, although, it is over, it being Monday. She sleeps soundly in our bed... she has been happy lately, finding some sense of comfort in her work, and enjoying the time she spends exercising... when she is happy, the whole world seems a better place.

The coffee is freshly made... I am drinking it black, with a good amount of sugar... no soy this morning, for that would only temper the coffee's heat and effects of the caffeine... with each sip I feel more pleasure. I must go outside to smoke... Ania does not appreciate the smell of lingering cigarette smoke... we do though smoke cloves in the house... last night we watched a film, smoking the cloves to help time pass.

I have begun to feel a sense of contentment as well... Ania and I are settling into the season. Ania loves the autumn, as do I. Most days are gray, overcast... there are a lot of muted yellows and oranges at present... so far it is not a very colorful fall; but, we are not yet at the height of the season. The air tends to be comfortable and cool... and, although the afternoons might be somewhat hot, by evening we must don long sleeved shirts and jeans to stay warm.

Outside, the crickets sing their songs... this must be their mating time... they are alive and chirping. They must have been making such music long before man ever existed... a primal song.

Although our cottage is not in the woods, it is on the cusp of the wooded land. I have, since childhood, always wanted to live in a cabin in the woods... now, to be close to the wooded land, tucked away on the edge of a farm's property is wonderful. My ears ring... echoes of the crickets' song.

At times Ania misses the city environment, but, now she is realizing that it is not bad here... that our animals will not be happier anywhere else is significant to her. She loves our Leo, and her cat, Lalunia, is precious to her. Lalunia tends to spend most days, all day, outside, catching crickets and grasshoppers. Ania brings Lalunia in for the nights, afraid the coyotes might one night hunt her. For a long time I have been letting my cat, Wookie, roam the farm day and night. He has only one good eye, but seems to keep himself safe, always returning to the cabin for food and water... there he is... scratching at the door, wanting in so he can fill his little belly.

Life here might seem simple, but it allows one to think and ponder... allows one to work on art... there are no distractions. It is uncomplicated. . a peaceful place. Although I would love to live in a city someday, for now this is perfect. I must take advantage of this time, for when we do move, all will change and I will no longer have quiet anymore as company, feeding my creative process. On the couch next to me, Wookie cleans himself... he is wet from the rain that dampened the grass early in the night.

OF NOD

I just stood outside, smoking, on the front porch, noticed a spider climbing a thin strand of web... delicate. The crickets have ceased chirping. Dawn will be aglow in a matter of minutes... all is quiet, in expectation of the coming light. I have woken early and am already at the height of emotion... all will be a slow descending through the rest of the day's course. The bed is calling and I will go to it, I will lie down beside my wife and our dreams will entwine— two mating serpents... until she must rise, and ready for work. It is Monday, and the hectic nature of work and life is upon us again. We are one force, she and I... we are riding this wave of autumnal bliss, loving each other day by day... she is beautiful, as this quiet before sunrise... and instead of the sun, her face greeting me when we wake is the dawn's glow.

Part 13

Ania and I had a wonderful conversation last evening, talking about the drive or inspiration that she and I have— to make some mark on the world... to leave some impression that will survive beyond our lifetime. It seems this is a human need, that we, as humans, know our time has an end, but want to live through words, or paintings, or photography... after our last breath is taken... want to leave a mark which will take the breath away from those who appreciate our creations. When one considers our time here is limited, that no one can be truly sure about the existence or nonexistence of an afterlife, it seems only natural for us to want to survive in some form or other, beyond. Ania is anxious she will never create anything of lasting value. I suggested she start attending the writing groups that I am a part of, for, she used to write poetry when living in Poland— but she said, "I feel unable now because of my struggles with the English language... but, I know you'll be famous someday, you will leave something behind."

It is afternoon, hot outside. I would be walking Leo but am going to wait until the day cools. He sleeps on the sofa next to me. Inside, the cottage it is cool, comfortable. I slept the better part of morning... it is my time off from work, so I am catching up on rest, readying for the business of the work week.

This morning, on crawling back into bed, before the light of day broke, I lay looking at my Love, there in partial light shed by a nightlight. She was sleeping on top of the blankets, her half naked body visible... and she breathed, but so quietly, that I thought her dead. No, it was merely a deep state of rest, for

~ 239 ~

when I stopped arranging blankets and pillows to feel comfortable, and my ears adjusted to the quiet of the room, then I heard, barely heard her subtle inhales and exhales. She means the world to me, and, although she rarely believes that fact, I am hoping one day she will understand. She makes me strong... I was thinking that I rarely see my psychiatrist any more, and realized that is because I am doing much better with Ania in my life. That she brings me happiness is the least of what she instills... it is more the constant presence of her— physically, or in my heart when she is at work— that is healing me day by day. I hope she reads these words sometime, and knows then how much I care, that I have come to depend on her, that I am growing and made more whole from her attention, from her beautiful healing sharing of spirit.

Ania is Polish... she is a redhead... she is filled with emotion, brimming over... so much so that she cannot contain her various emotions, whether they be positive or negative. She is a gift to my life... she helps me grasp hold of each moment and search for meaning and purpose... Ania strives to make some indelible impression that will survive her, but she has not found the means that will allow her to do this... I encourage her to have patience, tell her that what she is drawn to focus on today will someday— maybe five years from now, or longer— end up becoming something that does hold meaning, that might even be that which enables her to leave her "mark." I believe life is like that... we are on a journey, a path... that meaning and purpose is hidden through much of the endeavor, but one day it all comes clear.

Part 14

I drink the last sip of espresso... it is four o'clock in the morning, another short night of sleep that was fraught with various intense dreams. I am alive, and wandering through the field... the espresso cup sits, empty on the deck of cards in a country home, located outside of Warsaw... in this field, all is dark. I feel as if I have directional sense, but am not sure... I walk gently on this ground. I am making my way toward the little town that is close at hand, but am aware I have a long way to go before I arrive. The moon is a crescent hung in the clear night sky. I am half-drunk yet, the residue of vodka crawls through my veins at a seething pace, burning my childhood dreams... the hopes and cares I have rarely seen as different, regardless of what lens I gaze through. The present lens is one I discovered in a little wooden box... found on my father's work bench in the basement of our North Carolina home... it is a magnifying glass that would generally be used to examine the print and art on antique stamps... my father collected stamps when a youth... now I hold the magnifying glass up to my right eye and gaze at the heavens— the darkness is visible, now distorted, and bent... the stars are bursts of great suns, their long lived life reaching into the matter of my mind, each as a finger— searching, probing...

I am on a beach of New Hampshire... it is the fall; cool, windy... the wind whips and tears over the water and the sand. We guard the flame so as to light the marijuana in our pipe. Both of us take turns, taking long drags, holding the spirit within for a span before letting it loose, exhaling into the salty sea's wind. Reality takes on a different shape... you, my young love, seem to change, realizing a possible future… and we sit there, as day fades, making vague plans to run off together into the great world, to make a life for ourselves— I can see us now, drifting in the shallows of that tidal spread… two bodies which have given up breathing… we then take a different shape— we are as one, a monster with four legs and four arms, crawling out of the surf, onto the beach, to patter and slither toward the unsuspecting lovers huddled together half way toward the road… later, when driving, we pull off the main road and bring the truck to rest somewhere up a barely used dirt drive… it was with some sense of adventure we found ourselves in a corps of trees, for we were two drifters. We copulate during the evening light, in the shade of the forest's leafy bowers… the quiet… the danger of being on someone's property that we do not know… the drug that pervades our attention… all became etched in memory. You were a dancer… I wonder, do you yet dance upon the shores of some distant beach, racing through the nothingness, with your lips pursed, kissing the night's stars?

When a youth, I spent a year or so, on Sundays, as an altar-boy, at a church in the suburbs of Wilmington, Delaware. I would arrive early, before the service, and, with the minister, dress in the ceremonious robe, place the black drapery upon myself— then, I would feel a sense of importance… and, as I walked to the front of the congregation, while the organ was played, I would with unshaking hands, light the three candles on the table in the center, under the immense cross to which we all prayed… then, I would go and sit, behind the bouquets, on the left side, and quietly hide… singing hymns, repeating the minister's words, and rising and sitting, praying out loud in unison when appropriate… I did not think at all about the pros and cons of organized faith... I was ust there, worshiping with the rest, understanding my own faith in my own way.

I went to college eventually, and met a group of people who thought very different than me... it took time, but I was able to open to their ways of thought and living, was able to begin to comprehend more than the simple nature of this life-experience... but, thinking and being different seems to come with its own cost. There are questions now that have no answers; there are thoughts now that explode within my mind, wreaking havoc. We would sit in the dark of the cemetery— where the street lights' radiance could not reach— talking over matters that had no direct beginnings or ends. The subjects of meaning or purpose seemed to weave through all the conversations we had— we were searching, trying to grasp hold of the big answers, not knowing that resolution would be long in arriving, if ever... that we asked "Why?" was maybe a mistake... for there is no end to the "Why."

Part 15

Leo and I just returned from taking a walk in the field off of Hearts' Lane… the day is progressing, and I find now that I am lonely for Ania's company. Today is Friday, my last night of work for the week. I am looking forward to a relaxing weekend spent in Ania's company.

I had a sparse lunch, consisting of a couple of bananas and a hunk of cheese… I feel content though, and am happy I do not need to go to the Lodge to eat. By this time in the week, I appreciate my time away from the business of Farm community, preferring to spend time alone, or with Leo, or with Ania when I am able. When one lives where one works, there is pressure to be at work on a constant basis… here, one's life can tend to revolve around working and being present at meals and community events… I have gotten better, over the years, about not spending all my free time at work.

It is another overcast day… the leaves are though beginning to show bright— colors… the yellows especially becoming significant. I am grateful for the changing of seasons… and, therefore am happiest living here in New England, where we see all seasons, for good or for bad… meaning, the terrible heat in August can be just as daunting as the bitter cold of January and February; but, the pleasant mildness to the weather during the rest of the year is a gift. I am one that changes with the seasons, becoming different in my heart during different points of the year.

There are wispy cobwebs surrounding and covering, attached to the deer skull that sits on the little table on our front porch... by the skull is a clay bowl for flicking ashes into, a place to extinguish spent cigarettes. Dawn, my stepmother, gave me the deer skull one spring, after the waters of the river by their home had receded, leaving such a finding for her to discover during that season. The clay bowl was a gift, given to me one Christmas by a friend named Nate— he was a housemate during my first year or two here at the Farm. Out in the front yard, sits a rubber ball— a play toy of Leo's, left there some time recently... there are yellow and brown leaves scattered on the porch steps... there is the fact that Ania just called from her work to say "Hi," and, there is more life now to my existence. I am noticing subtleties, beauty. I am wishing Ania was home, but am resigned to looking forward to the weekend, hoping we will enjoy the time together, it being precious.

Late in the day... the sky is clouded, so dusk has arrived early. I am tired, but I must go to work in half an hour. I just sat outside smoking, contemplating... now, light is precious, the days short... Ania regularly arrives home after dark. She will have finished her work week by six o'clock. I am happy for her, and a bit envious. She will not be going to the gym today, but will be coming to have dinner with me while I begin my evening work. We talked this afternoon and I could hear in her voice that she was somewhat wrestles to be done for the day and the week, that she was looking forward to being home, and that she was missing me, wishing I could spend this evening at home.

Last night I had an odd dream just before waking... there was a court of people from the Farm in a great hall... the judges presiding were people from the Farm's Board of Directors. It was told to me that every person in the room would have opportunity to ask the judges one question... when it came my turn to ask a question, I said, "What differentiates between the various voices one imagines when reading a novel and the voices a person whom has schizophrenia hears?" There was a hushed silence in the hall after I posed the question... then, I could tell everyone was shocked and upset by what I had asked and that the judges were not going to answer such inquiry... at that moment I heard the alarm clock, and woke to the start of my day.

Part 16

Three o'clock in the morning… I am at work… I just had to wake to give someone medication… again, I am up at an early hour, and, regardless what I do, I will be tired the rest of the day.

I smoked a cigarette… there is a cool dampness to the night air… when returning to the inside I said "Hello" to one of the house's new residents, wondered what he was doing up at such an hour… the TV was on, an image frozen on the screen, as if someone had been watching a film. . the image was one of an Asian looking through a large window into dark night, his reflection visible… the Asian had a staid expression, as if he was expecting something to occur, something that was inevitable, perhaps irreversible.

Somewhere, outside, in the clouds the moon shines… somewhere, within my heart, there resides a little puppet of a man, sipping his coffee with a little Irish whiskey added to the morning… inside his heart, resides the Buddha, contemplating the great mystery… this labyrinth that is the heart, where are caverns delved by the coursings of blood from centuries past, this labyrinth where the souls of so many of my ancestors yet roam, and groan, and swoon— there in the darkness visible only to me… there I have focused my attention for the time… where shadows resided, there the mysteries are held… there the secrets are shared, there we live so we might wander unseen, riding the wave of dark blood…

The slightly lit corners of a room

OF NOD

        Tend to be most interesting,
        Holding mystery...

        Then there are the slightly lit
        Corners of my mind...
        Which seem to hold secrets
        That I have kept
        From myself over the years,

        Maybe even through lifetimes...

        Perhaps if I were to pay
        More attention to one dark and dim
        Space— such as the heart's realm
        That I do not give reign to—

        Then all places of little light
        Would become illuminated...
        And I might begin to struggle
        Less in this world.

I shine yet in the dark night... a star flashing across the horizon... the world turns; the mystic shore wants me to return... when will I live close to the ocean again? This land locked region is stifling... I feel sheltered, almost hidden... as if my time has not yet come, and so these ankles are shackled.

Again— but different— older, wiser maybe... I sit on a large drift-log to gaze upon the night sky as if it is the ocean, spend many hours then, peering downwards, into the crashing waves of my soul— for there, at least, the churning water can be found. The lighthouse spreads a sweeping arc of light over the peninsula's point. I sink into myself... the wind and the ripping sounds of waves my only company. I enter the blackness. In my mind's eye, I move into and through the darker regions of vision... then fly, fly toward that which in its depth is more of the hushed shadows.

Shaded in the realm of this state... I realize that one must find happiness within before one is able to appreciate life's beauty fully... that being said, perhaps I need only to truly see the sea within, feel its ebbing and flowing, splash in the pools of water that have collected in the low parts of the beach... I must gaze within to see the boats sailing out further into the blue, or dipping and bobbing where they are tied close to shore to some unseen mooring... I must wash my hands and face in the morning froth and cold salt currents... I must swim, there in the darkness, with the moon's light splashing on the living surface... I must swim deeper and deeper into the far reaching ocean before I can arrive at the distant shore... where all is a dreaming, a quiet pulsing of the star strewn heavens, where all is peaceful, calm, where there are no storms that pervade awareness, where the light of the sun is waiting, that which— when morning arrives— will strive to reach its zenith, and then plummet, plummet toward the western horizon, there to fall like a mad ball of fire in the illumined city that rises, rises out of the mud, its concrete pillars stark against the setting.

Part 17

I sit; in our cottage drinking beer... night has begun. Ania woke late today... it was after the noon hour that she finally rose. I prepared us a lunch and then mowed the front lawn, something I have been meaning to do for the past couple of months. Hopefully this will be the final time it will need to be tended this year, for winter will not be long in arriving. Toward evening, Ania and I made our way into Great Barrington, so that she could use the gym and I could shop at a local health food market for our weekend meals. We have recently arrived home, and are sitting in the living room of our log cottage, enjoying sipping on the beer bought, and watching our mastiff as he devours a rawhide bone. We had not been getting along through the better part of the afternoon, but, with the fist sips of Allagash, all is easier. We have suddenly become lovers again.

The first bottle I opened now sits beside me... empty. I can feel this night pressing upon the windows, somewhat cold. The porch lights to our and our neighbors' cottages are *on*, lighting up the crest of this little hill. It was a busy week... no time for resting... much work was accomplished. I am now enjoying this time, when I might relax and not worry about needing to be at work for the next couple days.

Tonight, we started making plans for a trip to Portland, Maine, which will hopefully occur two weekends from now... it will be Ania's birthday weekend. We are hoping to visit that coastal city in order to investigate if we'd like to move there in the future. I, at one time, lived in Portland for a matter of three months… it was after working at a camp in Oakland, Maine for a summer. I met a woman at that camp who I lived with for a matter of nine months, the first part of which was spent in Portland, in a large apartment on Congress Street. During the second half, we lived in a little wood-heated house, located in the woods of West Bath, fifty minutes north of Portland. The relationship was disastrous by its end… for, when all transpired with such unending arguing and discontentment, then it was that I packed up my truck and headed first south, then west, stopping for a time at my parents' home in West Hartford, eventually making the trek to Iowa— in order to put as much distance between Mona and myself as was possible.

I believe Mona and I destroyed each other that year… although we loved each other, we were yet young and immature, and did not recognize that patience concerning a partner is an essential part of how relationships survive. And we were both so impatient, wanting to change all that we saw wrong in the other. We berated each other unendingly, as the changes were so very slow in happening. Perhaps we were too different from each other… perhaps we were only young and needed to maintain our independence, and so would not change or even try to be different when the troubles arose… but the sex was good, and so we continued the destroying in order to have such an encompassing sexual relationship.

I had always wanted to live on a back road, surrounded by pine, close to a river that would become a serpent of ice during the cold months. Now, the white siding, the basement and its wood burning stove, a bedroom with its slanted walls and one window where the sun shows its face every morning, all of this seems to shine... the peach blanket and the fawn mastiff who stretches himself out, he who would have to be pushed and shoved during those early hours of sexual pleasures. Your blond hair would tangle to knots as I thrust myself into the cave— the furthest place of retreat. The back of your head, that place of arched bone, worked against the pillow... then, while we closed our eyes, and once again pushed against each other— the forging necessary to give the structure enough strength— outside of us, there were still the roses, those that I bought before we had even come to place ourselves in the spring of Maine's country... they hung from a string tied to their stems beside the closet, their heads pointed towards the floor.

Tonight I bought Ania flowers… I am not sure what variety they are, but the man selling them said they were of the hearty sort… would last long before wilting. On arriving home, Ania placed them in a wine craft that my father had given us last Christmas— she had to discard the wilted, moldy sunflowers that had been in that makeshift vase for the past week… the craft she set back on the kitchen table in the same place as before, new flowers a dark rich red.

I woke… it was two in the morning… hungry. We had some sushi left from our dinner, which I ate, thoroughly enjoying having sushi at such a late hour… Ania came and stole a piece from me… now we are both up and not needing sleep. We smoke clove cigarettes… a window is cracked so as to let in the cool autumn air… as we take drags, there are the little crackling noises heard while the cigs burn. Wookie meows, sitting by the front door… he wants out.

Ania just closed the window and is readying for bed… there is a quiet surrounding this cottage… the Farm sleeps. Soon I will ready for bed. I feel though as if I could stay awake for some time, wanting to live long through this night, not wanting dreams— for, at this moment, I live the dream… I am, and that is all that matters. Leo sleeps, as he breathes deeply and slowly, curled on the couch next to me… eyes partly open.

Part 18

Prehistoric labyrinths are believed to have served as traps for
malevolent spirits or as defined paths for ritual dances. In
medieval times, the labyrinth symbolized a hard path to God
with a clearly defined center (God) and one entrance (birth). In
their cross-cultural study of signs and symbols, *Patterns that
Connect,* Carl Schuster and Edmund Carpenter present various
forms of the labyrinth and suggest various possible meanings,
including not only a sacred path to the home of a sacred
ancestor, but also, perhaps, a representation of the ancestor
him/herself: "...many [New World] Indians who make the
labyrinth regard it as a sacred symbol, a beneficial ancestor, a
deity. In this they may be preserving its original meaning: the
ultimate ancestor, here evoked by two continuous lines joining
its twelve primary joints." Labyrinths can be thought of as
symbolic forms of pilgrimage; people can walk the path,
ascending toward salvation or enlightenment.

(Wikipedia: Labyrinth— Cultural Meanings)

Part 19

The Land of Nod (Hebrew: *eretz-Noa*, דונ ץרא) is a place in the Book of Genesis of the Hebrew Bible, located "on the east of Eden"(*qidmat-'Eden*), to which Cain chose to flee after murdering his brother Abel. According to Genesis 4:16:

And Cain went out from the presence of the LORD, and dwelt in the land of Nod, on the east of Eden.

"Nod" (דונ) is the Hebrew root of the verb "to wander" (דודנל) and is possibly anetymological etiology intended to explain the nomadic lifestyle of Cain and his putative descendants, the Kenites. One interpretation of Genesis 4:16 is that Cain was cursed to wander the land forever, not that he was exiled to a "Land of Wanderers" otherwise absent from the Old Testament. Genesis 4:17 relates that after arriving in the Land of Nod, Cain's wife bore him a son, Enoch, in whose name he built the first city.

(Wikipedia: Land of Nod)

Part 20

When I was a child, my grandfather would light his cigarettes
with a match that he'd hold out pinched between his thumb and
forefinger (fingernails cleaned by a pocket knife) for my
brother's pursed lips. To me it seemed that he, who had entered
the world through the same crevice as I, he, the younger, would
always be given the chance to put out the flame. Even though I
did not know then, I felt the magic that was gently held, that
gift which had allowed primitive man to survive, that which
Prometheus had been bound for giving and one might say
bound to give; so, in my need, one difficult day, like the feral
cat, I reached into the sky to draw my nails across the face of
Heaven, for, when the match had been discarded in the tray
twice, before my chance was made, I took my turn to rise and
blow the ashes like snowflakes— a gray dust over the two of
them. And, oh how quietly the old man stood, brushing my
brother and himself off, then, with a folded piece of paper,
scraped the mess into a pile and put it back where it belonged,
leaving only the wooden surface for us to look upon.

Part 21

Ania and I have decided— at this point— not to have children... the other day though, I realized that it is through having children that most people in the world survive beyond this life... they live through their progeny... and I am growing older, and this life is short... but that being said, the thought of having children seems to be something that I both wonder about and am paralyzed by, maybe not having enough faith that I would be able to provide for a child, or fearing I would not be able to live long enough, at this point, to be a fatherly figure through the large spans of a child's life... this saddens me.

My brother and his wife have brought two children into the world... maybe I will have to be content with being an uncle. I pick up the remnant of a clove that Ania left for me before going to bed, and smoke, forgetting this, my failure... we met so late in life... we both needed to wander far and wide in order to find each other... and now that we hold each other, this holding will be short lived... a tear comes to my eye.

Relationships seem to be as much about finding as losing... we found each other... and so we must hold tight, now, fingers entwined... and find our way out of the confusion, of the daily searching, of the great loss, and of the daily drudgery. There are many branches off this path we have chosen... she could choose to walk her own path in time, or I could do the same... but, somehow, someway, we need to hold to each other, never releasing the grip... and find our way out of this maze. Maybe that is why living by the ocean seems so appealing to us... there, in a fashion, we would be at the edge... no longer locked in by land... as if the escape would be near. There are shores to this life, where one is able to rest and find peace of mind... there are tragedies that have endings, and places of new-birth, new beginnings... we would like to live the new beginning, we want to somehow find peace, here, while yet living... we want to lie on the sand, during a pulsing summer day and remember the parts to this life that have been beautiful, while living the life of two lovers basking in the sun.

Part 22

Ania and I just ate a dinner that I prepared— a pasta with smoked salmon dish... we are both full and content. Our dog slept through dinner, in the bedroom, having had a good run in the field the hour before. Usualy Leo pesters us while we eat, begging, very pushy about wanting our food.

It is early yet... only five o'clock. I spent the early afternoon napping, tired after having had beer and Jameson last evening. It is good to catch up on sleep. I usually burn like a candle, but on both ends... waking early, and staying up late. Now, I am renewed... I will be strong heading into this next work week.

The light of fading day filters through the front windows, into the living room where I sit. I recall now how light has entered into other rooms of my life.

In Connecticut I lived in a farm house, close to Storrs... it was in the second floor of the backside of the house where I lived, renting a two room apartment... then I would spend many days during that winter, hunched over a make shift painting table, made with large sheets of plywood, two small desks as supports... there I would create watercolors. Light came from all angles, reflecting off the white of the outside snow... that light, blinding at times, was wonderful to paint by, especially for watercolor. In the middle of the desk, for a time, was a white rose given to me by the horse trainer of the farm... she with raven hair, and dark brown eyes. I painted the image of that rose into one watercolor… its thorny stem went past the margins I had drawn.

There was a time, in Iowa City, when I used to sit and meditate by the kitchen window that let in light of the morning… so warm, there, with the sun beating on my brow, during that winter. I would eat oatmeal that I had cooked the night previous, with a little soy and raisins added, maybe some walnuts… and sit at the kitchen window, eating that pleasant dish before meditating. I found an extreme pleasure in spending my time in such a way… in the living room, around the corner, there was an acrylic painting that I had done on a found-section of a door… red, aqua, and black being the most apparent colors in the piece.

A painting can be a window into an artist's mind… how I would paint in many mediums when living in my father's and stepmother's basement, during another winter… and then I had an exhibit of the windows to my mind in West Hartford Center, sometime around the first of the year… and soon after found that I could no longer survive in the world without psychiatric help. The space in that basement that I used to paint had little natural light… the windows were small in that game room / bar, so I had numerous lamps as light sources… even using a large interior painter's light I found in the garage— that which would make me sweat, because of its heat, when I would paint by its glare.

I stand outside on the porch… small rain drops suddenly begin pattering the ground… somewhere towards the north, a jet is heard streaking though the heavens. Back inside, Ania closes the window... for it is getting cold... a single candle burns and glows on the coffee table...

Part 23

I can hear the rain... it falls heavily. Ania and I have tried twice today to be with each other... she is nervous, not comfortable in bed today. I am hoping that now it is dark she'll be able to be more carefree... there is the scattered light of an overcast sky showing through the trees and through these windows... Ania is in the basement doing laundry... I am hoping that, when she comes back upstairs, she'll want to try again.

Part 24

I remember when I went to Poland— something I have not related thus far— I was trying to give up cigarettes, for it is difficult to travel as a smoker, in this day and age, it being illegal to smoke on planes or in airports. In total, before, during, and after returning from Poland, I went two months without having a cigarette. I was on the patch, chewing gum, and puffing on my tobacco pipe in the meantime, to cope... but, it was not the same, not enough...

I am only relating this presently, seeing as it has been over a year since that time in my life... for, I do feel safe now... that time is past, like a leaf that has fallen and been caught in the coursing stream... washed, washed downstream .. maybe to find a river eventually, to be carried out of memory and immediate time.

When in Poland, although it was a beautiful time in my life, I struggled... I heard voices... the voices were in the Polish language much of the time... I do not even yet understand that language, so I do not know what the voices speaking within my mind were saying, but I doubt it was a pleasant conversation that was taking place... for, at the same time, I was feeling as if I did not have complete control... as if I was being inhabited... that the owners of those voices could control my actions was pressing... for the most part, there was not any impending danger... but, when I worried and became most anxious was during the times we spent in Ania's parents' Warsaw condo. I cannot remember now... I believe their apartment was on the ninth floor... when standing on their little patio, then I felt most unsafe... I not only experienced vertigo, but it was of the most insipid nature of vertigo... for I felt a compulsion to jump. And then, not only when I was on the patio... it was hot that vacation, and so the windows were open... and the Polish do not have screens in their windows... and there are no screen doors either... so when the windows were open, or the door leading out to the patio open, then when sitting inside, there was also that urge... that I felt not in my own power, that someone else's spirit dictated my actions... that I might, at any given moment give up the fight, and so be made to jump to my death.

This is all so disturbing to me, even now... I am not sure what was happening. I do believe that giving up smoking made me not myself... beyond having the urge to leap to my death, during that two months, I argued vehemently with Ania, on many occasions... so unlike me... I am usually calm, a caring person... I could not control the anger and frustration though, on many levels... and it came out directed toward Ania most significantly... this is sad to me, thinking back to that time in my life... it was a great adventure to go to Poland with Ania and visit with her family... that I had such trouble was unfortunate... I was though able to push down the terrible compulsion... for I did not jump, for I yet live, and am strong, a year later... and, the voices have almost faded from memory.

A month or so after arriving home, when the arguments were becoming unbearable, then I rolled myself a cigarette from a little tobacco that I had saved... and smoked the Drum, coming back to myself with each inhale... I have heard that nicotine helps to control symptoms of schizophrenia... now I do not question that fact, for maybe if it was not for that bit of tobacco I had saved, I would not be here, recounting the darkest period that I have experienced in fourteen years.

Addiction is an extremely complicated beast, that I know firsthand... that we come to depend so much on a substance seems frightening for various reasons... that, when trying to give up such a love in my life, I would lose my perceived security and independence of body and thought... well, that makes me want to never go back to *that* labyrinth and fight the Minotaur ever, ever again... for I became not myself, for I lost a great deal of control... for I might have ended my own life... all of this makes me feel it is better to just smoke, to take that burning herb into my lungs time and again, throughout the day, throughout every of my remaining days, so I will be in control, at least, of my own destiny... in as much control as the next person... so that I have a choice, for that is what was so disturbing... I was losing my ability to choose whether I wanted to live. I was feeling such loss, maybe, and I had given up something that had been a source of sanity, and comfort for over ten years... maybe giving up that love too quickly, too abruptly, caused me to lose an essential part of myself in the process— my identity, my individuality.

A large portion of people whom suffer from schizophrenia commit suicide... that I know as a fact... the percentage is frightening... I though, at least for now, am safe... I feel comfortable in my own flesh and bones body... I am centered, and have much to live and continue striving for... my life is precious to me... always has been... and that I have Ania now to comfort and hold, that brings a whole different, satisfying,

experience to the mix... that I smoke cigarettes might seem
folly to some, well I will let those people in my life have their
own beliefs regarding that matter... but, for the time, I have
found my way out of that maze... I destroy myself daily in little
ways, so to not destroy myself in complete— the compromise I
have made... and am comfortable with such decision.

Part 25

Minos aspired to the throne [of Krete], but was rebuffed. He claimed, however, that he had received the sovereignty from the gods, and to prove it he said that whatever he prayed for would come about. So while sacrificing to Poseidon, he prayed for a bull to appear from the depths of the sea, and promised to sacrifice it upon its appearance. And Poseidon did send up to him a splendid bull. Thus Minos received the rule, but he sent the bull to his herds and sacrificed another... Poseidon was angry that the bull was not sacrificed, and turned it wild. He also devised that Pasiphae should develop a lust for it. In her passion for the bull she took on as her accomplice an architect named Daidalos... He built a wooden cow on wheels, skinned a real cow, and sewed the contraption into the skin, and then, after placing Pasiphae inside, set it in a meadow where the bull normally grazed. The bull came up and had intercourse with it, as if with a real cow. Pasiphae gave birth to Asterios, who was called Minotauros. He had the face of a bull, but was otherwise human. Minos, following certain oracular instructions, kept him confined and under guard in the labyrinth. This labyrinth, which Daidalos built, was a "cage with convoluted flextions that disorders debouchment."

~ Pseudo-Apollodorus, Bibliotheca 3. 8 - 11 (trans. Aldrich)
(Greek mythographer C2nd A.D.)

Part 26

I was in my friend's car... outside was pouring rain. The car was not running... I was alone. I had been there for I don't know how long, needing to get away from the house where the party was occurring, needing to be alone, for it was only by being alone that my mind could do what it needed to do...

My friend had stayed with me for a while, but he wanted to get back to the party, so left me there... in a way I did not mind, and, although I was a bit frightened, I felt that I could ride out the drug that I had taken, the acid that seemed to have torn a hole in my consciousness.

I alternated between looking at the wonderful intricate patterns that the heavy rain made as it hit and washed down the windshield, to closing my eyes and seeing Dali's painting, *The Hallucinogenic Toreador,* evolve and mutate within my mind's eye... that painting we had spent some time looking at earlier in the evening... my friend who lived at that beach house had a large print hanging on the wall of his room... now, later, when the drug was roaring through me, the matador had come alive and was tearing holes, ripping, becoming me in a fashion... the visions that I saw as this was happening are completely indescribable... I will not even attempt to paint a picture with words to help a reader's understanding of the moment... suffice it to say, it was as if I fell into a black hole within the universe... but the hole was not black... it was Dali's painting in its entirety of colors, shapes, mutations... and the color that was most present was the red of the cape being waved in front of the bull, that which would tempt the bull to charge... would disorient the bull when he thought he had speared, with horn, the waver of the cape... that which coaxed the bull to come forward, so the matador could pierce its shoulders with the barbed, sharp sticks...

I think, at times, the friend who owned the car I was in came and checked on me, wanting me to come inside... it was only after the visions of the matador ceased, that I did come inside and went into an upstairs bedroom. There were some very strange events that occurred between me and some people that were in that room... a guitar player seemed to be playing a song that was about me... the lyrics seemed to be depicting my life, and my journeys, my loosing contact with friends and family... it was all so disturbing... a woman about my age, who I had befriended earlier, before all the craziness, came into the room with pastries... she asked if I would like one, and what kind... I then realized I was famished, and asked for a cruller... when she gently put it in my hand, I thought it was more than a pastry... and she seemed to look at me with caring eyes, telling me that yes, it was more... I thought then that it represented the guitar player's heart, or was his heart in a fashion... and I, being upset that the song of disillusionment, and loss, somehow representing me, was still being played and sung, bit hungrily into the gift from the maid, devoured it... and the guitar player seemed injured... he ceased playing the song, made some comment to the young lady that seemed angry... most everyone left the room... other events occurred, but I will not relate them here, or maybe ever... eventually though, I tried lying down on the floor and then fell into some sort of trance, staring at the ceiling and not really seeing, not feeling anything... later, in the

OF NOD

early morning, while we were driving back to my friend's home,
I felt somehow that I had become more animal than human... I
had changed.

Part 27

The entire scene is contained within a bullfighting ring, submerged under a barrage of red and yellow tones, alluding tentatively to the colors of the Spanish flag. In the upper left section we observe a representational portrait of his wife, Gala, to whom he dedicated this piece. Her serious, rigid expression could be interpreted as a pictorial representation of her deep seated dislike for bullfighting. In the bottom left section there is a pattern of multicolored circles. This rectangular-shaped burst of colors immediately grasps the viewer's attention and steers it down towards the visibly emerging shape of a dying bull's head (probably Islero), dripping blood and saliva from its mouth.

This pool of blood transforms itself into a sheltered bay where a human figure on a yellow raft comes into sight. The lower section of the bay takes on the shape of a Dalmatian. The slain bull slowly rises to become the landscapes of Cabo de Creuss (Cape Creus), Dalí's beloved birthplace. It was said that concern for an increase in tourism led Dali to embrace its features in the painting. The mountain is mimicked on the right; however, this time, the mountain bears greater resemblance to the precipitous mountains around the town of Rosas, near Dali's studio.

An old anecdote lies behind the painter's desire to represent the sculpted figures of Venus de Milos, seen 28 times in the painting. Dali decided to incorporate these particular silhouettes in his paintings after a visit to New York, where he purchased a box of pencils with a reproduction of the goddess on the cover. Dali uses negative spaces to produce an image, alternate and complementary to the Venus de Milo. This complementary image encourages the eye to contemplate the painting in such a way as to introduce the quasi-hypnotic array of forms that inhabit the canvas. Examined from a distance, the body of the second Venus reveals the face and torso of the toreador (bullfighter, likely Manolete). Her breasts as his nose, while her face transform into his eye. Their long skirts make up his white shirt and red scarf of the Toreador. The green layer makes up his necktie. His eye is found within the face of the second Venus. The soft white area unveils a tear slipping from his eye.

The gadflies of St. Narciso (patron saint of Catalonia) march over the arena in seemingly straight and parallel lines, forming the cap, hairnet and cape of the toreador. Situated on the lower right hand corner, the whole spectacle is being watched by an infant boy dressed in a sailor's suit who is said to represent Dali as a youth.

(Wikipedia: *The Hallucinogenic Toreador*— Description)

Part 28

My wife will be home within a couple of hours… her long day at work ending soon. First though, she will go to the gym to work-out, find some peace and sanity, the workday fading from memory with each weight lifted. When she finally arrives, I will hold her in my arms and tell her how much I love her, how much she means to me… how happy I am with her in my life… I will hold her complete then, knowing that we are going to live life together… for we are happy now, and there is no reason for that to change, regardless of what tricks life plays… then, soon after, I will need to leave, and make my way to the Lodge on this farm, where a writing group that I facilitate will occur… there, I will read the villanelle that opens this work… there, I will probably realize its meaning and truth… there, I will listen to other writers share their villanelles, and love life all the more because of being exposed to others' creations of the heart… and, I will, after the group has finished, come home, then being embraced by Ania… she will though first hide in some closet, or behind some door… and we will play hide-and-seek, with me saying to Leo, "Where's Ania… where's Ania…" until he sniffs around and shows me where she has hidden… and her and I will laugh great big laughs and kiss and hug while the mastiff jumps up on us, crazed by the excitement of finding her… biting at the cuffs of our clothing… wanting to be the center of our attention, but us never minding him, and going along with the hugging, knowing that we are good in each other's arms, that we need, that we *are* all that we will ever need.

II

PACT

In the center of the labyrinth lies the glade:
Path gently turning, wandering; mind ever burning—
Where the Minotaur roams and the pact is made…

Lion cubs and lovers languishing play—
Song sung out by maidens a-yearning—
In the center of the labyrinth lies the glade.

The wise and young, both digress to say
One should not live life a-worrying
Where the Minotaur roams and the pact is made…

I've been anxious long, lying in shade—
Lost, all lads and maidens, the sacrificial yearlings—
In the center of the labyrinth lies the glade.

You and me, we both must fade
From memory of world forever turning; wandering, burning…
Where the Minotaur roams and the pact is made.

May we never digress; never lament the path we make—
The long coursing maze; Earth a wondrous place of learning…
In the center of the labyrinth lies the glade,
Where the Minotaur roams and the pact is made.

Part I

One rarely travels into the forest to hunt solace; modern man is lost in growth of paved roads and torn ruins of yesterday, scraps and tattered pages of love poems... as years slip by with each revolution... I take it upon myself to wander.

Then remembering the slow movement which enabled us to come so far, leaving this body... pushed by the wind, I push myself who is but nothing to regain what has been lost of the day.   As I go, I bury a thought or two between some unsuspecting roots to forget with whom or where I have been that the load will be lightened as I search for another path from which I may, if need, wander again... always meandering haphazardly as if by fate.

Music will sometimes surge forth with emotion, or might become quiet with regret. Words were becoming meaningless, I tossed a dead branch into the fire and watched it catch... it was now out of my reach and all I could do was stare at what I had done... I thought how the morrow was already beginning... I stood and walked down the beach, toward a dock where I would sit with my head cocked up to the fulness of the lunar face. As I took each step, I knew the further I left those friends of summers behind, the more I would walk toward an ending unwritten. Wind forced itself into my ears so that only through its howl could I discern the black waves that came to rest...

It was after graduating from college, the journey to Europe... in my childhood all I wanted was to walk and climb and so through wooded glades, over fences dividing sheep pastures, upon bridges spanning currents, to the height of Old Man Coniston, and beyond, towards the clouds, the granite steps of Skafel, until I looked down upon England— a furtive glance; then, descending the backside, disappearing in mist of that winter month. Towards those heights I climb even today, quiet mannered, looking up at what is hidden, bandages upon blistered heels— a heavier weight upon my back, never telling anyone where I am heading, never calling unless the cry from the height of preponderance can be considered warning…. This manner of thought best suits the spirit I am… no longer delving through cavernous Iowa… embittered by what I have seen… the bones of sheep scattered beside this path, pecked clean by scavengers, bleached by the sun, no more sour smell…. But, is this not truth… casting off of fleece and flesh, exposing one's self to harsh reality?

And from the Lake District the train did not stop until Amsterdam. There, to walk through homes of Jews, there to see paintings of the Dutch master, there to walk the streets at night, moon blotted out by each red bulb… night and day so the saying goes, the peaks of England to the sloth of Deutschland, the sores on my feet healing rapidly, each eye a window, but I am timid and would rather gaze into the paintings, the chiaroscuro charred upon my mind… stand on the precipice and, in the quickness, look into those prostitutes' eyes and wonder at the god that lives within.

While staying at a Catholic youth hostel, close to the Red Light District, I befriended an ex-heroin addict… he had been sober for about a year… in addition to using heroin, according to him, from the age of sixteen, he had been involved with smuggling heroin internationally, but had since ceased such illegal practice. He was born and raised in Switzerland, and again, according to him, his father was a great composer and his mother was a doctor... he though had chosen a different path, and at the time I met him, he was attempting to put his life back together as best as he could. He had no money and seemed to not have any friends, was about the same age as me, and was more than happy to spend the days with me, showing me the sights the city had to offer, or going along with the discovering I was doing. I really only remember a few specific times we spent in each other's company, but I was only in Amsterdam for a week, and stayed first at a different hostel in the western part of the city, before deciding I'd be more comfortable at the Catholic hostel, where he and I met.

One morning, as we were just getting to know each other, he shared his breakfast with me— a soft loaf of white bread, with copious amounts of honey spooned on top of each slice... it was a delicious breakfast. We sat, in the dining hall of the hostel, talking, while eating bread and honey... later that morning, we rented bicycles, and toured the city, riding over many little bridges that spanned the canals, eventually making our way to the central park of the city and biking on the winding walking trails through the sparsely wooded land that was dotted with benches... places to sit and rest for those whom were walking that spring afternoon.

I had found a friend. He was kind, and although there was a sad look in his eyes most of the time, he smiled often in my company... seeming to enjoy the brief time that we had to

~ 277 ~

spend together. He told me a lot about his adventures... unbelievable stories mostly... he also told me about how many of his friends from the times that he had used, or from when he had been living on the streets— resting his head on concrete— had died of their addictions... that heroin had gotten the better of them in the end. He used to roll his cigarettes deftly, and smoke quite often when relating these stories... I remember that I wondered why he continued living in such a city, seeing as the culture seemed to be so focused on drug use there, marijuana being legal... there being many tea shops where much of the population would spend their days and nights.

I was enjoying my time with him, and so when he mentioned to me his love for watching dance performances, one afternoon I bought us both tickets to see a ballerina dance. He was quite taken aback... could not at first understand why I had done such a thing... felt I had gone overboard in spending such money on a ticket for him. At first, he refused to go... but, then, when I said the ticket would go to waste, he ended up accompanying me to see the performance. It was a beautiful show... that was the only time in my life that I have been to such an artistic dance... on walking out the doors, after the performance had ended, beyond both of us expressing our enjoyment of the event, he also commented that my taking him to see the dancers was the most kind thing anyone had done for him in an extremely long time.

Later, that evening, almost as if to repay me for my kindness— the only way he knew how— he asked me if I would like to see the Red Light District. I was hesitant, but eventually agreed that I would enjoy such an experience... when he saw that I was

hesitant, he said "We could walk through the district quickly...
you should see what it is like there, regardless."

To begin with that evening, we went to a tea shop close to the
hostel... he seemed familiar with the place, as if he had been
there in the past. When we walked in the front door, one could
choose to go up a few steps and enter the ground floor of the
establishment, or go down steeply into the basement... he
brought me down the flight of stairs to the basement, where, at
the base of the stairs was a single framed window... that was all
there was to the basement... a small standing place, with a
window that slid open. The person on the other side of the
window asked what we wanted. When my friend talked to him,
explaining what was needed, the salesperson brought out a large
tray with many buds upon it. The odor was significant, as the
sales person had slid open the window so that my friend could
examine the herb. With some talking back and forth, and a
little—enough for two cigarettes— was put in a plastic carrying
bag, I then brought fourth my money, and paid a modest
amount for what we were given. Then, my friend and I went up
the long flight of stairs, turned the corner, and entered into the
ground floor of the tea shop... sat down at a table, and talked.
"Jesus weeps, but it's been paid for," he said as an aside. I
thought he was referring to the fact that we were staying at a
Catholic youth hostel... for he continued on by coaching me
about what I should do when we arrived back at the hostel that
evening... "Let me do the talking," he said as he took some
rolling papers out of his tobacco package. My acquaintance
proceeded to roll two cigarettes— a mixture of Drum tobacco
and a small amount of the marijuana in each, and gave me the
sparse remainder to keep for later. While I was smoking, a

queer look shown in his eyes— a hungry look… he then asked if he could just taste the smoke, wanting to take the smoke merely into his mouth, then let it go, without bringing it into his lungs… I let him do such, for I saw no harm in such action… and, when dragging from the cigarette, he did just as he said, taking the smoke into his mouth, then releasing it into the air of the tea shop— a taste.

We soon left the tea shop, turning right out the front door, and walked the two or three blocks to where the Red Light District's borders began. My cohort was quiet during most of the way, but, when the walking traffic began to become somewhat thicker, he said, in a hushed tone, but with a tension behind his words, "Don't talk to anybody, don't look anyone in the eyes… just keep looking straight ahead." I soon realized that it was good advice, for not two or three steps further, and someone passed me closely, saying under his breath words concerning various narcotics he had for sale. I kept following my friend, not acknowledging the other man whom had passed. We turned a corner and were suddenly in the red lights' glare. There were only men, dark and in shadows, that thronged… the women were all behind glass doors, or windows, lit by more red lamps, mostly naked, or scantily clad in mere undergarments. I saw various men approach certain windows, talk quickly to the woman of their choice, then enter through a door close by each particular window… and there were many inviting looks that were gazed in my direction from the faces of the women whom peered from behind glass… but, I, although being tempted, did not partake of such pleasure… for I was fearful, young, and innocent mostly at that time… and something inside me said, "Marc, don't."

Part 2

I am sitting here at my desk in this cottage... it is early in the morning... I just came in from smoking. When opening the door to initially go outside, there was an interesting turn of events. Tug, an old tiger cat, which used to live here with Ania and me, suddenly ran indoors— it was the last thing I was expecting to happen. Over a year ago, a friend from the Farm took over care of Tug, for he and Leo did not get along, and it was always a battle trying to keep them from being at odds. Tug had not been back to our cabin for a year's time, so when he just ran indoors, I was surprised to say the least. Fortunately, Leo was sound asleep in the bedroom with Ania... I believe he would have gone quite berserk if he had been aware that Tug was in the cottage. Tug, as he always did long ago, went immediately over to the food dish, but then saw Leo's bowl and must have gathered that Leo is yet living here. Perhaps frightened for his life, he made a quick exit on my opening up the door for him.

It is yet dark... the night is as a black curtain on the windows. The depth of fall has arrived... cold and windy, for I must be careful on extinguishing my cigarettes, not wanting the ember discarded to blow and set anything aflame.

Lately, I have been taking many long walks with Leo. I am enjoying the cool of these days... I have been loving the sound of my feet stepping on the fallen leaves... and, Leo does not tire easily at this point in the year... when it is hot, during the summer months, he is somewhat lazy, for he gets overheated easy, and on our walks will tend to take many breaks, lying down in the shade of trees. We have wandered far and long over this farm's property… I am grateful for the companionship, especially during the weekday afternoons when Ania is at work.

This morning, after the sun rises, I will go to work, needing to help with wake-ups here at the Farm, then man the Nursing Station for a couple of hours… there, at work, I will most likely be tired, only having five hours of sleep during the night… but, the chill of fall is upon us… the cool, crisp air, blowing through the window while I am in the Nursing Station, will keep me alive and invigorated. I am actually looking forward to this morning… the eating of homemade pancakes and the connecting with work-friends. I will ride the wave of these present emotions throughout the beginning part of this day, arriving home by eleven o'clock, to lie down with Leo, curl under the blankets, and fall towards the sleep of one who is at peace.

Part 3

I just woke… it is two in the afternoon. I went onto the porch to smoke, now am inside, trying to warm. I turned the heat down when first arriving home, currently there is a chill to the air, felt especially seeing as I slept, partly clothed, on top of bedcovers. I am trying to wake… the day getting late… soon I will need to head to work, again.

One by one, my friends left the Farm to pursue a degree, or other work, far away… and we did not stay in-touch, we let life slip by, and no new friends were made… suddenly years have transpired since I have felt close to anyone outside of my marriage to Ania.

As one becomes older, it seems more difficult to make close ties with others… we become set in our ways, and the reaching out to let others in happens less and less. I have a lot of work relationships, but no one whom I walk the muddy trails with during this fall, no one to talk to, to look in their eyes and witness the colors of yellow and orange reflected therein. I have heard said that the artist must have solitude to create… I feel though, that one needs to be in-relationship with people to see better the beauty of this Earth… and, yes, I do have Leo to walk this land with… and I, of course, have my Love, Ania, to spend much of my free time with, but I seem to have a need for more— I must find friends whom would share their time willingly with an artist such as me I will begin my search today… I will start by lifting up a few of the fallen leaves and maybe underneath the yellow, or the blood-red, there I will find

OF NOD

a companion or two hiding from fear, whom might need and want the sort of friendship that I would offer.

Part 4

Last night I dreamed an old medicine-woman, a Gypsy of sorts, pinned me to the muddy ground, and was probing my body— looking for some ailment perhaps that she would somehow cure. I could not stand... the sky was dark... she was elderly, but strong as an ancient tree, her groping fingers as roots that search, deep into the soil for water and nourishment... and she eventually found the entryway to my heart— that which was locked with a combination— and she turned the huge dial that was in the middle of my chest, knowing the number-sequence intuitively. Before she was able to open the vault door, just as she was turning the dial toward the final number, I woke, frightened... and I did not know where I was... then realized I was in my own bed, at home, but could not see Ania on the other side of the bed... Leo was there though, by my feet, snoring... and I crawled out of the blankets, and walked unsteadily into the living room to find Ania preparing to go to bed. It was late, sometime after one in the morning... I then bundled up in a sweatshirt and jacket and went out on the porch to ponder the nightmare.

The dreams of fall are always of the sordid variety... they hint at beginnings and endings, simultaneously... Ania's father's mother is presently sick— Ania's family is anxious that she may not survive this present illness. In my waking mind, last night, I thought that somehow she had visited my dreams... that she and I have never met, was a present thought within my mind... that she probably hopes the best for Ania, and that she would wish to have me love Ania with all of my heart seemed to be quite possible. I know that, consciously, we do not visit others

OF NOD

through the dream-world; but sometimes, I imagine such might be possible... there, on the porch, in the dark cold of night...

Part 5

A little Irish coffee, starting the fire in the woodstove, and the day begins. Today is a day off from work and responsibilities. Ania yet sleeps... morning scrapes the surface of canvas— the bristles of a painter's brush... the first strokes of the pigment black— night-black... and all other mornings fade... there is only the dark shadows of this bliss, there is only the color of flames lighting this room— the walls of my consciousness burn— this is the process of being born— all is ash, red coal, and flame.

There is a window to the front of this wood stove... I see the beauty of fire consuming the kindling, the logs. I wish Ania was awake to witness this first burning... it is a ritual... the summer, and early fall being consumed in the whipping, dancing flames. I can see therein the beauty of this life... one must destroy in order to create .. we must set flame to the past, so the past turns into other than it was before— the smoke that billows from the chimney into the right air might be my old-self, my early adulthood, my love of sobriety, my love, etc...

I go outside to smoke, there in the cold I take quick inhales, letting the remnants of a cigarette sate cravings— for life and love, and the mysteries of spirit... it is not that those things are not present in my daily living, it is merely that they are muted, dampened... age has taken a hold.

The cottage begins to warm— warmth that seeps into the marrow... I am renewed. I smoke a clove, the perfume of this

morning... I wander, and quickly lose myself in the labyrinth...
I am hunting the man-bull, fire is my sword.

Last night Ania and I united, in the half light of this cottage,
around midnight. Today I feel at ease, as if I have shed, and
now walk naked into the next day. Ania is good to me, she is
willing to indulge my fantasies... our love is like this autumn
fire which burns, warming, making me sleepy so that I might
rest soundly, and wake, rake the coals, put new, seasoned
kindling on top, and watch the fire catch again with the draft
open, and the door to the stove cracked... and seasoned logs are
put on top of the flaming kindling... there is a moment when I
wonder if the flames will die, but then, as the door is partly
closed, letting in just enough of air, the fire catches yet again
and pops and hisses... yellow light dances in the shadows of
this room, and in this room I know that Ania loves the man I
have become, made to be more than I was before— with her to
accompany me along the shaded path that I must tread.

Perhaps, for me, love is the Minotaur— which has been caged,
lost for so long a time. There were so many hurts I endured,
needing to be loved; the losing of my father at an early age
began this process... and presently, the lions are tamed— now,
to be wed, I have become my own enemy... that which I seek to
kill is only my own self... not by means of suicide, but by the
slow, enduring means of sleepless nights and the constant
examining of my intensions. If I were young, I would just be
living and enjoying the peace of this moment... instead, being
at midlife, I tend to press and probe my emotional states, not
trusting even my perception of the moment... not wanting to
be young again... more yearning to be as I was, mentally...

before schizophrenia bit its fangs into my soul and sucked the lifeblood of my youth and sanity. I look in the mirror, and there see the man-bull who has been exiled to wander this maze of the Earth, in search for his mate... then, finding her he has become tame, wretched in his mediocrity... his boiling blood has been cooled, and life no longer is a burden, but at the same time is no longer a quest, a puzzle, a misfortune that must be overcome.

And so I wander yet still, searching for the way out, for the path that leads to God... perhaps he is hidden in the glade of my youth, that which the labyrinth has been constructed to hide. I am entrapped by my own fate... I am urged forward by my own will and compulsion to succeed... I have worn the mask of insanity, and have visited the costume party, being well received and admired for my faults as well as my passions... I can see from out of the eye sockets of this mask— for it has its own vision of the world which I have needed to adopt— and what I see is a world of pain, glory, and death... there is no more... love is a passing emotion... it is more a decision... and so I decide to love Ania, and am able, in her company, to show my original face, to don the mask when I please, and to be wretched or her lover when different moments allow... in her presence, I am able to forget, and so be at peace with my life... in her presence I am able to love, and in loving be renewed.

All fades, the night has broken into a thousand shards of blackness, dissipating... and morning light spreads its great wings over my reality... I have discovered something else exists beyond the pain and glory of death— my childhood peers at me through the mind's eye... its own entity... surviving all misfortune... there, deep within, lies a memory, as a memory within a memory, just before the separation... as a lion slayed:

I remember the cold draft which came from the window, the light of the full moon shedding itself upon the cots where we lay... oh how our faces were white, the blanket that covered my lower parts, its soft edge quietly rubbing against the tender place beneath my chin as I turned my head to look into the shadows of my friend's face, then back again to that white sphere shining through the screen and the pane, how we dwelled upon the vastness of space with our barely spoken words... I remember how it felt to be that child alive in the night already curious about the things I would struggle to comprehend throughout the rest of life. I believe now that this was the first I had ever let myself be amazed at such a glow. And how awake we were and how we both realized that we had never seen the sunrise. It is difficult to explain, but I fell asleep after we made the pact to always be friends... without seeing the sunrise... and perhaps he did the same as I, just as the night began to fade, and in a way, I must tell you, it seems I have been asleep ever since, dreaming about what it is to grow old, what it is to become distant from a childhood-friend, but, in this dream, I have been given many sunrises and sunsets, many moons to gaze gladly upon; I still sleep and dream dreamily and one day will wake and begin to slowly remember this, my life.

EPILCG

OF NOD

CHOSEN WORDS

Looking out upon this world: the long stretch of sky, that place wherein the young hawks circle, where the sun burns like a fiery face of a drum, where the streams that lead away from the lakes have carved their courses, here and there the hill where could be buried the warriors of a tribe, the universal rules all taking place, walls of rain, the dark clouds which move like a herd of wild horses over the distant fields... the hawk, stands firm, waiting, expecting— this storm will unload... it will cover the sun in its decided path... and if it brings lightning, all the more... he will wait, upon this cliff's edge, for the cry of his mate.

I may be the driftwood in the stream; I may be that which journeys upon the consciousness of others, dreaming to be what they already are; or the part of a tree which has broken off simply by the force of gravity, that which didn't require wind of a storm or weight of ice to disconnect it from its source. I may be that which is supposed to no longer bear leaves, that which will likely become entangled with other fallen souls such as mine, to help in holding the flow of a river back, becoming a part of the structure of the natural dam. I may be all of this, but this would not be unworthy— for I once was that which grew toward the sun, that which created shade, that which made a safe home for the birds and their young, a place for song.

Entering into the fog of wilderness, the time of thought and weary spirits, the precious hemispheres, the bridges surrounding, the lone bird upon the branch of a great tree: this is a world in which one must struggle to survive. I might pass into different realms by digging deep into the ground, searching for my childhood, and then may find that there is nothing to fear. My internal clock has struggled to overcome the rampant surges of time, by courting what has passed but rarely what is to come. I have laughed to find some sense of myself and have then spent myself in fear discovering, beneath the thin surface, a mirage of identity. I have breathed in the fresh scent of a passing woman— the purple flowers that grow in spring. I have let myself lie upon the hay or upon my back in the fields of madness… I have found sincerity and watched it fall from the spaces between the leafy bows. I have groped and searched through the darkness of man and have lost the sense of security which I had always believed was shackled to my being. I have struck the palm of my hand against the drum and called the tone good. I have waited for all that I have waited for and I have sold that part of myself which some would think to be most important— and so, the account has become settled.

A minister touched me, laid hands on the wound…
there, in the Psych ward, recovering
from the strange sickness of heart and head…

I do not remember much of that time,
it is held in prayer-palms of those who believe,
like a flower, or a singing bird…

my life has been spent trying to find what was lost—
the ultimate goal being wholeness,
the surf and sand still meet, there in the darkest thoughts.

Years later, the beauty that caressed my forehead,

in a tent on the shore of a lake in Maine, North Pond...
she brought a love of being, touched again

my long loneliness... her fingers yet dance there,
or sweep away past mistakes.
I found myself in the sways of adulthood, not knowing,

breaking the calm with stones thrown into the still
surface of the waters of childhood... that which was taken.
And, last night, my hands, two gifts... orchids

brushed, petting my wife's head and hair—
the giving up of the ghost is a difficult task,
the trying on of different forms until the fit is made

and so time and again my heart is remembered
and I feel, now, as if I am able to be the man I was meant
to become, if only for you, Love.

About the Author

MARK ALAN MURRAY was born in Dearborn, MI, March of 1970 to Elizabeth and Alan Murray. Throughout his early childhood he lived in Delaware and then in North Carolina with his mother, father, and younger brother. His parents divorced when he was the age of seven. Following the divorce, he and his brother moved back to Wilmington, DE to live with his mother's family, consisting of his three cousins, his aunt, his uncle, and, of course, his mother. All eight people lived under the same roof for a number of years. During holidays and summer vacations, Mark spent time at his father's and stepmother's (Kathy Murray's) home, first located in Pittsburgh, PA and then in West Hartford, CT. While in Wilmington, Mark attended John Dickinson High School; there, discovering his affinity for English, he eventually chose to enroll as an English major when he attended the University of Connecticut in Storrs, CT. In 2007, Mark self-published a significant volume of poetry which contained two books, titled *The Red-Tailed Hawk and Pierced by the Cry of Swallows,* simultaneously with the printing of a book entitled *The Dismantled Moon,* and one which he called *Dark Content.* Throughout his twenties, he self-published, in a rough manner, three books of poetry, including *Scrawlings of a Beast, Climbing the Red-Rusted Ladder,* and an earlier version of *The Red-Tailed Hawk,* called *Inventions of the March Hawk.* All of those early publications were printed in limited quantities and were mostly given to his friends and family. Beyond writing poetry and prose, Mark Alan Murray is an accomplished recording artist, concentrating on the flute and harmonica under the project name of *Earth's Seductive Haze.*